CARGO & CHAOS

FRANKIE STYLES BOOKS 1 & 2

COOPERATIVE REALM

NICKY PENTTILA

I

CARGO & CHAOS

CARGO TROUBLE

CHAPTER ONE

THE SNAKE, apparently, had conveyed with the ship.

Frankie stumbled upon Little Minnie as the pale giant reptile was recharging—basking, if another snake were doing it—under the grow lights in the starship's garden room. She'd come in for a sprig of mint, but that thought vanished under the weight of her surprise. She slowly knelt by the long, soft nest that had seen better days. Old Peters had made Minnie a new nest but she hadn't taken to it, so now that one was serving as a cushion up in the rec space. Old Peters had been fond of cushions, and most of those had conveyed, as well.

But they didn't need care and feeding.

One of Minnie's eyes was partly open, but looked as if it wanted to be closed. Frankie wasn't sure how an eye could communicate like that, but didn't question it. She respected Minnie's boundaries. As she stepped out of the room, the door whooshing shut, she started the call to Old Peters. While waiting, she squatted down to see if she could see any snake prints on the extra button panel by the jamb. Minnie knew how to press these to gain entry to places all over the ship; how long that had taken to teach her, Frankie couldn't even guess.

"Frankie!" The voice was a warm scratch on an unacknowledged itch. "Miss me already? How's the Spear?"

"Spherical as always." Why the bulbous cargo ship had such a sharp name was yet another mystery. Frankie wasn't about to spend the time or the credits to rename her, though, so Spear she would remain. "One question, though. Didn't you forget somebody?"

A pause at the other end. "Oh, you mean Minnie. No, girl, she's yours. She'd never leave the Spear, her bones wouldn't take it. We're both at the ends of our useful lives now."

Frankie rolled her eyes. Despite his nickname, Peters wasn't so old. Sure, he had serious mobility issues from the wars, but the ship was modified to help with that. He had retired because he could afford to.

Lucky for her, since that meant she could afford the awfully reasonable price he'd named for the ship. "You're sure? Isn't Stackfield low-grav?"

"Don't think my new neighbors would be too hot on a snake that was taller than they are. And she'd find precious few little mousies scuttling down here."

"She is good for the ship, yes," Frankie said. "But seriously, she's going to miss you terribly." Frankie and Minnie were on live-and-let-live terms, not really cuddle buddies the way Minnie and Peters were. And Minnie could be moody, and hide when feeling low.

"She'll be fine. You will, too. Gotta go—it's time for my water-dance class. My friend who got me this place says it's like happy hour for us geezers."

Frankie blinked at the idea of Peters in a waterdance class, and then remembered to blink the call off. Her stomach rumbled. Mint, for the porridge with the weird smell. She tapped the lower open-door panel with her foot, whispered an apology to Minnie, grabbed a sprig, and took it back to the kitchen. While heating up the porridge, she opened her shopping list for when they got to Rosing Station and added frozen mice.

There was always a chance that the cargos of grains and other foodstuffs the Spear transported wouldn't attract mice or other invasive critters this run.

But it hadn't happened yet.

NO PROBLEMS AT ROSING STATION. Frankie had seconded to Old Peters for two full cycles before taking the Spear out on her own, so she knew all the port stewards and how to get around. The Spear had a portering contract for organic materials needing fast shipping to the inner ring of planets in the system. It was a steady job and usually took up only part of the cargo space, so she could freelance cargo for extra credits.

Rosing Station, the biggest and newest in this system, sat in the Lagrange Point between two top-producing agricultural planets. Frankie always picked up seed here for the less-blessed worlds on the route. Seed packed tight, so half the hold was free for extras. Frankie had drained her account buying the Spear outright, and needed to rebuild her safety net. And to buy some insurance, at least collision.

She sauntered into the economy section of the station's lower ring, looking for the ramen shop she remembered. She liked sauntering, that saucy sway of the hips. It made her feel captain-like, not like what she used to be.

The section, two stories high with a narrow bridge-deck all around, hummed and burbled; people of all sorts walking and talking, haggling, slurping noodles. The noodles here were stellar, of course, so close to the source.

She stopped at a specialty grocery, noisy with birds and people shouting. She checked out all the types of mice before making her order. She'd forgotten to ask Peters how much Minnie needed to eat, so she ordered fifty. That must be enough, for one haul.

With her short hair a new red, and her identity not triggering to anyone here at the edge of Cooperative space, Frankie felt free to roam. The people who needed to know where she was knew it; everybody else could find themselves stuck in a broken airlock.

The shop was still there, the noodles still delicious. So much better than porridge. She was on her second bowl and thinking about asking the proprietor if they sold freeze-dried servings when her message light blinked.

A local call.

She did not panic. She did not answer the call.

She slowly slurped her noodles, savoring fresh coriander and chilis. It was probably someone wanting something shipped. Speed-of-light response to her open-cargo posting, though. Maybe they were desperate. So let them stew, and they might not notice if she boosted the standard fee.

She had many options, and the best one was the ability to say no.

CHAPTER
TWO

"NO," she said.

The message had been from Skoll Shipping, the biggest cargo hauler in the sector. Proudly family-owned: Two younger Skolls sat across from her, taking up all the space in the small booth in a nondescript cafe in the inner ring of third section. Even seated, they were tall, and wide, and a shade of gray that indicated a once-darker complexion that had been in space too long.

Frankie was short and squat in comparison—planet-raised. Her skin was only starting to take on that sheen, and even just a week on-planet would wash it away. A lot of rich spacers used the sun booths to look planet-raised. The Skolls proudly did not.

They also did not eat or drink in front of people, which made meeting in a cafe less than comfortable.

Peters had told her to steer clear of the Skolls. They held most of the portering contracts in this sector, for the big hauls. She was just a little fish. She should be beneath their notice.

"It's a reasonable offer," the one in the green sari said. They hadn't introduced themselves, so she wasn't sure what the hierarchy was. Neither talked much, probably taking advantage of their prey's nerves.

Well, she wasn't prey. She took a sip of her real-bean coffee and savored it. Matcha was fine for everyday, but sometimes you just wanted a rich, thick blend to savor. When someone else was paying. She held the small saucer a shade longer, breathing in the steamy goodness.

"We're not in competition. I don't see why you need the Spear."

"We don't need the Spear. Only the contract."

"You're a new captain," said the one in gold and blue. "This route will go dull for you in no time."

"You're right, I'm new. So how about we postpone this conversation for a rotation and see how it goes?"

The one in green crossed their beautifully bangled arms. "We thought we had a deal with Old Peters."

Frankie tried to hide her surprise, and probably failed. What deal?

"Then you came along," blue sari said, "and we didn't hear from Peters again."

Frankie took another sip, larger, draining the saucer. This was trouble, and she didn't want to leave any coffee behind if she had to run.

She set it down, keeping her hands on it to capture the last of its warmth. "Captain Peters swore there was no other claim to the Spear when we registered the sale."

Green sari sighed, looking toward the service counter. Must be tough to smell all the delicious pastries and know you can't eat any of them. Too bad.

Blue sari set their clasped hands on the table and stared steadily at Frankie. "You don't know how it is around here, I see that. Here on the edges, we do a lot of things that aren't exactly by the book, if you know what I mean. There's agreements, and then there's agreements. And there's tradition, and precedent."

That was plain confusing. "Tradition?" she said tentatively.

"Exactly. Skoll Shipping traditionally"—hard emphasis on that word—"has right of first offer for all cargo transport from this station."

"Ah," Frankie said. "Peters should have offered. And you would have turned it down, because it is such a small contract, compared to the loads you haul. And we would be in the same position."

"We would not be in the same position. We would have purchased the contract. And for more than you did." They opened their hands like giving up an offering. "We offer the same price to you we would have to Old Peters. An immediate profit."

Now Frankie crossed her arms. She had spent two years setting this up. Learning the ropes, getting comfortable with a lot of quiet time and a giant snake. She needed something to do— something far away from everybody else—and this was ideal.

But she didn't want to be owned. Even if Skoll would keep her and the Spear on, and they would have to, for a cycle at least, she would not be in control of her life. Again.

"No," she said. "Thank you."

The one in green hissed in a breath. But the one in blue held up a hand, stalling them. "I understand you need to stay distant from the capital."

The one in green couldn't hold it in. "We know who you are."

Frankie went still. It wasn't a secret, of course. She just didn't want to be paraded around anymore. She didn't want to be known as a Child Orphan of Wala one second longer.

That life, traveling Co-op space collecting pity and uncomfortable pauses, was another kind of death. Let Beth keep doing it; she liked it. Frankie was out.

But she wasn't above using it for her own benefit. "You would take advantage of someone who's already lost so much?"

Blue sari sat unruffled, like an auntie who brings you sweets and then swipes them off the table to eat herself when you're not looking. "It's a good deal. You should take it."

"Thank you, no. If that's it, then?" Frankie stood up.

The two Skolls also rose, faster than she'd expected. The one in green loomed over the table, over her. "Take the deal."

Frankie nodded her head in farewell. "Safe travels," she said.

They did not give the familiar response back. They said nothing at all.

Bullies, plain and simple. They had no power over her.

CHAPTER
THREE

FRANKIE WAS BARELY through the airlock and into the dock where Spear was tethered when she heard the argument.

The voices, one high, one low, and one screeching, were three or four slips down the pier, so they must be really loud. Even with only their stern tied to the dock, most haulers were huge. Just to walk to her slip from the last station airlock would take most of an hour. Frankie looked longingly at the little red mini-wagon floating beside her. She could have ridden it to her ship, except it was full of spare parts, boxed ramen, and a bag of dead mice.

It would be good for her to walk, and the dock was lovely, for a dock. The pale gray ceiling so far away you couldn't even see the rivets gave her all the space she wanted. The gigantic outer portals in the distance promised adventure. The constant rattling and banging of folks getting their ships spaceworthy sang in her ears.

But the argument sounded a sour note.

Frankie dawdled, hoping they would finish whatever their discussion was, but even at half-speed she came upon them mid-battle. The captain of the ship, a boxy hauler, stood blocking the entrance to the cargo ramp, a true-to-life parrot on his shoulder. The parrot seemed to have much to squawk at an amazingly blond person draped in multicolored silks. This person was gesticulating wildly at the stoic shipper, and then at the shipping box twice their height that filled the entire width of the pier.

Frankie would have to shimmy to get past that behemoth box. Her miniwagon needed a floor to hover above; if the shimmy space was too narrow, the wagon might plunge to the port floor, far, far below.

No way that cargo should be here. There were rules about moving cargo, the chief one being always keep it flowing. Never block the route.

Now she was mad at the all-colors person, too. She didn't even wait for a pause in the overloud conversation to shout, "Excuse me."

The shipper was the captain, a friend of Old Peter. Punter couldn't be his name, but it was the only thing she knew him by. Maybe it was the bird's name? He nodded to her.

The stranger spun on a heel and glared at her, but stopped talking. He was one of the pretty ones, who probably never had a major problem in their lives. No wonder he was overreacting to whatever was wrong.

"Are you going to move this box?" she said. "People need to get by."

"I'm trying," he stretched out the word. "But my good man here refuses to honor our contract."

"The contract says pay up-front." The captain spread out his hands. The bird spread its wings behind him. "I'm waiting."

Typical. It was only a few days until the new month. Sir Pretty had probably blown through his allowance.

"I told you, good sir, that the funds are at the destination. Here, the proof." He flicked at something on his wristcom.

The captain did not look at his comm, or at the tablet in his hand that probably held the ship's manifest. "And I told you, it needs to be here, with me."

This argument would not end soon. Frankie nodded to the captain and started toward the box. How narrow was that shimmy going to have to be?

"Wait!" The colorful person approached her. She stopped her wagon, again. "Perhaps you could assist me where this captain will not."

He had a beautiful face. Big dark eyes like a cartoon character. Wide mouth that surely needed to smile a lot. Clear brow crowned by perfectly cared-for waves of hair in all colors of blond. The one piece of jewelry he wore was a pendant—black onyx?—that signaled masculine gender while looking rather feminine.

A player.

She jammed her hands in the back pockets of her tunic. She'd forgotten there was a dead mouse in the right pocket, thawing for Minnie. At least it was in a wrapper.

"Sir. The captain is a wise man. If he finds fault with your contract, I believe I would find the same fault." She was not going to extend a player any credit.

"Oh! He is so unreasonable. We've shipped many, many times with him, and he knows we're always good for it."

The captain snorted. "After months of dunning."

Something smelled … odd. Frankie frowned and took another whiff. Organic, but not the right kind of organic. Not exactly rotten, but something.

"See. She smells it too. There's something wrong with your box."

"There's nothing wrong with my box. It's carrying organics. It's going to have an organic smell." He fiddled with his wristcom, a fancy model with a gorgeous black band "It's cleared all customs, see? There is no problem."

The captain shook his head. "No credits, no portering. No problem." He turned and stomped up the ramp.

At least the argument was done. Frankie powered up the miniwagon again and stepped toward the edge of the dock. She wished she had a safety line, but who could have known one was needed in port?

"Captain, please, a moment. Please."

She sighed and turned back to the annoyance. She wished, again, that her parents had not trained her to be polite to all people.

"I'm Morgan, uh, Cloud. Morgan Cloud. It's very nice to meet you, captain?"

"Styles."

"Captain Styles. You're new here?" He leaned against his box as if they were having a conversation in a shopping court, not blocking the entire pier. "I haven't seen you around."

Frankie had no time for this, whatever it was, flirting? "We're done."

"No, wait. I know a way you won't have to risk your life trying to get around this box." A sound came from the top of the box, a shuffling. Three dock crewmembers peered over on the edge. The player stepped out of the way as they lowered themselves down to the dock. The dock's cat, a massive, scraggly, lumpy thing, remained on the top edge, eyeing the parrot.

"You could ship it."

As if. "For free? I don't think so." She put her hands on her hips.

"Of course not. I have the credits. I'll show you." He looked her up and down. "You look hungry. How about I buy you dinner and we can talk about it?"

"Not hungry. Not interested."

He looked over the contents of the miniwagon. "I know a great ramen shop up on the top tier. Noodles to die for. And the dining room has a view of the big park, too."

Frankie paused. "Peppermint ice cream?"

Morgan considered. "Not there. But nearby."

It wouldn't work. But, a free meal?

"You won't stiff me?"

"Me?" He held a hand in front of where his heart should be. "Never."

She could eat on his credits. And there must be a good story about this smelly box.

"I need to drop off my supplies. Meet you there?"

"Excellent! How about I give you a hand up?" He saw her confusion and pointed to the top of the box. "Like those good service workers."

Frankie scoped the jump. Might be done. Morgan must have seen her approval. He backed up to the box, bent his knees, clasped his hands, and held them out to her.

She set a foot on his hands and a hand on the box as high as she could reach. He stood and pushed. Easy scramble. On top, the smell was stronger. It reminded her of a visit to the country when she was little.

Frankie reset the miniwagon to float higher. It rose halfway, but started to struggle. In the end, Morgan gave it a boost, too.

"Perfect," he said. "See you in an hour?"

CHAPTER
FOUR

FRANKIE HAD CHANGED her mind in the time it took to stow the supplies. Minnie snubbed her nose at the mouse but then looked affronted when Frankie started to go without leaving it behind. So now there was maybe a dead mouse carcass in the greenroom.

Another prima donna. She only needed one. Less than one.

She should call this meeting off. Pick up some farm implements or something simple like that. No more organics. What if they infected the seed? Sure, the containers were supposed to prevent that, but if mice could find a way surely some virus or whatever could.

She got the ping from "Morgan" with coordinates to the shop, which she'd never heard of. The reviews were stellar.

She couldn't be always saying no. The sad echoes in her empty credit accounts were forever clanging in her thoughts. Just do the shipping, get it over with. Clear the nagging worries out of her head.

She changed out of her everyday and into the navy tunic that Beth said made her skin glow—at least when she had planet tan

—and soft boots that matched her leggings. Her hair was fine. She reminded herself: Peppermint ice cream.

Someone had shoved Morgan's cargo so the longer side ran along the walkway, opening a third of it up to travel again. As she passed it, she tried to place the smell, but nothing reasonable came to mind. Nobody needed to transport milorganite—people made waste on every planet.

The trip up to the third ring was a parade of fashion. Economy featured sturdy fabrics in bright colors. At second ring, the elevator doors opened to a sea of muted colors and smoothed-down hair and clothing. At third ring, she stepped out into a smaller crowd with louder taste: asymmetric cuts, hard and soft fabrics, colors that changed. And a lot of wrinkling; she felt tempted to bunch up her tunic to match the style. The fabric was rich enough to pass, barely. She was glad she hadn't worn the tan one.

There wasn't much anyone could do about the architecture of the station. Each ring was built the same, triple-contained space worthy. So the main difference walking the shopping courts here was the ornament on the same five styles of boxed-into-the-wall stores and freestanding carts. But they really did it up here: Each shop had a subtle scent, all of them alluring to humans, apparently. Frankie found herself at the threshold of a high-fashion store before she realized it. Only the shocked affront on the face of the human assistant inside brought her to her senses.

The restaurant did not look like a noodle shop. The wall facing the walk glowed amber. If she didn't know better, she would have thought it was solid amber. Light from inside seemed to highlight fossils in the wall. What a marvelous illusion.

And expensive.

Morgan wasn't waiting inside the restaurant. He lounged against the faux-amber, his multicolored tunic alternately matching and clashing with the wall behind him. His multi-hued hair, which did not change, fit perfectly in the setting. He was messing up his pretty face by scowling at his tablet. As soon as he saw her, he slid the tablet into his pocket.

"Captain. You're such a restful sight. No, seriously—I mean that in a good way."

"Mr. Cloud. You look well." That seemed safe enough to say.

"If you like, I can turn off my tunic for dinner, so you don't have to watch me swirl. One more thing." He reached for her, maybe to take her arm.

Frankie jumped back.

"Sorry, sorry. This isn't starting well, is it?" He smiled, a soft thing that somehow communicated regret, warmth, and calculation. "This is the thing: I know the proprietor here, Stella. We're friends. I helped design this wall, in fact." He waved toward the amber.

Frankie could not help herself. "It's astounding."

"Five-scan illusion, yeah. Anyway, Stella is prickly about how people order their meals. If it's all right with you, I will order for both of us."

Frankie crossed her arms. "You think I don't know how to order in a high Co-op restaurant?"

"Do you?" He obviously thought not.

Frankie did. She'd been partly raised under the supervision of the regent of the Co-op herself. But it wouldn't do to let that out, if she wanted to remain merely a captain here. She would need to make mistakes with all the glasses and implements, too, to keep the false front.

This was why she didn't like to be with people. They just kept pushing at her jammed doors.

"No," she said. She wasn't that hungry, anyway. "Let's just go get some ice cream."

The relief on Morgan's face was fleeting but obvious. He probably didn't have the credits. That's why he was taking her to a friend's restaurant. It wasn't to impress her—he probably thought she didn't know enough about fine dining to be impressed.

Fancy-pants player.

Morgan also sauntered, but he had to slow it down so much to stay even with her short legs that his gait looked like he was walking through water. The ice cream place was apparently back toward the elevator she'd come up in. How had she not noticed it? Morgan directed her toward a short alley between buildings. He did not try to touch her.

She gasped. There was a park back here!

A narrow strip of green ran behind all the buildings on this side of the ring. Small plants and flowery bushes flowed down the strip, with benches and soft ground seating sprinkled about.

"Pretty great, huh? All the restaurants are on this side, so they can take advantage of the view." Morgan turned right, and she could see the snack kiosk right away. The sweet and spicy scents of the blooms filled the air. It really did smell good up here.

Morgan did have the credits to obtain a crunchy saucer of peppermint ice cream and another of plain chocolate. They sat at one of the ground-cushions, side by side, and dove in. Frankie turned a little away from Morgan so his swirling clothes wouldn't distract her.

Bliss. Smooth and creamy, sharp and tangy. After the second spoonful, she sighed and lowered the saucer. She needed time to savor.

The last time she'd had peppermint was—what?—twenty years ago. Her eighth birthday.

Her last on Wala.

Peppermint was considered a weed among most of the Co-op planets. It was pretty invasive, but could be tamed by using pots. Old Peters hadn't wanted it in his greenroom.

But it was her greenroom now.

Morgan seemed to consider her pause in eating an opportunity for conversation. "So. My cargo. It must be at Smithson Station in ten days. Earlier is better."

Frankie frowned, and then took another spoonful of ice cream. Letting it melt on her tongue, its sweet tang rolling through her sinuses, she had to admit: She was not always free to say no. Being a businessperson meant making deals whenever they came up, melting ice cream or no.

"Show me the manifest," she said.

It was on the surface of his tablet immediately. His hands were free—somehow, he'd finished all his ice cream already and was chewing on the hard-cookie spoon.

So *that* was the smell. She did remember it, from visiting farms near her grandparents.

"That whole big box for only two horses?"

"Racehorses," he said, pride in his voice. "It's a whole stable, with space for months of fodder and a self-contained reclamation system. A veterinary setup for minor injuries. Plus capsule space for the jockey to sleep, when it's settled at the track."

She had to stare at him. "You ship racehorses off-planet?" The cost of doing such a thing was astronomical. He wasn't a player. He was insane.

He grinned at her. "Eat up. These aren't merely racehorses, captain. They are winners. My family has raised horses for generations." He shrugged. "They move where we move."

"And you're moving to Smithson Station?" It was an older station—only two levels—but it was on her route. Old Peters's Stackfield Base was nearby.

"Gods, no." Morgan actually shuddered, which set his tunic into hurricane mode. Frankie hastily looked away. When she looked back, he'd done something to it; now it was nonmoving swirls of red, pink, and white. "That's where all the horses are going. They have to be there for a week before the race, so everyone can see there's no doping and all that. Then they'll join me down on Hondichi, where the track is."

Somehow, all her ice cream had vanished. She lifted the saucer, eyeing between its waffles for even a bit more. "You think they've run out of peppermint?" she said.

He chuckled, a honeyed sound, and reached for her saucer. She handed it to him and sat back, leaning on her hands, as he went to get her more. The curve of the outer ring up here even had portholes, regularly spaced at adult chest height. What a job that would be to make sure none of them leaked.

"Okay," she said, after her first—second—initial hunger had been slaked. "But still, how is it economically feasible?

"It isn't, always. You need to place in the top three in a race and win some credits to cover the cost. If you win, or place in multiple races, that's when you make a profit. That's why most people bring two or more horses. Double the chances."

"And if you lose?" He seemed like someone who did not consider that he would lose.

"I have insurance. I have a contract to sell the pair: one price if one of them places, one price if they win, and a base price no matter what happens." He shrugged. "It's not even really a gamble: If we win, I win. If we place, I win. If we lose everything, I'm covered."

"And this base price. This gets paid up-front?"

"Exactly. As soon as we get there, and the horses pass inspection. There's your fee."

Frankie crunched on her saucer. She'd need to see this contract. She did not need to see the horses. That would bring up too many memories.

Did she trust this man? She had plenty of experience with fancy boys, and he didn't strike her as one of the mean ones. Or one of the hidden-mean ones.

"How much could you give me right now? As security."

He sighed. "Well. All the peppermint ice cream you can fit in your freezer?"

She had to laugh.

"Deal."

Morgan made one more push. "And might you take passengers, as well? I could bunk in a crew cabin, nothing fancy."

Frankie bristled. She was a businessperson now, sure, but she didn't need to sell all her space. It had taken her a while to warm to Old Peters, and he was the nicest they came. She wasn't ready.

"No. Not this trip," she said to soften it. "Don't you have a ship of your own?"

"Not exactly," he sighed. "But no worries, I'll find a way to meet you there. And the sale can go through, with or without me."

***

MORGAN CLOUD WASN'T THERE for the loading of his box. The dockworkers wouldn't move it down to the Spear, but the parrot and its captain had departed earlier, so she hopped the Spear down to that slip and used her own drones to wrestle the thing aboard. As they were securing it, the dock's older undersupervisor came up the ramp, lingering in the doorway. Frankie enjoyed the inspector's sly sense of humor when she wasn't its target.

"Thank you for removing the impediment. Your ship is in the wrong slip."

"Thank you, chief assistant dockmaster. I'm ready to cast off."

"Do you have room for another small cargo? Also for Smithson Station. Double standard rate."

Frankie hadn't known you could pick up cargo on the fly like this. But it was the assistant dockmaster, so it had to be legit.

"Sure. What is it?"

"Adzuki, they tell me. A half-ton."

Beans? To an agriculture planet?

"Standard contract?" She saw it on her wristcom in seconds. Nothing out of the ordinary.

She signed the contract and sent it back. "More the merrier."

A half-hour later she had a portal time. An hour later she was off the dock and under way to Smithson Station.

CHAPTER
FIVE

MINNIE MUST HAVE EATEN the mouse. Frankie didn't see it or her lengthy friend in the greenroom. She flicked her wrist to show the ship's map. Captain's suite.

Where Frankie was headed anyway. The Spear could pilot herself, although Frankie had widened the parameters for when she needed to sound an alert. Old Peters had been more sanguine about those things than Frankie was. Maybe when she was Old Frankie, she'd ease up on the controls.

The captain's suite had three rooms: the center one for meetings, one to the left for sleeping and washing, one on the right for whatever else. The last room was bare: Peters had taken all his collections and musical instruments with him, and Frankie didn't have anything to put in its place. She'd always traveled light.

But now she did have the space, she wondered what to put in it. A game room? There already was one of those, up by the kitchen. Not a music room—her little guitar would look mighty lonely there, and she liked to play it in bed, anyway. Maybe a reading room?

For now, the room would stay empty. She walked through the

office and into the bedroom, also rather severe at the moment. At least she had the navy and silver fuzzy blanket Beth had sent as a gift when she bought the Spear. "In your colors!" the note accompanying it read.

Minnie was here, draped along the top of her wardrobe. Her "stick"—more like a tree without branches or an overgrown coat rack—was still in the whatever room. Come to think of it, that should have tipped Frankie off that Minnie was still here.

But of course, Minnie wouldn't want to hang out in an empty room, so here she was. Frankie suspected there were still whiffs of Old Peters about here, to a sensitive nose.

"Okay, Minnie," she said. "We need to set some boundaries. This is my room now."

Her words did not move the snake, though it did give her a look, and a slow blink.

Well, if she was going to stay, it couldn't be on Frankie's dresser. The stick would have to come into the bedroom. Then later—or sooner—she would see if Minnie consented to having the stick in the office room.

Frankie had to summon the littlest hauler bot to help her even lift the thing. It helped a lot when it pointed out that the stick was bolted to the floor; Frankie had seen the bolts on the wall and thought the stick must spin when the gravity went out. Between them, they wrestled it into the bedroom close by the door and secured it with what she hoped were temporary, easily removable, bolts. Frankie thanked the bot and sent it on its way.

Almost immediately, Minnie dropped to the floor and launched herself onto her stick. She settled into the familiar loops Frankie remembered from evenings of music with Old Peters.

"I miss him, too," she said, resting a hand on one of the loops. Minnie's skin was dry and warm, comforting.

Frankie changed into her comfy mid-space clothes: soft pants, long sleeved Galactic U T-shirt, a thick navy-and-silver cardigan with big buttons and pockets. She kept her grav-boots on. She'd learned that lesson hard.

Passing Minnie on the way out, she tried to remember: Weren't horses afraid of snakes?

———

THE CAT WAS in the kitchen.

The one from Rosing Station dock, with the perpetual just-shocked-looking fur. Striped, sort of—tufted, mostly—in grays and blacks. Its gaze was unusually steady. A solid, sturdy body, it looked too heavy to lift. Maybe it wasn't a cat? But it had the pointy ears, complete with black tufts on the tips.

It perched on the back of the three-sided nook-bench with the orange cushions, above the spot where Frankie usually had her breakfast. Actually, all her meals now that she was on her own.

Did the cat know that?

"Good morning," she said, assuming the cat was on Galactic Standard Time. The cat did not acknowledge her as she passed to the smaller galley to start the morning brew. Frankie reached for the cupboard for porridges, and then stopped. Her belly wasn't feeling it.

She sat on the bench across from her usual spot, facing the cat but with her back to the open doorway. Foolish choice, a long-gone security instructor whispered in her thoughts. Stand down, brain, it's safe here. She stared at the cat-thing. It stared back.

She blinked first. "How did you get here?" Okay, that was a dumb question. "You chased something, and got stuck, right? You better've caught it."

The cat—she was going to call it a cat—jumped down to the seat cushion, spun twice, and settled in a circle shape. It blinked at her.

"Great. Well, I hope you like frozen mice. It's at least a month till we can get you home."

It set its head on its paws and closed its eyes. Frankie sipped her caffeine and decided that she would skip the gruel this morning. Would she find some other creature, one by one, in every room on the ship? Could add up to a lot of mouths to feed.

She scanned the ship's log—no problems overnight. When her cup was empty, she clicked her wristcom to scan and stretched her arm across the table. Time to read the cat's chip and tell whoever cared for this chonk where it had gotten to.

Before she could get a reading—almost before the scan's beam could have touched it—the cat squawked. It vaulted off the cushion, under the table, and away. Only the light breeze of its movement past her shin indicated which direction it had gone. And the growl from outside the door.

She swiveled in the seat to look out the door. The cat was on the far side, close to the wall. "Stand down, fuzzy head. I'm just trying to find out who to call. You don't want your people to worry, do you?"

The door slid shut.

Rude.

It must have bumped the lower open-button. It should have taken two intentional pushes to close a door at remain-open setting, though.

Frankie opened her to-do list and added check kitchen slide button. Top of the list was the ever-delightful cleaning of the filters. She promised herself the last of the fresh ramen for a job well done. And tried not to think about how much fur that big-pawed stowaway could shed.

CHAPTER
SIX

AFTER A LONG, dusty shift, Frankie was ready to play. She passed from the living/piloting sphere into the cargo hold, grabbed a hand-hold, and slid the second door shut. She waved the soft lights on. The vast space always reminded her of images from biology class, objects of various shapes and sizes growing out into the center from the smooth walls of the hull. Maybe a cross-section of an intestine? Except way, way drier.

She extended the retractable walkway/ladder across the diameter of the hold. No need to stow it; there was plenty of space on this trip. The port bots had done a good job, balancing the load and making sure all was secure. She clicked on her grav-boots and walked among the cargo.

Minnie was in here somewhere. Frankie checked her comm. Down a ways, by the somewhat-smaller containers. There, just below the walkway.

Frankie loved to watch Minnie swim in no-G. Most snakes tied themselves in knots, confused by the absence of their inner sense of place. Minnie's senses were modified to ease the stress. She swam through the air the way others swam in water, only the curves turned into spirals here. Minnie also liked the walkway, an extra object to rebound from in the center of the hold.

Sometimes, she sped around the space, ricocheting around corners and zooming from wall to wall. Today, she was taking her time, going from carton to carton, spinning like an otter sometimes, other times bouncing in great arcs like she was the path of a child's rubber ball. Must be getting familiar with all the cargo.

Frankie didn't smell anything besides the usual ozone and a vague mustiness. Soon it would be hard to smell anything in the chill. No cargo that needed warmth, so the heaters were off to offset the extra solar charge she was using to get to Smithson Station early. The hold would get colder and colder during the trip. Neither she nor Minnie could stay that long.

The bots had secured the horse stable container, which had its own heat pump, by itself at the far end of the hold. From the walkway, it looked vertical. Did horses adapt to no-G?

Most mice couldn't—they would spin and spin, until Minnie caught them right away. But a few strains could, due to random mutation. Minnie caught them later. The port could scan for and kill the smallest virus and bug, but had to be careful around live plants and larger animals. So, mice.

Frankie reached the far wall and clicked her grav-boots off. She held the railing and pivoted to set her boots on the wall, putting new boot-prints over the boot-prints already there. Minnie had been keeping her in sight. She knew what boots on the wall meant. The snake twined itself into a spring, holding onto one of the cargo handles near the center of the hold.

Frankie used the railing to push herself into her own version of a spring. She let go, kicked off the wall, and went flying. A moment later, Minnie pushed, and by the time Frankie was flying by, Minnie had reached her. Perfect timing: Frankie reached for Minnie's long middle, and pushed, so gently, downward. The snake ricocheted toward some cargo, while Frankie kept her trajectory but tumbled head over heels. The game was to be facing the door by the time she got to the entry wall.

She was facing the door, a ways above it and upside down, when she got there. She grabbed one of the safety lines tacked along the walls and spun to land on her shoulder. Hand over hand, down to the walkway. Brilliant.

She could only make the fly once at a time, because Minnie would try to do it again, too, and tire herself out too much. Once was enough—Frankie's shoulders had relaxed, her breathing was good, and she was smiling.

FRANKIE WAS SAVORING the last of the fresh noodles and staring at that dustmop of a cat who was again lounging in her spot in the nook when the call came in. Not even a message, an actual voice call, beyond expensive when mid-space.

Morgan.

"Styles. What's wrong?" She knew to keep it short.

"Yeah, this is Morgan. You know that. I mean, it says, right?" The strain in his voice could have cracked glass.

"Why are you calling? Where are you?"

"Funny thing about that, heh heh." The tension ratcheted. Frankie could picture his lean, handsome face, shiny with sweat. "I'm in a bit of a pickle."

"You're in trouble?"

"Not trouble, really. Well, yes." His breathing was ragged. He wasn't making any sense.

Frankie panicked. She didn't care about him, not really, but what would she do with his cargo? What did she know of horses?

The cat, watching her, stretched slowly. It walked around the bench seat and plopped itself down on her cushion, its shoulder on her thigh. Its shoulder had some heft to it.

Morgan blew out a long, loud breath. "Okay, it's like this. I'm here, in the stable."

"You're in the ship?" Frankie couldn't stop her voice from breaking. She thought she was safe here. Her own ship.

Without thinking, she set her hand on the cat's flank. "Get out," she said. "No, I mean, what is the deal?"

"Okay, okay, I know you're mad, probably. There was sort of a problem with my berth on the passenger ship, and I had to get to Smithson, and there is space here for the jockey to travel with the horses, if necessary. So I took it."

Frankie scowled. Under her palm, the cat rumbled softly. "You didn't have the credits for transit. You stowed away. On my ship."

"You're cleared for passenger transit. I checked."

He hadn't checked. This call wasn't costing him anything.

What a prince.

"Well, thanks for telling me. See you at the station."

"No, don't hang up! Please. Please, I need your help." If anything, he sounded worse now. "Thing is, capsule berths trigger my claustrophobia. It's not long enough, for one, and I have to pretzel myself just to get in."

"You're afraid of enclosed spaces?"

"I thought I was over it. Look, I'm climbing the walls. I'm heaving, and my chest feels like it's going to burst. I'm scaring the horses, and they need to stay calm to pass inspection."

Just his description made Frankie's heart speed up. But what did it have to do with her?

"You know you're okay, right?"

"That is so not helping."

"Fine. How about, get out, roam the cargo hold. Plenty of space there, and good air. It's cold, so bundle up."

A pause. "I was hoping I could come inside?"

"No."

"Just for a little bit? Until I calm down."

Frankie's last wonderful noodles had gone cold. This was her space. She already had unexpected roommates, first Minnie and now this cat whose name she didn't even know. That was enough.

But she also knew the blinding terror of panic attacks. She did not wish them even on her enemies—well, except maybe one of them. This thoughtless man, with his colors and his betting and his all the rest of it, was suffering. He did not know how large a gift he was asking for.

"Captain?" The voice a soft, sad peep.

"Fine." Frankie clenched her hand in the raggedy-soft fur of the stowaway next to her. "I'll meet you at the airlock."

CHAPTER
SEVEN

"I BROUGHT GIFTS." Morgan slid out of the hold, landing neatly on his feet, a duffel bag in one hand and another cross-strapped to his torso. His hair did not gleam, his face did not glow. His hands shook. If Frankie hadn't seen him days ago at Rosings, she would have thought he had a terminal illness.

She was going to have to let him stay.

"Give me that." She reached for the bag in his hand. "Tough enough getting used to gravity again." As she took the bag from him, he grasped her wrist, briefly.

"Seriously. Thank you."

She shrugged it off. "I'm absolutely going to scan your cargo now, contract or no. No more stowaways."

He followed her up the spiral ladder and onto the main floor of the ship's middle segment, only huffing a little. "Actually, the stable has its own gravity."

She stopped mid-stride, turning back to him. "What?"

His head bumped her elbow, and he had to grab for the railing to steady his teeter. "Yeah. I didn't tell you?"

"You know you didn't." Micro-grav systems were known to overheat. And explode. As cargo, they were a must-declare.

"I forgot," he said. "Honest. We're always hauling it around. Never a problem." He did not look contrite. Probably considered it the least of his deceptions. "Anyway, it's freezing in the hold. Nothing's going to overheat in there."

Frankie sighed and stepped the rest of the way up. "No more surprises. Okay?"

He made a big deal of resting on the landing, hands on knees. Marking time. There were more surprises to come, she was sure of it.

"How about this?" he finally said. "You agree not to look me up on the nets, and I'll agree not to look you up." He spread his hands. "Then, no surprises."

"I have nothing to hide," she said, and stopped.

A corner of his mouth pulled up. "A young, obviously university educated, perfect High Galactic speaker, piloting a cargo ship on a backwater route. Nothing to hide?"

He had her. What hay he could make with her checkered history. "Fine. Agreed. What did you bring me?"

"Show me the way to the mess hall, and I'll tell you."

On this floor, two pairs of crew cabins faced each other. She'd stow him in the one across the hall, farthest from her. She didn't look forward to keeping her doors closed, but so it would be.

As she stepped through the inner airlock, she heard that cabin door whoosh shut. Another panel-break? She bumped the floor panel to open the door, stepped in, and looked around. Nothing weird in the main room. She started to back out, and stopped

In the tiny bathroom, the cat was perched on the toilet seat. It scowled at her.

She backed the rest of the way out, crowding Morgan and blocking his view. She would think about that later.

"Change your mind?" Morgan's voice was getting smoother, brighter.

"Already taken. We'll put you here." She kicked the panel by the door across the way and stepped in. No cats, no snakes, no creatures of any kind. She dropped the duffel on the sofa. Morgan lifted the strap from his other bag, and placed it beside the first. He dug around the first bag, and pulled out a brown-wrapped parcel.

"Kitchen?"

"This way." She pointed out the crew showers, the gym, the open room, and the media room. As they neared the open door to her rooms, she saw a row of eight small brown packages lining the wall.

Mice.

She stepped up her pace, and had closed the door by the time Morgan got too close. He bent down to inspect the gruesome display.

"That must be the work of the other stowaway. Dock cat from Rosing Station. Guess it's trying to earn its keep."

He reached to poke at a mouse, and then thought better of it. "Seems like a lot." He was right—no way Minnie was eating eight mice a day. At least Frankie thought not.

She bent for a closer look. The mice didn't just look dead—she now knew what dead mice looked like—they looked aggressively dead. "Why do you think they have that stuff around their whiskers? Goopy ears. But I don't see any giant wounds."

Morgan cast her a glance. "Not my specialty. But I might be able to find out. Got a container?"

They continued to the kitchen. Frankie pulled out the outer bag from her frozen-mouse purchase—not really needed this trip, apparently—and handed it to Morgan. He waved his hand no, thanks.

"No rush. They're already dead. Let's do the fun part first." He presented her with the wrapped package.

Frankie untied the simple string around the plain paper. Inside was a giant bag of peppermint candies. Even the capital cities didn't have such luxury.

"Bought out the kiosk's stash."

She looked at him hard. "That must have been as much as a ticket to Smithson."

He shrugged. His shirt, colors quiet now, whispered with his movement. "I wanted you to be glad you took a risk on me." He leaned against the galley and grinned, more at himself than her. "Your face eating that ice cream. Such bliss."

"You like these, too?"

"I don't know. Never tried." That smile again.

Well. She knew exactly what to do with these. Frankie opened the bag and took two of the thumbnail-sized lozenges out. The rest she put in the freezer. If she wanted another one, she'd have to thaw it out first.

"Then I'll show you the best way to enjoy them." She searched around the cupboard for the special tea. "Thirsty?"

"Indeed."

Tea in pot, hot water in pot. Cups and pot and small dish for the mints, all on a tray. She lifted the tray and turned to head over to her nook. The cat was back, now lounging on the back of the seat in the middle, watching them as if taking measurements.

Frankie set the tray on the table. "Voila. High Tea on the cargo ship Spear."

Morgan, for once, wasn't on her heels. "That's a—" He paused, swallowed. "Cat."

"Stowaway Number One, yes."

"Oh," he looked relieved, who knew why. "It's not yours then." He slid into the seat the cat had taken up this morning as

Frankie prepared their tea. Looked like she had a new place in the nook pecking order.

"It belongs to Rosing Station, I guess. I don't even know its name. It wouldn't let me scan it this morning."

Before she'd even finished the sentence, Morgan had leaned toward the cat. Fast as laser light, he grabbed it behind its head, turned it along his forearm, spread away some fur by its neck, and released it. Both the cat and Frankie stopped, startled.

Then the cat started to lick its paw, all casual. Ignoring it, the move seemed to say. Frankie took its lead and slid into her seat.

"Here's what you do," she said. "Put the mint on your tongue. Don't swallow it! You can suck on it a little to get the flavor going. Take a sip of the tea, let it run over the mint, and swallow that." She showed him.

That first sip brought with it so many memories Frankie thought she might faint. Summer at the beach. Solstice holidays. Extra-special birthday treat, this time only—every time. She closed her eyes. That life had been so sweet.

"That's the face," Morgan said.

She didn't open her eyes until the peppermint itself was a memory.

THE TEA POT WAS COLD, the cat was asleep, and Morgan was reading his tablet when Frankie came back to the present. She straightened in her seat, startled.

Both stowaways looked up. The cat went back to sleep. Morgan glanced at his tablet again, turned it off, and set it down. "Welcome back to this sector."

"My mind did go far away this time." she clasped the tea saucer in two hands. "It was nice."

"So," he started. "About the cat."

"I know! Isn't it a monster. I didn't know they came that big. At least the domesticated kind."

"Right." For some reason, Morgan looked uncomfortable. "It's a girl, which is good because they are usually calmer. She's spayed, so no little monster kitties are coming anytime soon. And her name is Spike."

The cat perked up at the sound of her name.

"Seriously? Can you rename cats?"

"Not if they're not yours, you can't." He tilted his head, teasing. "Besides, your ship is called Spear, and it looks like a mecha snowman. I thought you would like it."

At Frankie's blank look, he lifted his hand and started drawing a picture in the air. "Snowman: big circle for his bottom, medium circle his middle, little circle his head." He punctuated the drawing with single-dot eyes and a wide smile. "What I can't figure out is why we're here in the middle and not in the head."

He didn't know much about cargo ships. "Engine and all the exploding parts are in there. That way, if boom, cargo is safe. Safer."

"We're the protective barrier? Great fun." He stretched his long arms and legs. "Guess I'll go get your critters, then. Take them to the stable. There's a mini-lab in there. It's calibrated for horses, but I'm sure we can dial it down."

He took the bag from where Frankie had left it on the galley counter. "Want to come with? You can see a live horse, up close."

Frankie wasn't ready yet to tense up her muscles to move. "I've seen horses."

"But have you seen galaxy-famous racing stallions? I thought not."

"Yes, I have." She shouldn't have said that, but it was true.

"Where ever did you— ?" He held up his hand. "Nope. We agreed. No delving into backgrounds."

She watched him pass, heard the soft groan of disgust amid the apparent shuffling of dead mice into the bag. "She could have eaten a couple," Morgan said.

"Who knows that she didn't? Eight's a lot." She rested her hands on the cushion to each side of her. Orange wasn't so bad. "You know how to manage the airlock, right?"

"Aye, captain." A pause. "You won't lock it on me, will you?" The waver in his voice was back. He wasn't as serene as he pretended.

"Of course not," she was in the middle of saying when the alarm claxon pierced the air.

Frankie jumped to her feet, bashing into the table. Spike at least landed on her paws on the seat cushion after startling herself aloft.

"What is it?" Frankie shouted at her wristcom as she dragged herself out of the nook, even though the room had good sound pickup. She swiped open the pilot screens, two panels of controls and a wide viewscreen, and searched for red across the gauges.

All green.

She widened the viewer to all cameras, and scanned for incoming trouble. She'd never moved so fast.

Nothing.

"Ship!"

"Cargo hold. Crewmember Minnie. Life signs red. Drone activated, sent for visual."

What could a drone do? Would Minnie even let it touch her?

Frankie was running for the stairs before she remembered Morgan was in the hall. He caught her before she barreled into him, spun, and let her go. "I'll follow."

Down the hall, down the stairs, quick, quick.

"Severe convulsions. Acidosis imminent."

Acidosis wouldn't be so bad, Frankie rationalized as she slammed her hand on the inner door panel. She slipped through before it was fully open and slapped the next panel. "Where? Map on my comm. Hold lights on bright!"

A moment of blindness as every light in the hold powered on. Frankie was nearly off the walkway before she remembered to stomp her boots grav-on. The map showed halfway along, but nearer the hull than the walkway. She got to the spot, and looked down.

Minnie's body floated, unanchored. Whipsawing, as if a giant child had hold of her middle and was shaking her back and forth. She was keening.

Frankie already had the closest emergency box open and was tying the line around her waist. She locked the anchor clip on the railing and stomped off her boots.

Minnie's flailing wasn't stopping. She should be way into acidosis by now, minutes after the claxon.

It was not going to be death throes.

Frankie gauged the distance and angle again, kicked herself over the railing and then turned her boots on. She dropped as fast as a blink.

Aim true, she had hands on Minnie, close to head, close to middle. Together, they landed on the hull.

Minnie wasn't stopping. The snake's eyes were glassy, but she was still keening. Not dead yet. Not going to be dead.

"She's hurt?" Ship had linked Morgan into the comms.

"Sick, I think."

"Bring her to the stables. I'll pull your line there."

Minnie must have roused enough to know Frankie was with her. As they lifted and started to swing toward the stables, the snake pulled its tail in, wrapping it around Frankie's middle. "I'm here," Frankie whispered toward Minnie's head, which she still held a bit away from her. The mouth had foam around it. "We've got you."

Morgan moved quickly, too. As he dropped onto the stable box, and then short-hopped to the hull nearest the smaller opening in his container, he was talking to someone. She hoped it wasn't her, since she wasn't hearing it.

He pulled her in hand over hand. At the container, she tried to grav-on as gently as possible.

"Double entry, but portals, not like yours," Morgan said. "You'll have to step up. He spun the wheel that opened the portal and then swung it wide. Minnie's head crossed the threshold first as Frankie stepped over the short barrier. Morgan held Minnie's tail out of the way as he wheeled the door closed one-handed. Then the second, inner door.

Frankie's gaze was on the snake in her arms and the portal she was stepping through as she entered the space, a bright, brilliant white.

"I've turned all the lights on, sir," a cultured voice said. "And closed the door to the stallions. They shouldn't be able to scent on her."

A synthetic person stood beside the largest examination table Frankie had ever seen. They had a cart of medical-looking implements at their side. Aqua-blue antiseptic gloves on their hands. The mirrored light above the table cast a halo around their head.

"Elvin, this is Captain Styles. Captain, this is Doc Elvin, the best veterinarian in the sector."

Elvin cleared their throat. "With horses," they said, but added, "who move just as much on the table as your friend, there."

Frankie didn't take the time to wonder at a fully-stocked veterinary facility hidden in her hold, nor at the fact that there was, indeed, another stowaway. She held Minnie's head sideways to Elvin, who took it gently. Minnie was still spasming, but more gently. Pulsing rather than thrashing. And still, barely, keening.

Frankie spun slowly in place to unwind her friend, keeping her hands on whatever part was nearby. With Elvin and Morgan's help, she got all of Minnie on the table. Good thing it was so big.

"Captain. you take the head, in case—"

"Minnie," Morgan said.

"In case Minnie can see or smell. She knows you best, and that would make her more comfortable."

Frankie went around the table to the edge closest to the horse-door. She put both hands on Minnie, sending all her most comforting thoughts. Please, please, girl, stay with me. Minnie's eyes were open and glazed. The green-white foam wasn't coming out of her mouth anymore. It had crusted along the sides.

Elvin deftly rearranged Minnie so her coils lay flat, if twitching. He pointed to two spots where Morgan should put his hands. After a moment's hesitation, he did as directed.

Elvin took a tool from the cart and waved it steadily along Minnie's length, starting at the mouth. "Big meal," he said. "I see three new mice at the top of the stomach. One part-digested lower down."

"I gave her that one yesterday."

Elvin kept scanning. "No internal injuries past the meal. Nothing wrong at this end." They set the scanner down and ran their hands along Minnie. "No reaction to touch, here where the meal is, or where it isn't."

Her breaths were slowing, now that the spasms weren't pushing air out. "Hurry," Frankie said.

Elvin nodded. "Something to do with the meal. I don't want to take the time to find out exactly what. We need to get it all out first, then clean up what's already in her system after."

Morgan slid a hand up to cover one of Frankie's. "What do we have to do? Reach down her throat?"

"Surgery. Faster and less invasive. We can get the three out through one cut, and the earlier one through another."

Frankie squeezed Minnie softly. "But can she stand that?"

"We need to sedate her, at least a little bit. She's out right now, but I don't want her moving mid-extraction." Elvin pulled an aerosol can out from the cupboard behind them. "I can't give her this—it will tranquilize a horse. But I think a little spray, and wave it in front of her nose, should do it."

They spritzed a bit onto a giant bandage, and handed it to Frankie. "Don't you breathe too much of it in, either."

Frankie took the bandage and waved it in front of Minnie

twice. Almost immediately, the spasms eased, and her breathing evened out.

Frankie's breathing was not evening out. She pictured the worst as Elvin laid out his scalpel, antiseptics, bandages, and an exceptionally sharp pair of forceps. She swayed. Elvin grabbed her arm.

"I'm fine," she said. "Just, Minnie."

"In process. Morgan, let's put the ether in a bag for now. Top drawer behind you."

Morgan had a bag in seconds, without taking his other hand from Minnie. He flicked it open and held it out for Frankie to drop the bandage in. Once sealed, he handed it back to her and took his place.

"We're going to start," Elvin said. "Captain, can you tell us a bit about Minnie, here?" They used another bandage to sanitize the surgical site.

Frankie looked up at the vet. "She... she conveyed with the ship. Old Peters and her, they've been together a long time. He left last week, and I think she really misses him."

As the blade neared Minnie's body, Frankie shut her eyes tight. She felt a slight pull, but Minnie didn't seem to react.

Morgan cleared his throat. "How can you tell?"

Frankie had to smile. She looked at him, but he shook his head. "One more minute."

"Right." She kept her gaze on him. "Well, I didn't move into captain's quarters until the second day we were on our own. Wanted to change the sheets, air things out, all that." Peters favored some ancient perfume that would only attract selkies.

"We keep most of the doors open, when nobody else is on-ship," she said. "So Minnie doesn't wake us up all the time going in and out of places. I don't know when she came in that night. There's a big tree thing she likes to drape on when she sleeps. When I woke up next morning, I was so comfortable, tucked tight, so warm and cozy. And then I remembered, I was on-ship, in a big bed, by myself."

Morgan choked off a laugh.

"You're right. Minnie was in with me. Under the covers! Snoring like the giant snake she is. Lucky I don't startle so easily."

"Done," Elvin said. "Sealing the cuts now, very small. Stomach sealed easily, and we'll figure something out about these scales."

Minnie's eyelids had closed. Frankie bent closer to feel the snake's breath. Still there.

Elvin swept up his tools and set them aside on the cart. "I think it's the mice. It might be hard to tell, because they're mixed in with gastric juices." They looked at Frankie. "But we'll try."

Frankie reached up to wipe her eyes; they were wet somehow. Both Elvin and Morgan grabbed for her hand. Morgan was fastest.

"Might want to wash the tranquilizer off first. And doc, I think I might have something for you." He pulled the bag of dead mice out of a pocket. "Ship's cat gave us these. No stomach juice: She wisely didn't chew on them first."

"Smart cat," the doctor said. As they went to a corner where the lab must be, Frankie crawled onto the table. She lay along Minnie, touching as much of the snake as she could. She closed her eyes. She was so tired.

A moment later, she felt a soft blanket settle over them both. The bright part of the light over the examination table winked off, but the heat part kept buzzing, sending warmth into the blanket.

She woke halfway to feel Minnie draping herself along top of her. She fell back into slumber, smiling.

FRANKIE OPENED her eyes to find two people sitting in straight-backed chairs, watching her. The human one spoke first.

"You spend a lot of your day with your eyes closed," Morgan said.

She pushed herself up and swung her shins down, and she was seated just as they were, except on a metallic table and with a giant snake draped across her shoulders and into her lap.

"You are not a serious person," she said.

"Captain," Elvin said. We think we know what happened. Approximately." They looked at Morgan.

Morgan rubbed his eyes, which looked almost bloodshot. His hair did not look perfect.

"You want the good news, or the bad?" he said.

CHAPTER
NINE

INFESTATION. Worse, the mice carried some sort of toxin—toxic even to them, apparently.

Elvin raised a screen showing their scientific findings, which only made Frankie's caffeine-deprived brain swim.

Morgan interrupted with words that made sense. "We found the box. The cat led us to it. It was some singleton labeled as coming from Stackfield."

"There was no Stackfield cargo. Is that a coffeemaker over there?"

Elvin rose gracefully and moved to the tiny shelf that must be their entire kitchen in here. They'd dimmed the lights, but the room was still super white and sterile. One room, two-thirds this table she sat on. Two portholes, one over the other, that must be the capsule beds. And a door behind which stomped and snorted two giant mammals. It was easy to see how a person might get cabin fever locked in here, unless they really loved horses.

Plus a synth. She'd think about that news later.

"Single box. Beans?"

She frowned. "Adzuki beans, weird. Last-minute add. Double

rate." Never take cargo you don't know anything about, Old Peters had said. And here she was, proving his point, stowaways galore. Some great captain. She hadn't even had the ship scan the cargo. "But the inspector herself vetted it."

"Did she say that?"

She couldn't remember. "I guess I assumed it was safe. Inspectors inspect, right?" The scent of coffee brewing reached her nose. The pain between her eyes eased. "Anyway, so this box," she prompted.

"The box, so it was designed with corners that the mice could gnaw through. Elvin thinks it took most of a day. Then the critters were free to roam the hold."

Elvin handed her a cup of the blessed brew. Frankie breathed it in, washing away a bit of the panic that was building inside her chest. She took a careful sip, but it was the perfect temperature.

"So the grain is ruined," she said. "Infected." And she was on the hook for its whole cost, since she didn't have portering insurance yet.

"Well, there's your good news," Morgan said, accepting his own saucer of brew. "Thanks, Elvin. Whoever set the trap up got their timing wrong. The mice hadn't made it far out of their cage before they started to die."

"Seizures and spasms," Elvin said. "Like this one, here." They stroked Minnie gently, away from her head. The snake sighed in her sleep.

"So—more good news—Minnie didn't eat any live mice. The toxin took longer to get into her system, even though she downed three of them."

Elvin stroked her again. "And she is clear of it. Temperature steady. Her color should improve within a day, and her energy."

"She's always this color," Frankie said, gazing at Minnie's scales. "Faded rainbow white."

"Even better," Elvin said. They patted Frankie's hand softly, and then turned back to their chair.

Morgan looked impatient at the interruption. "It's a rare toxin, actually plant-based, which is another link to Stackfield."

"But the grain?"

"The grain is fine. Elvin and I scanned it not an hour ago. Spike was guarding the closest crate, and batting any mouse that came near. But we didn't see any live ones there."

Frankie shivered. Close call. Too close. She lifted Minnie from around her shoulders and started the uncoiling process. "We need to check and doublecheck. Could I borrow your scanner? And Elvin, do you have another of those zipped-bags? I could use that for cleanup."

Morgan was faster, pulling out bags. "I'll help," he said. "Need to earn my keep, you know."

Frankie laid Minnie's tail across her coils. "Someone needs to stay with her."

Morgan bumped his fist lightly on Elvin's shoulder. "This guy can do it. Turns out, he doesn't have grav-boots."

"True," Elvin nodded solemnly. "I was quite the flight risk until we got me tethered."

Morgan laughed, as if they were going on a picnic instead of cleaning up a murder scene. "I swear, that Spike gave us such an evil eye when we went to scan the other cargo. Not only infringing on her territory, but in the flopsiest upside-down way you could imagine."

Elvin opened a lower drawer and pulled out a fleeced jacket. He handed it to Frankie, who only then realized she was wearing only her work tunic and leggings. And that she needed to remember Elvin was a he.

"Need to keep your body temperature up," he said. "For Minnie."

MICE WERE EVERYWHERE. Most floated near the box they had escaped, but an intrepid few were near the walls of the hull, bumping against other cargo. A few had even made it to the running lights, as if they were a homing beacon.

"Where are we going to put them all?" Frankie said, looking down at the box from the walkway. Tiny brown bodies everywhere. Farther down, she could see Spike, as advertised, tucked by a handhold on the nearest grain container. That cat deserved a raise.

"Put 'em back in the box they came in." Morgan said. "All the ones in there now are dead. We can seal the opening when we're through." He gazed at her, appraising. Did she look as stupefied as she felt?

"Captain. How about you go scan the cargo again? That will put your mind most at ease, won't it?"

Frankie glared. "Patronizing."

He shrugged. "Am I right?" He pushed himself over the railing and toward the box and its many brown-fuzz satellites.

She did not follow him. He was right. Below the walkway it was easy to tell which way the air currents traveled. Mouse corpses hung along an invisible line from the poison box forward, their numbers thinning the farther they traveled. Frankie dropped off the walkway with grav on, plummeting to the hull beside the first box.

Spike watched her fall, and then poked his head over the edge of the top of the cargo. The container was too tall for Frankie to reach the cat, so she just waved inanely. She should eat something soon. Then she took another look at the cat.

It wasn't shivering. How long had it been in here? Most cats had double layers of fur for warmth, but nothing that would stand against spacer chill.

"You want my jacket?" she said, looking up at Spike. She could have sworn the cat snorted. It moved out of sight.

She should eat something soon and sleep soon. She was starting to hallucinate. And she was talking to a cat.

All the cargo scanned clean. After reading the data on the last box, Frankie sagged against its side. She was okay. Everything, everyone, okay.

Water droplets floated out of the corners of her eyes. She stomped her grav on, and curled into a ball sitting on the hull. This could have gone so much worse. Her carelessness had almost killed Minnie! Frankie did not want any death on her conscience. Not in her life. Any more death.

If she wasn't cut out to be a simple cargo pilot, what was she good for? She'd had such advantages, everyone said. Everyone who didn't know better. She wasn't ready to go out on her own, that was what Beth had said. Did she—and even Morgan, a stranger—know Frankie better than she did herself?

Her comm pinged. Morgan. "We're clear over here. Meet me by the inner hatch?"

"Stables. I need to be with Minnie when she wakes up."

"Elvin has her prepped for travel. We used your red floater-thingy. Big warm horse blankets piled on and everything."

He waited for her to answer.

She couldn't.

Poor Minnie.

"Captain," he said, soft. "We need to get Minnie inside. Get her to her own space, comfortable. Tuck her into bed. Right?"

A shadow moved above her. They were passing on the walkway.

Frankie kicked grav off and went to join them.

She left her tears to float.

FRANKIE LED Morgan to the near elevator, but she took the stairs. By the time he and Minnie were at her suite entry, she had hit the toilet, grabbed a protein drink in the kitchen, and gotten to the bedroom to throw the covers wide enough for a giant snake. Together, they slid the semi-awake Minnie onto the bed, covering her to her chin. The snake tasted the air with her tongue a couple times, and then slid her head under the covers.

Standing by the bed, Frankie sucked down the drink and did a quick scan of the ship's status screens.

"How often do you do that?" Morgan said. He was inspecting Minnie's tree as if he were going to build one, but he must have heard the screens buzz into view.

"Couple times a day."

He looked at her, as intently as the tree. "You've done it at least eight times in the last hour. That I've seen."

She wiped the screens closed with a little more force than usual. "This is all ... a lot. We need to talk, right? But first I need to get my head straight. I'm tired." At the word, her eyelids started to feel even heavier.

He nodded. He ran his hand along one of the tree's branches. "Sleep would do us both good. And Minnie. All of us. Yeah." He hadn't slept much either. His face was pale from an hour in the cargo hold. And he had been in there earlier, while she was with Minnie, finding the mice. Helping save her hide.

But he'd also hidden things. Lied. And she needed to find out why.

Later. Now she needed his help. Again.

"Morgan?" She skirted around the edge of her bed, slipping to the other side. Keeping her eyes on the lump that was Minnie.

"Anything," he said.

"My doors are set to stay open. Would you leave yours open, too? In case I need to call."

He paused so long she had to look up at him.

"Of course," he said, placing his left hand over his heart.

"Thank you," she sighed out. "It's a long push at the top right of the door panel." Of course he knew that, it was standard. She should stop talking.

She sat—sank—onto the bed. After she set the empty shake bag on her nightstand, she didn't know what to do with her hands. They dropped into her lap.

The gray fog was coming in, thick and deep. She needed to divert the mood, not let it reach her. Not let it devour her like it did sometimes. What was happening now was not as bad as that first time, nothing to drop into the abyss for, she told herself. As usual, her mind listened but her heart kept sinking.

A footstep on the office floor. She couldn't even look up.

"I've got hot miso soup," Morgan said. "For people who take their boots off."

That sounded plausible. Frankie lifted a foot and set it on her knee. The lacings were icy but familiar, the touch fasteners zipped open fine. The boot fell to the floor. She dropped her hands into her lap, exhausted. Once she'd admitted how tired she was, the cavernous need for panic-processing, event unravelling, history suppression, opened up.

"Boots. Plural."

She must not have moved fast enough. Morgan was kneeling at her foot, lifting it by the heel, slipping the boot off. Handing her a mug of umami steam.

Miso soup had never tasted so good. Even with the borrowed jacket, she'd been chilled frosty. That must be why her thinking was so slow. She should give the jacket back. As soon as she unzipped it and started to pull an arm out, Morgan was there to make it go faster. Somehow he had taken the mug, as well.

Frankie dropped to her side and wriggled under the covers.

Minnie was so warm.

WHEN FRANKIE AWOKE, Minnie was draped along the higher branches of her tree, dozing. She allowed Frankie to inspect the two incision wounds, which looked fine.

Frankie rested her forehead on her friend's coils. This could have been so, so worse. Who would send sick mice across space? What were the chances a fully stocked veterinary facility would be in her hold at the same time? And where had she seen that white-cloud logo that was on Morgan's jacket before?

The ship's status screens were clear, and Elvin had sent her a message. She fetched the scanner from the miniwagon, which Morgan had left beside an office wall, and ran it down Minnie's length. She sent the results to the vet. Another message pinged.

"Elvin says you're cleared for food, Minnie-min. I'll go heat up a mouse for you." Frankie shook her head at herself. First she gives Minnie a nickname, now she offers to put a dead rodent into her reheater. Guess we're friends now.

She heard Morgan moving in his room as she passed. He did

not come to the kitchen while she warmed the mouse and left it at the base of the tree for Minnie. Giving her space? Hiding?

Whatever, good. Frankie needed to have a private conversation, and it might be better on an empty stomach. Well, except for matcha. She took the small pot with her down the hall to main navigation.

She could pilot the ship from anywhere using her screens, and most of the time it was in long transit it was on autopilot anyway. But sometimes you wanted to touch the panels and turn the keys. And sometimes you wanted a place that wasn't so personal.

Frankie programmed in the ship-to-satellite call, grimacing at the estimate of credits needed. It was worth it, to know. She had to check the local time before trying to figure out what time it was in Stackfield. Almost midnight! Everything off-kilter.

A pause, and the call connected. The first link—ship to satellite—would transmit faster than light. The second—satellite to ground—would be slightly delayed. Memories of trying to reverse-engineer how exactly the system worked threatened to bubble up, but Frankie stamped them down. She needed to focus.

"Frankie? What's wrong?" She didn't see Peters, but his tone was clear. "You know how expensive this is? This call will cost profit off an entire run."

He should stop talking, then. "Listen. How could you load a package of infected mice on my ship?"

"Mice? Is that what you said? I didn't order anything."

Now Frankie wished she'd paid for visual. That would have put her back a whole circuit's profit. "Addressed to you, your new address, in Stackfield. Labeled adzuki beans. Your favorite."

"Shit."

"Why, Peters?" She couldn't keep the hurt out of her voice.

"No! Frankie, no. Believe me. I would never do that to you."

"Minnie almost died." Now her voice did break. "Doing her

job. She ate the poisoned mice." She sniffed back a sob. "We had to cut her open to get them out."

Silence. Then, "My lord. My blooming lord. I know who did it."

"Who, then?"

"Where are you?"

What did that matter? "Halfway to Smithson Station. Ship hit deceleration eight hours ago." They'd been sitting in the kitchen then. So much had happened, in the space of eight hours.

"Two days out, then. Running fast? No, don't answer. That's good." Peters was talking fast, which meant he was thinking fast, which could be good or bad. "You'll be too early for the next pickup. Free a couple of days. Could you meet me at Stackfield Orbital? It will take me as long just to get out there."

She didn't want to see him, even if he didn't try to destroy her cargo and kill her friend. "Can't you just message me?"

"Wouldn't be prudent. Better to meet up. And Frankie?" His voice choked off. He cleared his throat. "I changed my mind. Begging pardon. I want Minnie here. With me."

She was such a fool. Of course, Peters would never harm Minnie. If he'd wanted to sabotage her business, he never—never —would have done it in a way that even hinted at putting Minnie in danger.

"Minnie is fine, now," Frankie said. "She's on her tree—no, she's in the greenroom, basking."

"I will bring her with me when I see you."

CHAPTER
ELEVEN

AS SHE RECONSTITUTED something that called itself NoodleBowlYum, Frankie caught herself checking ship's scanners again. How many times today, already? She had no idea.

She was halfway through the noodles, which had, surprisingly, lived up to their promise, when Morgan entered the kitchen. He, too, looked rested, if a little less put-together than usual. He was wearing the same tunic, still blessedly quiet, but had changed to thicker trousers and crew boots.

Spike followed at his heels. The cat was another puzzle. Why did she stow away? Surely she knew how ships at docks worked. And how had she known not to eat the poison mice?

Morgan opened the breakfast cupboard and inspected its contents. "Okay if I have some of this?" He pulled a packet out and read the label. "Porridge." He moved easily in the confined area, for such a lanky person. He should eat more.

"Have two," she said. "Tea's to the left, coffee's below. There's even some reconstituted juice in the cooler below you. Fruit, but I can't remember which. It's green, but tastes good. There's an open protein chow that Spike likes."

He fed the cat, and then brought her a glass of juice along with his own. Its sharp citrus bite made up for its lack of smell.

She let him eat in peace. She needed to recover from her first hard conversation. What did Peters mean, he knew who did it? Did he have some enemy from the past, shipping toxins without looking to see if Peters was still the pilot? No, the label and manifest both had his new address. She should have noticed that at loading. Should, should, should.

Morgan ate neatly. Capital City manners. She wondered if he'd noticed that about her, too. Deliberately, she lifted her saucer with her wrong hand and drank the dregs of her tea.

He'd already finished his. He lifted his saucer to her—want more? He poured for them both.

"So," he said. "Ask your questions."

Frankie held her saucer in both hands. Its warmth traveled all the way to her wrists.

"First, I want to thank you, and Elvin. Your quick actions and your amazing veterinary lab saved my shipmate's life. We owe you a great debt."

He opened his mouth to speak, but before he could start in, she held up a hand. "And I'm grateful, as well, for your help solving the mouse problem. Without you, and yes, you too, Spike"—the cat was rubbing itself against her shins—"my cargo would have been ruined. People would have gone hungry."

The cat jumped onto the cushion next to Frankie, settled in, and looked at her expectantly. Frankie stroked her head and the soft tufts of her ears. "Thank you, Spike." She leaned back up, and Spike started cleaning her whiskers. She looked at Morgan.

"But," he said.

"But. How did you know to bring a veterinary facility onto the ship? Why this ship? How did you know what was wrong so fast. Wait, there's more."

"No," he interrupted. "I can answer those right away. I did

not know anything about anything to do with your shipping. I swear to you. I got kicked off my transport and I knew you were young and hungry."

"How did you know anything about me?"

"I didn't! No, seriously. Everyone can tell. Your captain's tag is still shiny. You need to dull it a little if you want to be taken for an old-timer."

Frankie glanced down at the tag. He was right.

"I did not bring poison onto your ship," he said.

Right. "But you brought an undeclared micro-gravity device. Otherwise, the stable would have no gravity." Micro-grav units, some as small as a miniwagon, were extremely rare—and extremely prone to overheating and exploding. Frankie had never dreamed she'd encounter one.

"It's freezing in the hold. Nothing's going to overheat." Morgan stopped. Frankie waited him out in silence. It took a full minute.

"You're right. I should have told you. But I needed to get to Smithson. I had to! This deal is the end of my career in horse-trading. I need it to stay in the black. I absolutely need it." He turned his palms up, shrugging. "I regret the error."

She'd come back to that. "In addition, you contrived to bring onboard a person who is considered illegal in Cooperative space."

"Elvin's not illegal. He has papers showing he's part of an experimental cohort."

Frankie crossed her arms. "Of veterinarians?"

"No, of course not." He ran his fingers through his hair, both sides at once. It reminded Frankie of a swimmer pulling out of the water and onto the side of the pool, pushing the water from their face. But his face didn't look so serene.

"Yes, he shouldn't be out here. He's supposed to stay at home, on the compound. But he's still legal! Only, it's better if no one knows about him."

Frankie shook her head. "Then why is he even out here?"

"He's a great vet! I need him to, um." He paused. "Keep the horses healthy. Perfect."

"You're doping the horses!" She slammed her hands on the table. Morgan jumped. Spike opened an eye and closed it again. Frankie didn't know much about horse races, but she did know that many kinds of enhancement were forbidden in contests of that kind. "You're using Elvin's skills, and his precarious situation, to force him to do something illegal for you."

Morgan looked sheepish. "Kind of. But not really! It's not illegal, just a little to the side of the rules. You know, if you read them strictly."

"Elvin does it, and you have deniability. Your hands stay clean." Frankie didn't know why the idea made her so bitter.

"It's not like that." He was a bad wheedler. "Well, it is, but not exactly. I can explain."

She shut that off with a wave of her hand. "I won't tell anyone about your 'friend.' But I want that exploding grav-box out of my hold first we get to Smithson. And you, too."

"And you," she leaned over to stroke Spike again. "You get one more run, then off."

There were way too many beings on this ship. She couldn't wait to be alone.

CHAPTER
TWELVE

ONE COULD HAVE DESCRIBED the next two days aboard the Spear as calm if one ignored the undercurrents of regret and distrust that wafted throughout the ship.

Elvin had politely declined Frankie's offer to bunk in the main segment. He said it was because he preferred to keep a close eye on the horses. If there even were any horses. He probably didn't want to be around Morgan, who held the synth's safety in his careless, thoughtless, hands.

Frankie scanned the cargo three times a day, to be absolutely sure. She could not seem to stop herself from continually checking the system-scan screens. She'd deal with that compulsion after the trip.

Once, she found Minnie coiled up next to the floor panel for the outer portal to the cargo hold. The snake quivered. Frankie knelt and set her palms on her friend.

"Don't want to go in there? I don't blame you a bit." She stroked the white-of-all-colors length, so solid, so warm. She hadn't eaten the first mouse Frankie had left, rolling it underneath the miniwagon. But the second one, this morning, had disappeared.

"You're off the job, Minnie. I'm taking you to live with Old Peters. You'd like that, wouldn't you?" Frankie tugged Minnie gently to uncoil. "Up, up."

Minnie unraveled from the floor and raveled up Frankie's torso and arms. Thus precariously balanced, Frankie pushed to stand. She walked her friend to the greenroom. The humidity hit them both like a tonic.

Minnie dropped into her nest and settled in. Frankie looked at the nest enviously.

Where was her own safe nest?

FRANKIE WAS INITIALING the manifest for the assistant dockmaster when Morgan walked off the ship through the dock entry, together with his cargo. The cargo traveled on, but he stopped beside her and waited for her to be free.

After she acknowledged him, he bowed prettily. "Thank you for your hospitality—and generosity. I know I was not the most well-behaved guest." He gestured toward the cargo, now being diverted to a side pier. "Would you like to observe the inspection? Make sure you get paid, and all."

After all that had happened, Frankie was still curious about the horses. What were they like? How could they possibly put up with space travel? In her limited experience of them, horses didn't like anything out of the ordinary. Space travel was out of the ordinary to the Nth degree. She nodded, yes.

"One more question," she said as they walked side by side. Morgan had to hitch his stride so she could keep up. "That jacket I borrowed. It had a familiar logo, but I couldn't place it. Is it where you work?"

He winced. "Hoped you hadn't seen that. I used to work there, a while back. Not now. That company is long gone and best forgotten. I'm surprised you recognized it."

"I didn't, exactly. What was the name of it, again?"

Morgan was waving at a person even taller than he was, and in finer clothes. "My buyer. Excuse me a moment."

Frankie stopped, frozen for a moment. Her face went blank. A Skoll. Not one of the two who had harassed her on Rosings, but a more important one.

Morgan hadn't told her a Skoll was the buyer. She didn't care for that omission.

The Skoll saw her, and smiled. "Captain!" they said, closing the gap between them. "Pleasure to meet you. Such an improvement over that bent-back Old Peters."

A rude Skoll. Shocking. Frankie did not smile.

Morgan stepped up. "Frankie, this is Skoll Shara. I take it, Shara, you already know of Captain Styles."

"The captain has something that belongs to us." The Skoll's smile twisted. "We hope she finds herself ready to return it now, after—shall we say—such a difficult trip."

Frankie struggled to keep her composure. The Skolls. Steer clear, Old Peters had said, and she'd tried. They hadn't steered clear of her.

They could have easily bribed the dockmaster on Rosings— they owned half the station. They knew Peters was gone and could easily have found his new address. They knew the Spear was carrying grain.

They couldn't have known about Minnie.

The Skoll took her nonresponse as a cue to keep talking. "And your stalwart companion? Snakes make such good mousers, don't you agree?"

They knew.

Frankie saw red.

Morgan stepped directly between the two, holding a hand up at each of them. She glared at him. Didn't he see what they had done?

"Great to meet, everyone. And here's the examiner now. How about we go and get this done, and the captain can watch with the rest of the crowd?"

Frankie noticed the crowd for the first time. A good hundred people, seated to the side of what must be a viewing area. Drone cameras and two live reporters had the spots directly in front. Only the up-high rows of seats were still empty. She took the back stairs to get to them, avoiding Skoll Shara, who seated themself in the first row.

So these were horse people. They looked like regular people, with really nice boots. Maybe a little overintense in their expression. Their gazes were all rigidly fixed on the two horses stepping nervously out of Morgan's container.

And rightly so. Frankie had never seen such beautiful horses. Browner at the head shading to black at the other end, they were a matched pair. Morgan, tall as he was, barely came up to their withers. Coats so shiny! Elvin must have done something there.

At the thought of the synth, Frankie pulled her gaze away from the action and toward the container. The doors were already shut. Morgan had led the pair out, and stood alone with them as they were scanned, prodded, and, apparently, found acceptable. The inspector nodded and noted something on their tablet. They shook Morgan's hand.

Skoll Shara rose and joined them. Another handshake. Morgan handed the horses' reins to the Skoll, a process that took longer than it should because they had to wait for the photographers to get the shot. The Skoll quickly transferred the reins to a small person, probably a jockey, who led them toward a type of entry Frankie hadn't seen before, for animals.

Morgan was watching the trio intently. As they passed

through the opening, which was thick like it had a scanner embedded, his shoulders eased. He looked at his wristcom and nodded.

Show over for now, the people in the stands dispersed quickly. It wasn't all that warm on the docks. Frankie stayed where she was, browsing through all the horse-related products and services advertised in the local feed. She heard someone coming up the back stairs.

Morgan sat on the same bench Frankie sat on, a couple people's width away. He didn't look at her. He made a show of wiping something from his wristcom toward her. She felt the ping, and saw the payment notification.

Still not looking at her, Morgan leaned his elbows on the bench above them. "I've a bit of a problem," he started, and stopped.

Frankie looked away. So many beautiful personal craft in the near docks. The Spear had already been ordered to vacate their inner slip before the next shift, in a few hours. "Not my problem," she said.

"I understand. I do. But I fear for my friend. Our friend."

Frankie leaned back herself. She blew out a long breath. "Fine. I'll take the container, and all it contains, back to Rosings. Standard fee."

"No hazard surcharge?"

How dare he sound amused. "I studied up on that, ah, propulsion system of yours. As you say, overheating is the only risk. Not fair to charge you."

"Not fair," he said slowly. He sat up to use his wristcom. Another payment pinged to Frankie.

She stood, facing away from him. "I'll get it loaded right away. The Spear can't stay in inner dock, so I'm taking her to Stackfield system to wait until my cargo—my other cargo—is ready."

She heard Morgan stand, turn away, turn back toward her. "Captain. Frankie." Even as her brows rose at the familiarity, she turned without thinking.

"Thank you," he said. "I mean it. It was so … nice to take a trip as just a person, not an Infamous Name. Yes, even though half of it was in a terrifying capsule cabin." He held his hand out to her.

She had to take it. They were in business together.

"Nice while it lasted," he said.

"It was nice to meet you, too," she said, on automatic. Then amended, "Well, interesting."

His laugh was warm as ever. "Safe travels."

"Clear skies," she said.

CHAPTER
THIRTEEN

STACKFIELD ORBITAL STATION hadn't changed in the two weeks since Frankie had set Old Peters down on it. A tiny hub with giant docks attached and spinning, a geostationary albino spider. It was best to come in directly from above, if you were a spacer; below, if you were a groundling.

Frankie had already sent in all the many documents to allow formal entry to the planet for a pale giant snake. Minnie's head-only eyes-front-and-open photo was only a little blurry. Once again, Elvin and his lab were a blessing: He could perform all thirteen required tests and supply the results in the proper formats. Minnie was already conditionally approved for immigration by the time the Spear had moored. No quarantine needed.

The adjutant dock chief met them at their berth, peered briefly into Minnie's industrial strength carry crate, and signed off. He looked more askance at the tree.

"It's art," Frankie said. She and the very helpful little bot had managed to get it down into the hold and levered it rather precariously onto the red miniwagon. Minnie's crate had its own slight propulsion, little puff-jet boosters that kept her comfortable when the ship did slingshot maneuvers and the like.

Frankie signaled the hatch to close and lock. She hoped that this wasn't a place that scanned ships without permission. Most stations this far out were live-and-let-live. Closer to Central, you couldn't be sure. Elvin couldn't hide, exactly, he said, but he could stay very still and turn his temperature down.

"I do have the proper papers, remember," he'd said in the lab as he was busy convincing Minnie he did not have a needle and was not about to draw blood.

"Yes, but. Papers." She'd searched for words. "What if they don't ask before they shoot?" Synthetic humans like Elvin were banned, on point of death. For the first time, she wished Morgan was here. To talk her down. To talk dock security down. Just to talk.

"I understand." Elvin said, blood competently obtained. He turned away from her to set the needle in the test kit. "You would not be blamed if I were apprehended, in any case."

"Who cares about that!" Maybe she should, but he'd saved Minnie and therefore was the Hero of the Spear. "I worry about everyone on my ship." She squeezed Minnie so hard she squeaked in protest.

Elvin turned back. He set a rubber-gloved hand over Frankie's. "I am worried, too. But this is not the first trip like this I've taken. How does Morgan put it? Ah. The odds of success are stacked in our favor. It would be dumb not to play."

Yet again, he had politely declined her offer to bunk in the warmth and space of the center segment; this time he gave no reason. So she left him there, in his shining bright caravan in the cargo hold.

Frankie was barely past the gate into the station proper when she saw Old Peters. He didn't look so old now. Already his spacer pallor was less. He had a new chair that looked like it had little boosters as well as wheels.

He looked guilty.

He spoke first. "Frankie! And my so, so pretty Minnie, too," he cooed at the crate. Minnie launched herself at the latched opening. "Give us a minute to get away from the scaredy-cats. I know a place." He looked past the crate. "And the reptile stand, too?"

He did not look her in the face. His gaze darted everywhere else.

"I thought she should have it. I sure won't be using it." Frankie looked at it again from his point of view. "Might need to ship it separately."

"Maybe not. We'll call it art." He pivoted and rolled to the left. "Arboretum's this way. Best spot on the station."

Nearly every station had a greenroom, but few had devoted a full one-third of its area to plant life as had Stackfield Orbital. The station's profit came from selling healthy cuttings and seedlings to ships for their own greenrooms.

The arc of the hull here was made of some almost transparent material. The local sun shone down, bathing the trees and bushes. Deeper in, the flora grew shorter, grasses and flowers. In the center sat a pond big enough for small people to float in foot-powered boats shaped like swans. Peters took them slightly away from the families and toward a clearing of grasses between tall trees. He'd been here before—he beelined straight for an almost-hidden bench in dappled shade.

Frankie hadn't left the dock when she'd dropped Peters off. "I can't believe you didn't tell me about this. I would have hopped off for a minute."

"You couldn't slow down. I never saw a baby captain so eager to get to a grain depository." Peters pushed out of his chair and bent to Minnie's crate.

The latch clicked open, and Minnie flowed across Peters' arm, over his shoulders, around his chest, and back again. Her happy-scarf move.

Peters staggered at the force, but caught his balance, chuckling. He let Frankie take his arm and help him get settled on the bench. Minnie's head swiveled back and forth, tasting the mesmerizing mixture of scents. She even tasted Frankie's hair when she didn't get out of the way fast enough.

Frankie powered down the crate and the wagon, and then sat next to Peters. The clearing was almost empty of people; just a few nappers on a blanket in the sun. Moist air kissed her face. She breathed it in deep. The place was calming her.

She wasn't sure she wanted to be calm.

Peters wasn't going to talk, so Frankie started. "Tell me."

"I'm so sorry, Frankie. I didn't think this would happen. Never in a billion years."

She stretched her arms out, so the sun's light touched the back of her hands.

"The Skoll," he started, and stopped.

She waited, a slow count of thirty. "The Skoll," she said, looking up at a tree that appeared to be a perfect triangle. "Steer clear, you said."

"Already too late for that, I guess."

She dropped her gaze to Peters. He was trying to look at her, almost succeeding. "Did you really agree to sell out to them?" she said.

"No!" His gaze briefly met hers. "But the way they talk, of understandings, of agreements. I said I wasn't interested. I stayed under the radar."

She set her hands on her thighs and stretched out booted feet out to the light. "Why do they even care?"

"They don't. I don't think they do. Thing is, they're collectors.

They want everything. There were two of us, holdouts. We thought they'd forget. The routes aren't that big."

Minnie flowed down Peters's legs and out into the sun-warmed grass in front of them. She kept hold of his ankle, though. Peters sighed.

"The other one, Smalls, she sold out a little bit ago. The pressure on me went up. But you were here, better than the Skoll. They don't even like snakes."

"And you didn't tell me this—why?"

He faced her directly. "I talked to them, I did. Explained the situation. You were no threat; you weren't going to poach any Skoll cargo. They didn't need to worry."

They weren't worried. Frankie slid off the bench to sit beside Minnie. The smells were stronger here: grass, loam, wet dog. A hint of lavender or rose? Minnie must be in heaven, after all the years of dulled scents off-planet.

She looked back at Peters. Old Peters, kindly, solicitous, too trusting. "Why didn't you sell?"

His face went fierce. "Why should I? Why should they have such a monopoly? We're the Cooperative, right? We work to the benefit of all, or however that goes."

To one, to all. Frankie had heard the motto all her life. Nearly every day as a child, despite not living on a fully invested Cooperative planet. When she did move, all the way to Central Planets, she heard and saw it constantly.

It had never been true.

"You need to sell, Frankie." Peters sounded defeated. "They'll kill you, and make it look like it was your fault. Just like this time."

Frankie threw herself back on the grass. She had to cover her eyes with a forearm; already the sun had burned red spots in her vision.

"No," she said.

"You can't win. Now that I see how this played out, I can see that they've done this kind of thing before. They said Smalls had a heart attack and needed to retire. Suddenly, she had a nice place on-base, after her pacemaker surgery. There were other times, too."

"I don't want to. Like you said, they shouldn't win." She was sick of venal people succeeding while good people suffered. When would it end?

"They only want the contract. They'll give up the Spear. You could find something else. You're so clever. You can make it work anywhere."

Move systems? Galaxies? With what bankroll? She was in the black, thanks to Morgan, but only just. And nothing in savings. She could beg from Beth; her friend had her own settlement nest egg.

But once she admitted to Beth that she couldn't make it on her own, that would be it. Any help from that end would come with strings attached. Not just strings, but thick cables. Beth would insist that Frankie stay in Central system. Where Frankie absolutely did not wish to be.

Minnie must have sensed Frankie's shifting mood. A heavy coil thumped onto her belly like a friendly punch. "You too? Fine. I'll think about it."

Peters let out a breath. "Best I could hope for."

Later, Frankie walked with them to the departure lounge. Peters had to buy an extra one-way ticket for the tree, which, while art, also took up a person's worth of room on the shuttle and so counted as a person. Peters said his friend would pick him up at the landing with their own miniwagon.

"Creek still wasn't too sure about bunking with Minnie," he said. "But once I told him about the stand—I called it a tree, like you do—he's all onboard. Says it will be our conversation piece."

Frankie took the long way back to the ship so she could walk through the whole of the garden. She was tempted to swipe a couple blades of grass, but she let the lawn be.

CHAPTER
FOURTEEN

FRANKIE COULDN'T SLEEP. As the Spear piloted itself back to Smithson Station, she prowled the halls on main deck and upper and lower decks, too. She watched the bots clean the stairwell. She checked all the filters. She just kept moving.

She decided that the cat was avoiding her. She'd heard the door slide, and glimpsed Spike's tail heading toward "her" toilet. But that was all she'd seen of her the rest of the day and night. The half a gravy-boat dinner Frankie had left out was gone, though.

Once, she tried the cargo space. She left the walkway retracted, so it would be even more like flying in space. She kicked off near the entry door and flew, flew, flew to the far end of the hull. She stopped, feet first, on the hull, and then flew back.

Something was missing.

Frankie thought about inviting Elvin up for a game of—what? Synths were supposedly super geniuses. Besides, he'd been pretty clear about liking to be alone.

She liked to be alone, too. Or so she'd thought.

Doing the rounds inspecting all the escape pods, most of

which looked surprisingly similar to Morgan's jockey-sized sleeping capsules, a thought struck her. She'd never really been alone—absolutely by herself. Never, since she came to Cooperative Space. She couldn't remember much before then.

Even when she thought she was finally on her own, she'd had Minnie. And then the circus of stowaways. But now, finally, she had what she'd thought she always wanted.

The capsule in the pilot's station blinked green for good. Frankie opened the seal to check inside anyway. It opened along its length, like a coffin. She stared at it for a while, and then crawled in. Surprisingly plush, but it could use a pillow. Maybe a blanket.

She pulled the lid halfway down, telling herself it was a test to see how claustrophobic she was. She curled up, wrapping her arm around her knees.

She wasn't sure how long she'd been there when Spike jumped into the capsule. The cat lay where her legs should be, with its shoulder propped up on her butt. She started to purr. Soon they were both asleep and dreamless.

WAITING for a peppermint to thaw so she could have some tea, Frankie read through the Skoll shipping contract once again. The offer was still in the trades and offers database; the family had not retracted the one they'd sent earlier. Not even to lower the price. Clearly an oversight Frankie felt easy about taking advantage of.

The terms and clauses for the trade looked the same as those in the contract she had signed with Old Peters. This one was only for the portering contract, like they'd said. Nothing about the Spear itself.

She could sign it remotely, the database office person's

message said. They'd just seen her in the office a month ago, so felt confident she still was who she said she was.

They must also be in the Skoll family's pocket.

Frankie took a deep breath, signed the contract, and sent it. She checked the ship's sensor screens again, and then shut down all screens. She put the peppermint in her mouth and took the teapot and saucer to the greenroom. Minnie's nest turned out to be too disgusting to lounge on, so Frankie sat with her back to the wall, next to the baby-tomato vines. It was misting time for the tomatoes; she didn't mind being misted too. She savored the tea through her mint, and celebrated her return to solvency.

She'd pick up the Smithson cargo, and finish the route at Rosing Station. Drop Spike off there, and then… see.

The tea was gone, the peppermint melted into memory, when the comm pinged. Probably notice that the contract had been co-signed. Frankie turned her screens back on. Not just the contract, but notice that the Smithson shipment was cancelled.

No reason to go there, then. That much closer to the end of her glorious—meteoric, really—career as an outer rings cargo hauler.

She should change their heading to Rosing Station. Take Elvin home, all the way, not just to the station. What else did she have to do?

Have another peppermint.

She was at the kitchen counter staring at a single peppermint, trying to decide if she really needed to wait for it to thaw, when the satellite-to-ship call came.

WHEREVER MORGAN WAS, it was loud.

"Sorry!" he shouted. "Wait." The other sounds cut off abruptly. "Now I'm in the toilet. Connection still good?"

"Hello?"

"Listen, Frankie. Where are you? Want to come down to Smithson Prime? The race is tonight, and the place is already rollicking."

"Where are you? Why?" Frankie checked her charts. ETA Smithson thirty-five minutes. She'd moped the whole trip away.

"I'm in the Skolls' box seats here at the track."

"No. Absolutely not." Frankie said.

"Wait, listen! You are golden with the Skolls now. I talked with them, and they understand."

"Understand what? That I sold them the portering contract?"

"You did?" The surprise in his voice made Frankie wince. Some tough pilot she was. "Okay, never mind," he said. "We can sit in the regular stands, no problem. But you do want to see my horses race, don't you?"

She kind of did, she had to admit. See the culmination of this crazy idea of shipping horses around the universe. But it would mess with her schedule.

What schedule? For a moment, she'd forgotten that all her calendar days were now big empty boxes. A trip down planet would delay her inevitable return to the Inner Worlds.

Still.

"I don't have passage. And I can't afford it anyway."

"You just got paid! Hold on." The connection blasted noise again for almost a whole minute. Frankie used the calculator on her screen to determine how much this pause was costing Morgan. Almost the same as a shuttle ride.

The noise cut off. "I'm back. Skolls have an atmo-hopper at Smithson you can borrow. I said you were a pro pilot. You do know how to fly it, right?"

Frankie rolled her eyes. Atmo-hoppers were what everybody trained on. Except Morgan, apparently. "I'm coming into the station now. Where is the hopper berthed." Silence. "What are the berth coordinates?"

Morgan understood that, and gave the coordinates. "Go to the landing nearest the track, Smithson Number Eight. When can you be here?"

"What's the rush? You said I had a few hours."

"Ours is the last race, the marquee event. You'll want to see the earlier ones so you can compare."

Was she really a person who just ran off and went to the races?

She was now.

———

THE HOPPER WAS where Morgan had said it was. It was bigger—rated for twenty people, not six—but it flew like all the others Frankie had ever piloted.

Smithson Eight looked like a child's dream flycraft play set. Hoppers and standard planes of all shapes and sizes were parked along the tarmac and covering the dirt packed fields around the two landing zones. She pitied the poor person who had to keep track of whose was where.

She slowed and touched down softly. Easy. She powered down and waited for the tower to tell her where to park. She couldn't see the truck that would tow her. She could hop there, sure, but with this much flyware parked in, she expected nobody was being allowed to do that.

The hull door popped open, and Morgan fell in. She could smell the new burn on his palm from the superheated handle.

"Power up! I got the door." He scrambled to his knees and grabbed the inner handle with his unburned hand.

"What's the berth?"

"No! Take off! I need to get off this planet. Sooner is better, Frankie."

She powered back up. The craft was still warm, but the process would still take a few minutes. Then she stopped, and turned. "I thought we were going to the races?"

"Tell you later." He raced down the aisle of the main cabin and thew himself into the copilot's seat. He started strapping in.

"Tell me now."

His hair hung lank. The only color on his face was a mild burn from sun across his cheekbones and the hairline above his forehead. He stared out the side window toward the terminal.

"I don't see anybody," Frankie said. She flicked a lever, changing her scans. "No humanform readings nearby."

"Everybody's at the races. They left a bot in charge here, can you believe it?" His breathing had not slowed. Frankie thought she could see his pulse in the shadow movement of the skin at his temple. Now he watched the engine readings, tracing their rise into the green. He grabbed the copilot's headset. At speed, they were really going to need the noise protection.

"Go, go, go!"

Frankie set her ship's beacon to warn of liftoff. She scanned the skies with her instruments and her eyes. She reversed her course on the navigation screen and checked that it would work. Not three seconds had passed.

"Quick like a bunny!"

All clear. Frankie pushed the throttle, and the hopper actually leaped off the ground. She pushed the engines hard, to cool off the hull as much as she could as well as reach breakthrough velocity. The force pushed them both deep into the chairs.

Morgan still managed to run his hands through his hair, headset and all.

When they broke atmosphere, and all the noise had eased off, Frankie turned to him.

"Now."

He set the headset back in its cradle. "I told them I was expecting you in three hours, an hour before race time. So, we have"—he checked his wristcom—"two and a half hours to get out of this sector."

Chapter

Wherever Morgan was, it was loud.

"Sorry!" he shouted. "Wait." The other sounds cut off abruptly. "Now I'm in the toilet. Connection still good?"

"Hello?"

"Listen, Frankie. Where are you? Want to come down to Smithson Prime? The race is tonight, and the place is already rollicking."

"Where are you? Why?" Frankie checked her charts. ETA Smithson thirty-five minutes. She'd moped the whole trip away.

"I'm in the Skolls' box seats here at the track."

"No. Absolutely not." Frankie said.

"Wait, listen! You are golden with the Skolls now. I talked with them, and they understand."

"Understand what? That I sold them the portering contract?"

"You did?" The surprise in his voice made Frankie wince. Some tough pilot she was. "Okay, never mind," he said. "We can sit in the regular stands, no problem. But you do want to see my horses race, don't you?"

She kind of did, she had to admit. See the culmination of this crazy idea of shipping horses around the universe. But it would mess with her schedule.

What schedule? For a moment, she'd forgotten that all her calendar days were now big empty boxes. A trip down planet would delay her inevitable return to the Inner Worlds.

Still.

"I don't have passage. And I can't afford it anyway."

"You just got paid! Hold on." The connection blasted noise again for almost a whole minute. Frankie used the calculator on her screen to determine how much this pause was costing Morgan. Almost the same as a shuttle ride.

The noise cut off. "I'm back. Skolls have an atmo-hopper at Smithson you can borrow. I said you were a pro pilot. You do know how to fly it, right?"

Frankie rolled her eyes. Atmo-hoppers were what everybody trained on. Except Morgan, apparently. "I'm coming into the station now. Where is the hopper berthed." Silence. "What are the berth coordinates?"

Morgan understood that, and gave the coordinates. "Go to the landing nearest the track, Smithson Number Eight. When can you be here?"

"What's the rush? You said I had a few hours."

"Ours is the last race, the marquee event. You'll want to see the earlier ones so you can compare."

Was she really a person who just ran off and went to the races?

She was now.

THE HOPPER WAS where Morgan had said it was. It was bigger—rated for twenty people, not six—but it flew like all the others Frankie had ever piloted.

Smithson Eight looked like a child's dream flycraft play set. Hoppers and standard planes of all shapes and sizes were parked along the tarmac and covering the dirt packed fields around the two landing zones. She pitied the poor person who had to keep track of whose was where.

She slowed and touched down softly. Easy. She powered down and waited for the tower to tell her where to park. She couldn't see the truck that would tow her. She could hop there, sure, but with this much flyware parked in, she expected nobody was being allowed to do that.

The hull door popped open, and Morgan fell in. She could smell the new burn on his palm from the superheated handle.

"Power up! I got the door." He scrambled to his knees and grabbed the inner handle with his unburned hand.

"What's the berth?"

"No! Take off! I need to get off this planet. Sooner is better, Frankie."

She powered back up. The craft was still warm, but the process would still take a few minutes. Then she stopped, and turned. "I thought we were going to the races?"

"Tell you later." He raced down the aisle of the main cabin and thew himself into the copilot's seat. He started strapping in.

"Tell me now."

His hair hung lank. The only color on his face was a mild burn from sun across his cheekbones and the hairline above his fore-head. He stared out the side window toward the terminal.

"I don't see anybody," Frankie said. She flicked a lever, changing her scans. "No humanform readings nearby."

"Everybody's at the races. They left a bot in charge here, can you believe it?" His breathing had not slowed. Frankie thought she could see his pulse in the shadow movement of the skin at his temple. Now he watched the engine readings, tracing their rise into the green. He grabbed the copilot's headset. At speed, they were really going to need the noise protection.

"Go, go, go!"

Frankie set her ship's beacon to warn of liftoff. She scanned the skies with her instruments and her eyes. She reversed her course on the navigation screen and checked that it would work. Not three seconds had passed.

"Quick like a bunny!"

All clear. Frankie pushed the throttle, and the hopper actually leaped off the ground. She pushed the engines hard, to cool off the hull as much as she could as well as reach breakthrough velocity. The force pushed them both deep into the chairs.

Morgan still managed to run his hands through his hair, headset and all.

When they broke atmosphere, and all the noise had eased off, Frankie turned to him.

"Now."

He set the headset back in its cradle. "I told them I was expecting you in three hours, an hour before race time. So, we have"—he checked his wristcom—"two and a half hours to get out of this sector."

"WE?" Frankie said. She swiped the Spear's screens into view and started its ready-launch sequence.

"I sort of implied we were together. To get them to let you on the planet." Morgan rubbed his face with his hand. "I sort of implied we were a couple. Lovers. Sorry."

Frankie blinked that information straight into her brain's buffer. She'd think about that later.

"So, the deal is, the horses, their hearts aren't exactly right. One or the other may win this race, but if they do, they might have a heart attack before they get to the winner's circle. Or soon after. More likely they'll start to feel bad, and wash out altogether. When that happens, the Skolls will be unhappy. And we should be gone before that."

"But we're going to Rosings. Where all the Skolls live."

"Yeah, we should probably change that." He pointed out the window toward a gray circle in the distance. "We should take the jump-tunnel."

"Jump? Where?" Not to mention the usual backup at jump

tunnels. She would have needed to put in the request hours ago to get a spot soon.

"Doesn't matter."

"It really does, for a jump-tunnel."

"Dyad System, then. It's close but not Rosings." He watched her call up the tunnel authority and start the permission process. "I forgot that part."

"You are not a shit-together person," Frankie said.

The screen to Smithson station blinked green. "Prepare for dock."

She did not put the hopper back in its proper slot, but parked it at the pier right next to the Spear. There was no chance of hiding their tracks anyway. Frankie jumped and Morgan tumbled out of the hopper and up the pilot's ramp.

"Find the cat," she ordered as she sat down in the pilot's chair. "She needs to be secure by the time we hit the tunnel." She told Ship to send Spike's coordinates to Morgan's comm. "Tell Elvin, too."

Then all her attention was taken up arguing with tunnel authority that no, they did have a transit pass already and how could it have gone missing, and she had important live cargo that had to be moved at fastest possible velocity. The phrase actually was "fastest practical velocity," but nothing about this situation was practical.

Her Art of Persuasion class at university actually paid off: They had a "replacement pass" for only an hour from now. Barely enough time for them to get to the gate itself.

CHAPTER
SEVENTEEN

THE SPEAR WAS ten minutes from the gate, and third in the queue, when the Skolls caught up to them. The ship closing in on them was shaped like a Galactic Patrol cruiser, but wasn't behaving like one. But it could still override Frankie's too-basic communications locks.

"Spear: Stand down. Await boarding." The blast of sound rebounded through the halls and rang in Frankie's ears. She pushed her earphones down around her neck but kept the microphone close. She punched in the patrol transmit code. "Patrol: Assistance needed. Right at the gate at Smithson station." It was an open-channel call. The Skolls would hear it, too. She kept the Spear aimed straight for the jump-tunnel.

"Spear: Stand down or we will shoot. Show us the engines powering down."

Frankie cut the engines in half, which, since they had been decelerating to gate speed, actually boosted the distance between the cruiser and the Spear. They were going to rocket through the tunnel. If they got there.

The message was a full minute delayed. "Patrol acknowledged. Cruiser fifteen minutes out."

So much for that. "Acknowledged. Thank you." The Galactics would be able to cite the Skolls for impersonating an official patrol, maybe, after they cleaned the wreckage of the Spear out of the travel lane.

The second-to-last ship winked through the gate, and the one before their slot moved into position. Frankie was headed straight at that position, no side-tracking. She hoped the very nice midsize pleasure cruiser knew how to set up a quick jump.

She was programming the jump on one screen while keeping an eye on the fake cruiser on another when Morgan stomped in. "Give me communications," he said, dropping into his seat and strapping in.

"That panel has it already, top right. Where is Spike?"

"Isn't she here? I told her to come up. We were in the kitchen, and then she left." He was searching for main comms for the Skoll cruiser with one hand and holding a bunch of pita chips in the other. "Want some?"

Her hands were full, but somehow she managed to flick on all-call. "Spike the cat: Report to the pilot's galley now. Elvin the doc: Please strap in. You have full ship's-view access."

"You know the cat doesn't speak Galactic, right?" Morgan didn't wait for an answer. He cleared his throat and opened a channel.

"Patrol cruiser, this is the cargo ship Bubbles. Why are you chasing us?"

"Don't bullshit us, Spear."

"Seriously?" Morgan actually made his voice squeak. "Who would ever mistake my little snowman for something that deserved such a pointy name."

"What are you doing?" Frankie spared a half-second to glare

at Morgan. He waved his hands, and then signed "playing for time" in passable GSL.

"Stand by," the fake cruiser said.

Seriously?

"Toldja," Morgan said.

"We are powering weapons," the fake cruiser said. "Last chance."

The jump coordinates were set and double-checked. Frankie waved that screen to the side and pulled up a list of possible evasive maneuvers. Not a lot to choose from for a bulky cargo ship in a traffic lane barreling toward a jump-gate.

"Um. Frankie?"

"Spit it out." There was some kind of barrel roll she might be able to finagle, so long as the next ship in the tunnel queue didn't move. At all.

"What kind of shielding do we have?"

"Asteroid evasion. Steep-angle deflection."

"So, none, really. In that case, we should turn around."

"What?" Frankie pulled her fingers away from the screens so she wouldn't flinch and push a panel by mistake.

"Not surrender. But it would be really good if the stable's grav-coil didn't get hit. By anything." They were traveling engine first, as usual, which meant the cargo bay was closest to the fake cruiser's weapons.

Frankie pulled up another screen and started calculating. "If we do a tip-to-toe, we would take damage. And then we'd have our engines in their line of fire. Also bad. Which would be worse?"

Morgan held his hands out. "For us, it's the same. For the tunnel, a direct hit on the grav-box would knock it out of service. Maybe for good."

The last ship before them winked into the tunnel.

Frankie's fingers flew over the panels and controls. "I can do this," she muttered.

Spike jumped onto the pilot's board. Morgan grabbed for the cat. She slipped out of his reach, but away from the control panels Frankie was frantically manipulating. "We're doing this," she warned both of them.

"Target locked. Last chance, Spear."

She didn't have enough fingers.

"Morgan, listen! I need you to press this panel, the moment I say so." She pointed with her pinkie finger toward a panel too far for it to reach. "Pitch thrusters, there. It's all set up."

"Which panel?"

"This one. On my count. Three…"

The first blast went wide. Time seemed to stretch. She saw the moment Morgan froze. Only his gaze followed the powder from the blast reflecting the light as it streaked by.

"Locking target."

"Morgan!"

Spike jumped over to him and bit him on the chin. He shuddered, and came back to life.

"This panel."

"Okay, " he said, reaching over.

Everything under her hands was ready. "Now!"

Morgan pushed the wrong button. The hull's outer lights turned off.

Spike dragged Morgan's hand across to the correct panel and dropped it.

The Spear's under thrusters blew, tipping the ship ass over teakettle.

The second blast went wide.

"Hit that bleeping ship!" came roaring from the fake cruiser. Frankie, gripping her seat's armrests and trying not to throw up, had time to think how strange it was that Peters had put child-safety controls on the comms system.

Another voice broke in. "Aggressive cruiser: Identify yourself." Galactic Patrol. It really was as fast as advertised.

But not fast enough. The third blast sliced along the length of the two bigger bulbs of the Sphere.

They went into the jump-tunnel ass-first, bleeding air.

CHAPTER
EIGHTEEN

THE SPEAR CAME out of the tunnel tumbling.

Frankie did what she could with the two sets of thrusters that still worked, and managed to slow their roll. As soon as she caught her balance, she dropped the seat's safety straps. They had to get the hulls sealed.

"Stay," Morgan said, already up. "We need you here, keeping us steady. Tell me where to go."

"Biggest rip is in the cargo hold."

"Elvin here. I have the materials and am heading there now."

"Excellent, thank you. Second biggest is below us. Down the near stairs and listen for the hissing." Frankie pulled the cord on a trap door in the ceiling, and a cascade of patching materials and glues came down. "Take as much as you can carry. I'm calling the bots up to bring you more. Elvin, you too." She picked up one of the emergency breathers. As Morgan bent to scoop up materials, she pulled it over his head. She put another on herself, and a third for the cat.

As he left, she leaned over to palm the door shut, and then reconsidered. She sat back up.

The cat didn't look any worse for wear. Tufty and disreputable, but that was normal. Frankie didn't know how she had known how to help, but she had. "Spike, you clever girl. Would you run down the halls and close all our doors? Keep their air on the inside."

Spike leapt for the door, easily avoiding Frankie's reach. No breather, then. Frankie could have sworn it said, "sure." But that thought was quickly subsumed by the necessity of explaining simple hull fixes to Morgan, trying to balance the blasters against the torque of the air spilling in four places, and repeatedly assuring Dyad Tunnel Authority that yes, they were moving out of the lane right now.

By the time she got the ship evened out—only a little looseness in the yaw, like a giant drunk fish—Elvin and the box bots had the cargo breach patched. She felt secure enough to join Morgan among the water tanks and pipes and heating. She kept her scan-screens up.

Morgan made up for his lack of knowledge with an overabundance of energy. "I'm all adrenaline!" he said when he saw her. He was soaked, but the burst pipe had been spray-glued shut. The water at their ankles wasn't getting any higher.

Frankie checked her scans. "Water pressure normal. I don't see any more breaks." She looked at him. Droplets in his hair glowed golden in the orange emergency lights. "But we should keep main lights off."

"Agree completely! What's next?"

Frankie frowned at him. "You should go get dry clothes."

"No time! It's hot in here anyway. Why is it so warm in here, anyway?"

Frankie explained how water systems in space vehicles worked while they walked the length of the capsule. It looked like just the very edge of the scatter-beam had hit them; most of the damage was in parallel streaks and even in the center none of it went deep. Two bulkheads needed to be sealed off, but only one section of the inner hull needed an entire panel patch.

It could have been so much worse.

***

A LONG SHIFT LATER, the Spear wasn't hemorrhaging air anywhere. Morgan and Frankie collapsed in the kitchen nook with warm porridge and cold beer. Spike, who had stayed out of the water and out of everyone's hair, got an entire serving of reconstituted meat product and gravy.

And Elvin appeared. He bowed to her from the kitchen entry. "Permission to board, captain?"

Frankie waved him in. "Glad to see you, Doc." He must have borrowed some of Morgan's overalls; the cuffs looked like they'd been rolled three times. He unhooked a chair from the floor and brought it over, sitting straight while the two of them could barely sit upright on their cushions, even with the support of the back of the bench.

"About our destination," Elvin said, looking at her as if he wanted to splint her posture to the correct angle. "What is it?"

"Short term, we stay wobbling here on this side of the tunnel. Wait for news to come through. Comm links are free so long as we stay in a certain range."

"What news are you expecting?"

"I want to make sure our credits are still good. I would love to hear that that Skoll ship was apprehended, or at least detained."

Morgan frowned. "Won't that make us easy to find? Assuming the Skoll pay off the patrol. Or, more likely, have a second ship."

Frankie waved that problem away. Her balance was off. One beer was one too many. "I lied on the jump application. Everyone thinks we went to Rosings."

Morgan's face lit up as if she'd given him a priceless gift. "Brilliant! Then we'll go home. I mean the home planet in this system. Actually, it's a moon."

Then he frowned. "But once they know we didn't head to Rosing, won't they drone-bomb all the tunnels, looking for us?"

"That is a problem for tomorrow." Frankie lifted her bottle of beer. It was empty. Morgan pushed himself to his feet and got two more. Elvin picked up the empties and took them to the cycler. Frankie followed his path. How was she going to keep track of how many beers she'd had when the bottles disappeared like that?

"And how far is this moon?" she said. "On slow speed with fewest turns."

Morgan sat and pushed a beer her way. He started to write figures on the tabletop with his finger. "About a week, which isn't bad. Not great—we're already out of beer. But," he glanced up at her, "we might get a tow. I know the best collision shop in the sector."

She pushed the beer to Elvin. "Why am I not surprised?"

"Morgan has had his license suspended," Elvin said, pushing the beer back to Morgan. "Twice."

Morgan glared at him. "Thank you, Doctor Elvin."

Elvin shrugged. "Best to have all the data, up front."

Morgan returned to the subject. "My guy, he'll do you up good. And he takes all types of insurance."

Frankie gasped. She'd filled out the forms to get collision insurance, waiting on Morgan's payment. But she never actually sent them in.

She'd be in the red, again.

Way red.

She hoisted herself off the bench. "I'm going to bed."

"Captain, don't you want to weigh in on our destination?" Elvin's voice was simultaneously solicitous and cutting.

Frankie walked past him, lifting her hand to wave the question away. "You know, this past week, I've taken a lot of risks. And a lot of damage."

"So for now, I'm going to go lie down on my own bed with the door closed.

"And repent."

CHAPTER
NINETEEN

FRANKIE STARTED her day on the below deck, vacuuming up the spilled pipe water. At least it hadn't been a sewage pipe. The surface glistened yellow in the orange emergency lights. Safer to keep the main lights off until the mechanics could look at the circuit. The reclamation tank was going to be full, the filters busy, but the system could handle it. She couldn't get to the two closed-off sections. It would be ice in there anyway.

She tried not to hear the tiny, high-pitched drip, drip from somewhere. She'd already looked for it once. It could wait until they got to base. Or moon, or wherever.

She was going to have to ask for terms from the repair shop. Maybe they would agree to hold the ship as collateral while she worked to get the credits to pay for the repairs. But some places charged a fee to store vessels. That would add up fast. Maybe she could get the Spear space worthy, not for travel but for parking in orbit around some lifeless moon while she saved up to pay for the bigger repairs. But she'd have to figure out how to make it more secure than just a wrist-chip lock.

She was nearly done, the floor merely silty, when she heard

Morgan coming down the stairs. He wore work overalls that fit him perfectly. He seemed to be talking to someone, but when he came into view he was alone.

"You're right," he said. "Thanks."

"Who are you talking to?"

He waved up the stairs. "Spike. She told me where you were." The cat came into view, giant on the narrow emergency steps. She stopped high above the messy floor and started to clean her paw.

Morgan grabbed the mud scraper and started pushing the fine coating of gunk into a neat row. Frankie was glad to let him.

"Spike talked to you, too?" she said.

Morgan shot her a look. "No," he said slowly. "I asked her where you were, and she trotted over to the stairs. I figured it out from there."

Right. Of course. She'd imagined it. Maybe it was the adrenaline.

"I can't believe she bit me, though." He held his hand up. "Look."

Morgan leaned in. "Didn't break skin. You'll be fine."

He started pushing silt again. "It shouldn't be in her programming."

"She's a cat. Of course it's in her programming."

He looked about to argue, but stopped himself. "Watch out. She's taken over your chair on the bridge. Might be a coup in progress."

Frankie folded up the vacuum and set it on top of her helper bot. "Supply closet B, please. Why did you want to see me, again?"

"Right!" He grinned at her. "Guess what? We're dead!"

He wasn't making any sense. Her arms, suddenly free after having held the vacuum for the past few hours, definitely did not feel dead. "Pardon me?"

"Official story is we went into the tunnel at the wrong angle."

"We did not!"

"Stand down, expert pilot captain ma'am. Nobody blames you. We were being shot at, remember? By a cruiser falsely identifying itself as a Galactic. The cruiser and its commander are currently being detained. Indefinitely."

That part sounded good. Skoll Shipping couldn't have so many cruisers that they'd waste inventory to send another after them. She hoped.

Morgan kept looking at her expectantly, between pushes. What did he want her to say? The news was wrong.

"Captain." He drew the word out as if she were a slow student. "We're dead to the universe. What if we just stayed dead?"

His definition of death must be different from hers. "You mean…"

"Ditch the ship! Or rename it. Give ourselves new names, new IDs." He waited for the other helper bot to position the trash bag in front of the pile he'd made. "Push our old selves into the trash," he said, illustrating. "Tie it up and start over."

"Think about it, Frankie! Captain Styles. Stop running from whatever it is you're running from. Give the Skolls the slip. Be free!"

People did sometimes disappear and then reappear at the edges of Cooperative space. Refugees from a transit disaster, or a seed-planet project everybody had forgotten about.

Frankie thought she knew how to fry the ID chip in her wrist. That would disconnect her from her wristcom, practically disappearing her all by itself.

Who could she be? An astroarcheaologist, like her mom? She'd have to forge credentials. Or go back to school. How much more fun school would be this time if she had a different name. She could fail a course. Join a team. Go out dancing all night.

The Cooperative would be glad she was gone. Win-win.

But Beth would be devastated. And the others. So many of their group had died already. She couldn't do that to them.

Morgan and the bot had finished their mud collection. He bounced on his toes.

"So?"

She had to make him see. "What about your family? Your friends?"

"They'll never have to be disappointed in me again. My father even said 'gravely disappointed' the last time I saw him. How did he know?" His grin wobbled.

She didn't believe him. "They would miss you immensely. And you would never see them again. You couldn't risk it."

His face fell. "It's a trade-off, yes. But it solves all our problems. Debts cleared, slate wiped, future shining bright." He must have been able to tell she was going to say no.

"Frankie," he took her arm gently. "You could be whoever you were meant to be, before the bad stuff happened."

She jerked away from him. That wasn't possible. The Cooperative had seen to that. She would not give them one bit more of herself.

"No," she said. "I'm not running."

She might not be ready to shout her name from the top of CapCities Tower, but she certainly wasn't going to burn it to ash.

"I'm not letting the Skolls—or anybody—take my name away from me."

CHAPTER
TWENTY

BY THE TIME Frankie had sent all the free messages to all the relevant people and institutions, confirming that yes, she was indeed still alive, the tug from the repair shop had arrived. Morgan must truly be a good repeat customer: The shop didn't even ask for a deposit.

Eckberg Ship Rebuilding sat on the larger of a close pair of terraformed moons circling the twin stars of the Dyad System. In only half a day, they could see it coming into view.

More brown than blue, swirling with clouds, and packed with buildings and transit tubes, the moon looked happily prosperous, at least from space. Frankie chose to tie off at their orbital platform, just a few slips and a very chipper mechanic inspector. The inspector, a somewhat ruddy young person, sent her big drones around the outer hull and walked with the smaller ones through the Spear, starting far aft, in the cargo sphere.

"Big ship," she said. "Gonna take a while." After that, she pointedly ignored Frankie. Another spacer who obviously liked to work alone.

Frankie was halfway down the walkway back to the main sphere when she saw Morgan, leaning on the railing and staring down at his container. She stopped beside him and matched his position. "You're worried she's going to scan the stables?"

"No. A redhead, right? If she's who I think she is, her mom built the stable. No worries there." He shrugged at her surprise. "Home system, remember?"

He didn't seem that happy about it. Mouth turned down, arms all floppy, cuffs mussed.

Frankie changed the subject, as much as she could. She called up a map screen and homed in on Dyad system. "How can I help you get the container moved? Where is its final destination?"

His laugh tasted bitter. "You've done a bang-up job with that. Sorry about the pun, couldn't help it. The stable is housed here." On the map, he pointed to the second moon.

"Like I said. Home."

"Cloud," she read. "You're named for your moon?"

"It's my middle name, if you must know. And I guess you must, now that we're here."

"Here where?"

He looked directly at her. "You don't know this place?"

She shrugged. "Wasn't on my route. I don't know a lot about the outer sectors." She pinched the moon bigger. Looked like any other new terraform project. Not a lot of buildings yet. They must have started with the other moon, Silva. Forest. "Looks like they got the names switched. Cloud should be the big one."

A message blinked across her screen. The insurance company? She swiped it open, and gasped.

"Did you do this?" She looked at Morgan and pointed to the part of the message that said, "Fully Covered."

Morgan scanned the note, and shook his head no. "Guess Past Captain Frankie was looking out for you." She frowned at him.

"Maybe you did it in your sleep?" He shrugged.

She swept the screen to the side and called up her main credit account. "It's all still there. Wasn't me."

"Maybe you just haven't paid the premium yet."

Seriously? He'd never had to pay an insurance premium? She glared at him.

But it was clear he was deep in his own thoughts.

Morgan pushed up from his slouch. "Listen, Frankie. Captain. It's going to take a while before your ship is patched-up. Why don't you come to Cloud with me? Cheaper than a hotel."

"Not a chance."

"Why not? It's beautiful. Bucolic and peaceful."

"Bucolic maybe. Peaceful I am sure it's not." She poked him, gently, but in no-G it set him back on his grav-booted heels. "You are obviously the black sheep of your family. When was the last time you were here?"

He looked sheepish. "Four years."

"Right. Your family, do they know you're here?" He shook his head. "As soon as they do, you know they're going to be all over you. You want a distraction. I will not be that distraction." It was bad enough not having a family of her own. She was not going to suffer through the tempests of some stranger's family.

"It would be a blast. You could eat peppermints by the handful and watch the fireworks."

She crossed her arms. "No."

He sighed. "Worth a shot. Hey," he said as she started heading to the airlock. "What if I stay with you instead?"

She snorted. "I'm staying on the ship." No use spending money on some random bed when she had twelve perfectly nice ones. "But you might send me some of those peppermints." She kicked the panel to open the door and passed through, Morgan hard on her heels.

He followed her all the way to the kitchen. Thoughts of peppermint had reminded Frankie she hadn't eaten yet today. She rehydrated two ProntoPestos. He hovered as they cooked, helping get the water bottles and set the table. She dumped the contents of the steaming packets into two bowls and handed him one. She reclaimed her usual seat, facing the door. The cat, wherever it was, could claim a different perch.

Morgan let her eat in peace, at least. As soon as she was finished, a full ten minutes after he'd done wolfing his portion, he took in a breath.

She held up a hand. "No. Final."

He blew the breath out, defeated. "Fine," he said. "When do you want me off? Oh-sixteen-thirty-two?"

That wasn't even a time, and he knew it. "Why are you so mad? Just catch a shuttle and go back to Smithson. Or Rosing. Or anywhere else."

"My mom would die if she found out I'd been so close and not come by. My dad would kill me."

Their voices must have attracted Spike. The cat, even raggedier-looking than before, sat just inside the door and stared at her.

"You want a cat?" she asked Morgan.

"Not that one," he said.

Frankie looked over to Spike's dining area. Half a gravy-thingy remained. The water bowl was fine, too. "What?" she said to the cat.

Spike gazed at her steadily. She was not going to get into a staring match with a cat. Spike closed her eyes slowly, and then opened them, slowly. Frankie shrugged, clueless. Spike sighed and headed out the door. She turned, tilted her head toward the end of the hall with the piloting room, and left in that direction.

"I believe I'm being summoned," Frankie said. She rose, reaching for the empty bowls.

"I'll get this," Morgan said, still sullen. "It's the least I can do."

Frankie was starting to remember why she didn't like people like him. "Don't just run away. Say goodbye before you go."

"Goodbye, then," he said, facing the kitchen disposal and away from her.

CHAPTER
TWENTY-ONE

SPIKE SAT on the communications console, her tail waving side to side.

Frankie looked around the room, messy with burst patch-kits and used drink pouches. The arms of the comms chair were sticky. What had Morgan eaten in here? The consoles, on the other hand, were unusually dark and quiet. Screens off, engine off, solar sails out, no port chatter. Readings shunted to her comm screen.

She grabbed a wipe from the nearest patch-kit and cleaned her hands and then the arms of the chair. Spike waited, tail still slowly wagging. She sat on the now-clean chair and folded her hands in her lap. They gazed at each other.

Enough of that. Frankie raised her eyebrows. "You wanted something?"

Spike pounced on the call button. The connection came nearly instantaneously. A masculine-presenting person she didn't recognize appeared on the screen.

"Captain Styles. It's nice to finally meet you." He pronounced her name correctly—Stee-lay. She'd never heard anyone not from her home planet who said it that way. It sounded strange, after all this time.

"Sir." She guessed at the pronoun.

"Let's call me Bruce." He had a dark square face made more square by thick black hair that ended evenly with equally thick sideburns, connected by a sharply trimmed moustache. "I represent a firm that hires people like you to find … things."

She frowned. People like who? What things? "You mean, information?"

"Sometimes. Sometimes actual things. Or people." He chuckled, smoothing out his perfect moustache. "This must all sound rather mysterious." He shrugged. "Can't be helped."

She didn't answer.

"Captain, we've had our eye on you for a long time. Since university, in fact."

"You know who I am, then?"

"Yes, but it doesn't matter to us."

Frankie sat straight. "It doesn't?"

"We were delighted that you chose this line of work, and we will pay you to continue doing it. On top of that, we ask that you carry out occasional information-gathering assignments for us. Bonuses apply."

Frankie shook her head. "This is all very deus ex machina of you."

"The timing is coincidental. My agent had already started observing you before your little adventure. Closely observing. She's there with you now."

"Spike?" Frankie's gaze, horrified, shot to the cat, or whatever it was. It walked into the camera's field, and nodded at Bruce.

A secret agent had cuddled with her.

She'd slept with it!

"Unfortunate name, but she got it when she was little, and she likes it."

Spike tilted her head askance at Bruce, then started cleaning her shoulder.

They were getting off-topic. "Let me get this straight," Frankie said. "You work for a private company—"

"—Public-private partnership—"

"—that will pay me to ship cargo and also to … what? Hunt for clues? Spy?"

"On-site research." Bruce's sideburns moved apart when he smiled. His teeth were very white. "A recent assignment was to locate the mother of a little girl who ran away and then forgot her family name. Another was to determine if a certain family remained in possession of a certain artwork they had claimed stolen."

"Like solving puzzles. People puzzles."

"The best kind! "What do you say?"

She didn't have to say yes now. She could say no.

"There's a contract?"

Bruce looked down. "Sending it. Standard, for this kind of work."

The contract was relatively simple. A base income in the range of the second-to-top tier of the dockmasters' scale. Per-diem for the length of each special assignment, plus expenses. Guaranteed two assignments per year, 20 days minimum, paid even if unused.

One addendum: A nondisclosure agreement.

What was the catch?

Frankie looked up. "Tell me more about your company."

"Systems Analysis. Address on the contract. I'll wait for you to look it up."

It came up first in the search results, despite the mundane name. "Philanthropic venture funders. Truly?"

"Cross my heart."

"Based on Rosing Station." Her hopes fell. "I can't go to

Rosing."

"But wait. As a signing incentive, I've already managed your Skoll problem."

"It wasn't my problem." Well, except for the aiding and abetting.

"And that made it easier to manage the family, believe you me. But I do think we took care of the young man's debt as well. That part of the discussion was a little … opaque." For the first time, Bruce looked less than confident. It made her trust him more.

She'd lost her shipping contract, and this one could replace it. She would keep helping people not starve, and maybe reunite families. She loved solving puzzles.

She didn't want to lose her freedom.

"Sounds interesting," she said. "The Spear would need better shielding, and upgraded communications."

"Done. I'll tell Eckberg."

"And a ship-to-satellite credit account?"

"We'll see."

She smiled. So they did have limits. "Second-to-last thing. Can we agree to a six-month trial period? Six months, either party out, no foul."

Bruce had to lean out of camera range on that one. He leaned back in. "We'll get that out to you, soon as Scott is back from lunch. Last thing?"

"Is Spike assigned to me, or is she off to the next recruit?"

"For the six-month trial, she'll be with you. Barring unforeseen events." Spike perked up at that news, pushing her way on-camera again. "Think of it as a vacation," Bruce said to her, flashing another bright smile.

"We took fire." A simulated voice growled out of the fur at Spike's neck.

Frankie kicked the chair away from the console. The chair,

bolted to the deck, did not move. Frankie swallowed her shout of pain.

"I read the report." Bruce's smile vanished. "It shouldn't have gone that far."

"My fault? No. Absolutely no." Spike's tale whipped side to side. Frankie leaned as far away from it as she could.

"You weren't the only agent there."

"Talk to the union rep," Spike spat. She jumped off the console and stalked out of the room, only pausing to kick the door shut with a hind leg.

"Spike is one of our best in the field, Captain. But, as is often true with a diva, she has a few sharp edges. You'll work out fine."

Frankie turned back to Bruce, and caught him wiping his brow with a bandana. "Is Spike really a cat? Some special kind?"

"Spike is her own being. She will share her story in her own good time. So, captain," Bruce's smile was back. "Can we count on you?"

She'd traded a snake for some fancy secret-agent cat. She'd get her ship upgraded for free. She'd have guaranteed income for half a year, at least.

No need to say no.

"Deal."

"Fantastic. Here's your first assignment: You're off duty until Spear is whole again. Get yourself down to Silva and have a little fun. Expense it to Systems. Scott will show you how."

"Welcome to the team, Captain Styles."

The call cut off with a pop. Frankie leaned back in the chair, winded after doing nothing but sitting and talking. Systems Bruce was right. She did need some time off.

She pulled up a screen to see what sort of adventures Silva promised.

FRANKIE TAKES A HOLIDAY

CHAPTER
ONE

FRANKIE STYLES WAS GOING to relax.

Leave her poor, banged-up space cargo hauler to the tender care of Eckberg Ship Rebuilding. Get off this repair shop in orbit and down to the bigger moon nearby, Silva. Go directly to Silva's most gorgeous spot, according to the majority of subscribers to AllWorldsRated. Lay on the beach for a week.

Bliss.

She buckled herself into one of the bank of twelve passenger seats facing each other along the smells-like-new boxy bus orbital shuttle. The straps told the real story. Worn and prickly, the cross-strap snagged on the front of her best blue tunic. The one with the clever stitching that made it drape and swing like dancing.

So much for first impressions. Frankie managed to let that minor frustration go on the wings of a deep sigh. She closed her eyes and let the pilot do their job.

Her gut took note of the jerk and overcompensation on liftoff. Her ears—and her butt—recognized the scrape of the outer hull tripping over the garage-bay threshold on their way out the dock. The unfortunate cracks in the why-so-young pilot's voice forced her casual grip on the soft edge of her seat cushion into more of a claw.

But all the other passengers were still making the usual murmurs; nobody was hurling or even gasping. It was a quick trip down to Silva, and there was always autopilot.

She should have brought a peppermint candy as distraction.

It would be fine.

Her wristcom vibrated. New message.

Frankie did not open her eyes. She was releasing tension. Good news could be as stressful as bad, and she'd had a full shipment of all manner of news lately.

Her ship, the Spear, the best cargo hauler in the system, was currently in the care of Eckberg Ship Rebuilding, thanks to too much excitement on her last delivery. Somebody had shot at her! She still couldn't believe it.

She'd lost her main hauling contract earlier that day, and that had felt like the end of the world. But even that was completely overshadowed by the Skolls' laser cannon gouging the side of her poor, innocent ship. Spear would be out of the flow for a couple weeks, Eckberg's said.

Then the good news: A new job offer! Doing the same sort of hauling as her lost contract, with added bonuses for "looking into certain matters." Frankie wasn't positive what-all those matters would be, but the examples they gave sounded useful and helpful and easily do-able. Hunt for missing shipments. Find out if a painting is in a certain building. Take notes on which ships are at which ports.

Best, Systems Analysis, the forgettable-sounding "philanthropic venture funders," had agreed to her request for a short contract—six months. If it didn't work out, she'd walk. But she'd walk with a ship that had upgraded communications and shielding, thanks to the signing bonus. Win-win-win.

Then the strange news: The chonky, disreputable-looking cat

who'd stowed aboard the Spear on the last haul wasn't really a cat at all. Spike was a "field operative," whatever that was, for Systems Analysis. It was her recommendation that had gotten Frankie her new job.

Spike had also slept on Frankie's calves on a too-cold, too-dark night or three. Frankie wasn't sure how she felt about that. Kinda intimate for working colleagues, no? On the other hand, she'd appreciated the warmth.

Plus, she'd just discovered, Spike could talk. The baby-bear-sized not-cat used a simulated voice that growled out of somewhere near her neck. But rarely: Frankie got the idea that Spike didn't consider her voice-worthy. Their boss, Bruce, called Spike a diva, but not to her face.

Frankie also wasn't sure how she felt about Spike coming down to Silva with her. Her raggedly striped colleague sat beside her, hunkered down in a meatloaf shape with the lap-band clipped over her shoulders. Frankie had set her small duffel bag on the other side of Spike, for more cushioning in case of trouble.

Spike had given her that look Frankie translated as "is that really necessary?" Probably not. Spike had lived long without her help. But Frankie was here now, and she needed to help.

Well, Spike wasn't going to want to spend every day at the beach, which was what Frankie planned to do. Her coworker would have to find her own fun.

The shuttle bus banged to a stop, hopefully on a landing pad outside Silva's second-biggest city. Frankie let the ship settle, took a deep breath, and opened her eyes. Parcels were falling out of overhead bins, half the people couldn't unclip themselves from their restraints, and the other half were stumbling about as their bodies began to remember real gravity.

All was well.

She couldn't remember if she'd told Spike of her beach plans, but it didn't matter. The cat—she was going to keep calling it a cat until Spike told her what she really was—stuck close to Frankie through disembark, decontamination, and customs. But as they stepped out of the building into the mild light and light morning breeze, Spike did not follow Frankie to the platform for transit to the shore. Instead, she veered off toward one that would take her into the city proper.

For a moment, watching Spike lope off, looking confident and disreputable, Frankie felt a pang of loss. Neediness, her? She shook it off and turned back, toward her fabulous, all-expenses-paid holiday vacation.

THE SCENTS OF COCONUT, mesquite, and something astringent embraced Frankie as she entered the tiny tropical bungalow she would be calling home for the next ten days. Big open windows, faux-thatched roof, and bot-delivered meals. Hot tub in the bathroom. Beach chairs and giant umbrellas! What could be better?

She dropped her duffle bag on the teak bench next to the door to the bathroom, which was the only part of the bungalow that seemed to have sturdy walls. The place was more like a high-end hotel's honeymoon bathroom with a sleeping porch attached than an actual domicile. So much weather could blow in! She couldn't wait.

She'd have to share the beach—she didn't spring for total privacy—but this was the last bungalow in the row. A jagged cliff started only about a bungalow's-length away on her other side. She might see a couple of intrepid hikers, maybe, but nobody else.

Frankie waved away the stray thought that she, a cargo pilot who worked alone and sometimes felt lonely, had chosen a vacation spot that avoided almost all the people in the area. She would see plenty enough of them in the course of things. And she could always go to one of the restaurants or bars. Although, come to think of it, the resort offered drone-delivered drinks right to the beach, so maybe not.

She rummaged around the duffle for her second-best swimsuit, the one with the most coverage, and slithered it on. Maybe tomorrow she'd go short, but this long-sleeved, long-legged beauty would protect her tender spacer's skin until she got a true reading on the sun.

She switched wristcoms to her all-weather one, and set it to synchronize with her everyday one. Maybe in a day or two she would be able to commit to complete radio silence, but for now she needed the familiar tether. She grabbed two towels, one of the canvas folding chairs, and the most colorful umbrella, and hit the beach.

The view was just as the travel guide had described: pale skies, emerald-blue water peaked with gray, a thin strip of curving pale-sand beach as far as she could see. Hints of hot plastic, musty cloth, and marine life seasoned the air. Gull-like birds way offshore but still so loud. Frankie had no idea what season it was here, but there were only a couple dozen people at the moment.

Perfect.

The sand was already toasty at mid-morning. She grinned as her body woke up the memory of how to walk in the slushy stuff. How it sifted between her toes! She glanced at the bigger sun above and jammed the umbrella into the sand at the proper angle for ultimate shade. She had to fight with the chair to figure it out. Turned out it was one of the kind with the tiny short legs, the ones where when you sit on them your butt pushed the seat almost to the sand. She hoped her spacer knees were up to the challenge of getting up out of that thing.

But not now. Now she ran the dozen steps and into the surf.

The first crash of cold water on her thighs made her gasp. She caught her breath, and shallow-dove into a wave and under. All the reviews said you could see clearly under the waves, and they were right.

Frankie kicked hard to get to deeper water but kept herself above the layer that went cold. She had enough body fat to float on her back okay, but the best was floating on her front, just under the waves. Suspended in space and time, she used to call it.

It wasn't really like space, now that she'd been there. The water was far more substantial. More insistent.

She'd missed it so.

CHAPTER
TWO

AFTER HER SKIN had pruned up and her limbs started to shiver, Frankie dragged herself through the surf and back onto the now-frypan sand. The towels passed muster, and the chair didn't sag as much as all that.

Her belly grumbled. Time to test out those drones. She flicked her wrist, calling up the White Sands Resort guest portal, and looked for menus. The resort had sent her a message, welcoming her and asking how she would rate her stay on a scale of one to six.

She gave it a six, in case that would get her extra tomatoes on her eggplant po'boy. A raspberry smoothie and a refillable White Sands Resort water bottle finished the order. She wasn't sure the sandwich and the smoothie would mesh. If not, smoothie first and po'boy in a couple hours. She liked making decisions like this, with no lives at stake. Just a little indigestion, if that.

Thinking of the message, and why people wanted you to rate something when you haven't really even tried it yet, Frankie remembered the earlier call, in the shuttle. She flicked over to that screen.

Morgan Cloud. She should have known.

Last she'd last seen of the prince of blond highlights, he was bussing their breakfast table, mad that she wouldn't act the protective shield between him and what he expected to be a chilly homecoming. Cloud—Morgan's middle name, she didn't know his family name—was Silva's twinned moon. So Morgan's anticipated pain had been imminent, and he had been desperate. And then sulky.

Whatever. He probably deserved it. In the short time she'd known him, he'd brought aboard "regulation" cargo that turned out to be live horses and a synthetic human she couldn't be sure wasn't on the run. Then he'd pulled a scam on the Skolls (involving the horses) that led to the shooting—people shot at her!—that had ripped holes in her ship. How could he act so surprised that she didn't want to play another part in his schemes?

Problem was, he was such a cutie. And she was definitely in need of a cutie at the moment, if the swirl of sexy thoughts in the ocean of her mind was any indication.

But not him.

Frankie played the recording Morgan had left. "Captain. I'm hoping you'll reconsider my offer. This is Morgan." His high baritone voice made everything he said sound so pleasant. But now he spoke so fast she had to close her eyes and concentrate to parse out the words. "I may have been a little hasty in how I presented it, but it is a very good deal for you. You wouldn't need to meet the family at all. There's a little bungalow thingy on the other side of the pool—did I tell you we have a pool?"

A pause for a door slam, and he continued. "I know you're short funds at the moment," he said. Frankie rolled her eyes. He'd had a lot to do with that. "And I feel bad about you having to bunk on-ship when Cloud is right here. With a swimming pool. And peppermints. Give me a beep if you do reconsider. Please."

Too needy. Besides, she already had a little bungalow and an entire lively ocean right here.

In the time it took her to swipe the message screen off her comm beeped.

Before the "No!" in the front of her brain could travel back to her motor cortex, her wrist had flicked the link open. Ugh.

"Captain?"

"Hello, Morgan." He must have set a tag on his message to ping him when it was opened. "Things have changed."

"What do you mean? Wait, is that a breeze I hear?"

"Good ear. I picked up a new gig, and they even gave me a signing bonus. I'm spending it here on Silva, gazing out at the Pearl Sea. Mechanical doves are going to bring me a sandwich soon. Can't beat it."

The longer-than-usual pause made her smile and settle deeper into the hammock of her chair. Still not touching the sand.

"I see," he said. "Whelp. Have a nice time."

"Enjoy your reunion."

Two seagull-sized drones buzzed in, carrying what looked like an entire picnic. They shared nothing in common with doves other than a vague gray-white coloring. One drone carried a clever folding table, a chill-bucket-thing, and a napkin it spread as a tablecloth. The other held the universally familiar cardboard four-cup carrier, holding two tall, insulated cups with straws, and the sandwich, wrapped in a giant napkin. They came, distributed their cargo within reach of her left hand, and departed. The whole thing took less than a minute.

She took a sniff of the sandwich—heavenly—and wrapped it back up tightly. She swigged some water and then got down to business with the smoothie. A person could get used to this.

At the first tang of raspberry in the drink, everything changed.

Frankie was thrust back into memory. Age eight, promised a smoothie if she got back to the tent from swimming before having to be called in. But it was so fun at the beach. Beth in her candy-apple green suit, Frankie in her sapphire blue. In and out of the water at the campground's sandy shore. Going deep, diving for treasure. It was a lake, not an ocean, but a big lake. Artemisia, named for the shrubs that lined the edges of the woods nearby. From the shore, you couldn't see the other side, if you were eight.

Barely making it in time, gasping deep breaths, hands on knees in front of the wooden picnic table. Mom sitting on the opposite seat, laughing, baby Jo in her special chair, smiling for once. She was teething that summer. Raspberry smoothie in a wet-waxed paper cup, along with the usual hummus and pita. Even busy with Erik, Mom had remembered.

Cut scene, and the usual nightmare stormed right in. The view out the window of the orbital platform. Her planet. Blue and gold and beautiful greens. Puckering in. Exploding out. Everyone in the station falling as the shock wave blasted the platform out past the moons.

Then, nothing to orbit around.

Nothing, nobody, at all.

Frankie set the smoothie down, wiped her eyes, and went back into the water.

CHAPTER
THREE

WHEN FRANKIE EMERGED from the sea, equilibrium restored, someone was sitting in her chair.

Morgan Cloud, forelock as blond and bouffant as ever, handed her the dry towel. He was not dressed for the beach. The long tunic in a lime green that made his eyes look even darker and khaki skinny pants were going to soak up sand. He must have left his boots with his transport; his long pale feet rested half-submerged in the sparkling sand.

"My sandwich better still be there."

He waved a hand at the still-bulky napkin on the small table beside him. "Captain. Marvelous to see you. And covered in so much cornflower blue. Not wanting any sun at all?"

Frankie didn't answer at first. She toweled and then finger-combed her dark chin-length curls, hoping to avoid snarls later.

"How?" she finally said.

"Elementary. Only one resort on Pearl advertises fake-dove delivery. I should have known you would choose the quietest one."

"Nobody needs to play disc golf. Or hit small balls at other people." Dried off enough, Frankie folded the towel and dropped it on the sand on the other side of the table. She sat cross-legged on it and grabbed the sandwich.

The first bite was bliss.

She opened her eyes to see Morgan watching her. "You do enjoy your food."

"You owe me a smoothie."

"There's peppermint smoothies on every countertop on Cloud."

"Give it up." She reached for the bottle of water, then paused, glaring at him. "You didn't drink my water, did you?"

"Didn't touch it." Morgan made a show of thinking, even to tapping his chin with a lovely, tapered finger. "Strange, how the resort just let me come right up here. It was as if you were expecting someone."

So he knew that, too. "Spit it out," she said around a mouthful of eggplant and sauce.

"If you want sexytimes, I'm your man." He waggled his eyebrows, which was more goofy than sexy. "I know you like me. That way."

"I do like you, Morgan, that way. Which is why I won't be scratching that itch with you. I'm a one-and-done kind of gal. You are a walking, talking example of strings attached." He didn't need to know more than that.

"One other thing," he said. "Have you looked at the weather forecast?"

She watched a tiny brown bird inspect the soggy new length of beach as the tide rolled out. "Clear skies," she said.

"Not for long. On Cloud we never have such nasty weather. We're still under domes. But they're really big domes."

"Give it up."

"You'll be missing out." The usual teasing lilt held an overcoat of expected disappointment.

Despite herself, Frankie leaned toward him. Morgan's disappointment could act like honey to a bee.

But she had free will.

"Tell me the real story, then. Starting with your family name."

They'd played this game on board her ship: I won't tell you mine, and you don't have to tell me yours. It had been such a relief for Frankie, whose name was famous systemwide: The Pitiful Orphan of Planet Wala.

She'd thought he was hiding his because he was acting the part of a careless wealthy party boy. But if his family had pools and extra houses maybe that wasn't it. Time to know.

Morgan slurped the last of the smoothie. He tucked it back into the carrier divot.

"Fine. Morgan Cloud Orr."

Shock lightninged up Frankie's spine, exploded across her mind.

"Orr? Like Konrad Orr?"

"Of Orr Enterprises, yes." Morgan drew himself in, shoulders hunched, as if expecting a blow. "He's my dad."

"You can't be serious." Frankie had to put her hands on the sides of her face to stop the spinning inside.

"Yeah, sure. He sells munitions. He captured the market on tech a couple decades past. He's handing it all off to my brother." He shook his head. "I don't have enough of the killer instinct. Like that's a bad thing." He glanced at her, and away. He hunched in more.

Frankie stared at him. She had to close her mouth and swallow before she could make a sound. How long had it been hanging open?

"You really don't know who I am?"

"We made a deal." He shrugged. "You obviously kept the bargain. So did I."

Frankie pulled her hands over her head, pushing the curls out of her face. She laced her fingers and cupped her neck. "My full name is Fridrika Styles Faldasdotter."

Now Morgan's mouth dropped open. He shut faster than she had, but so hard his teeth clicked.

"From Wala. Stop my breath. What are the chances?" He looked around, as if spies were circling them. "Who else knows?"

Frankie frowned. "Nobody. Wait—my new boss. He said they were negotiating with the Skolls, trying to patch up relations for me and maybe you. So Systems Analysis must know."

"That the son of the 'Butcher of Wala' and its most famous orphan are a thing?"

"We are not a thing. Never a thing, now." Frankie was trying hard to sit still. Every muscle screamed *run*.

"Right, right." Morgan was still thinking. Adding up the damages, or whatever. He stopped, and looked at her. Stared. Squinted.

"I do remember you. I was twelve. You must have been nine, ten, but you looked like you were six. So little. Your hair went out to here." He held his hands a meter away from the sides of his head.

"Nobody knew how to manage my hair back then." And Frankie was never going to tell them. She was never going to speak to anyone ever again.

Now was not the time for those memories.

"You were at the formal apology?" she said.

"Yes. First row, behind my dad and the other executives. Boy with the hair plastered to his head. You don't remember me?"

Frankie did not open that door to memories, either. She tucked the napkin back in the cardboard container and pushed herself to standing.

"Have a nice visit with your family," she said. The one you still have, she did not say.

"Wait!" Morgan reached for her arm and then stopped

himself. His hand dangled in the air a few centimeters from her wrist, and then dropped back into his lap. "This doesn't change anything. A storm is still coming. You are still welcome to use the in-law cottage."

She took a step back from him. The sun slapped her in the eyes. "Seriously?"

The skin at the corners of his eyes pinched, bitter. "I wasn't the one who killed your family."

"Of course not. But that still doesn't mean I want to enter the lair of the killer of Wala."

"He's not even there! He's allowed back in Central District now. We never see him." Morgan sounded bitter about that, too. "Worst is you'd run into my crank of a brother. Neither of us look anything like our dad."

"Thank you for the offer, Morgan Cloud. I'm happy where I am."

But she couldn't stop herself from making stupid concessions. Solving other people's problems. "How about, spend a couple days with your mom, then finish the week here?"

The light came back into his eyes.

"Share a bed?"

"Bring a hammock."

Her lustful thoughts will have dissipated by then. Sooner if she did something about it.

It would be safe again.

CHAPTER
FOUR

TROPICAL CYCLONE ALVIN not only jigged when it should have jagged, but it broke all speed records coming across the unseasonably warm ocean. The first rainband hit the shore just hours after Frankie, sun-tired, swim-tired, and finally, finally relaxed, had fallen to sleep.

She woke in the storm's strobing light to find the beachside wall of her bungalow bending over the bed like a blade of grass. Sounds bad, her dream-addled brain came up with to describe the banshee wails and ominous crunches coming from all around her.

She had only enough time to roll off the bed and hit the floor before the winds ripped the wall out of its supports and away. Now the wind howled, the water whipped, and who knew what debris was blasting her way.

In the three seconds it took to crawl to the bathroom and the three more seconds it took to fight the heavy door closed, Frankie was soaked and shivering. She'd never seen such angry water.

But she knew about wind, and tornadoes. Get to the sturdiest wall, low. She'd spent a couple afternoons on Wala reading storybooks while bundled with all her bedding in the downstairs tub. You just had to ride it out.

Luckily, she was a lazy traveler. She'd left her whole duffle in the bathroom after swimming, since that was the place where all the clothes and toiletries would eventually be needed. So she had dry clothes and her toothbrush. She pulled yesterday's tunic off the top of the bag.

Even with all the noise, she heard something big go thunk behind her. She spun, gasping, holding the tunic in front of her bare chest.

Just the hot tub, losing its water. The wind must have pulled the plug.

The angry water wanted more?

Good news for her, though. Frankie used a towel to dry off some of the tub, and then jammed it in the space where the drain-pipe used to connect. She put on the rest of yesterday's clothes and pushed everything else that was dry back into the duffel. She brought it into the hot tub with her and settled on its floor.

She could barely think for the screeching of the wind. But for now, all the bluster and crash were outside. The walls and ceiling here were intact. The tub was another piece of solid, and that was the best she could do.

The tub was made for lounging, which was good because all her pillows were soaked. Gone, probably. She rummaged in the duffel for her kit bag, and found the earplugs. They shut about half the bluster out. She pushed the duffel into the pillow spot, and snuggled under the soft weight of two of the bigger towels.

The silence woke her. Either that, or the buzzing of her wrist-com. She'd left it on the nightstand, but that was the sports one. The main one was in the duffel, apparently directly underneath her cheek.

She slapped it on her wrist and felt it pull warmth to power up. She moved her arm from side to side to help before calling up the message screen.

The quiet was eerie. Anticipatory, not conclusive.

Messages from the resort ran down her screen. *Are you there, Mx Styles? Come to the main building. Do you need help? Don't go anywhere, shelter in place.* And the newest one: *Don't move. This is the eye. More storm imminent.*

She texted back that she was sheltering in the hot tub. She got an immediate reply: *Awesome. So glad to hear from you. Comms will go out again, when the eyewall hits. But not for long. More news later.*

They didn't ask if she needed anything. Or send one of those messages inviting her to rate her stay.

It would not be a six now.

FRANKIE NEXT WOKE to a persistent buzzing around her belly.

Stupid wristcom.

She pushed herself up to sitting on the floor of the hot tub. At about the four-hour mark, the tub had lost any semblance of comfort. She was stiff and sore.

And mad.

The call was from the address Bruce's assistant at Systems Analysis used. Work? At a time like this? She growled and flicked the channel open.

Bruce's square, dark face, framed in scouring-pad sloping sideburns and bisected by a perfectly trimmed moustache, popped up. "Frankie. Heard you got swamped out of your vacation place." He frowned at her. "Woah."

She grimaced and pushed her hair into something that must look like a bird's nest but maybe a slightly neater bird's nest.

"Still here, actually. Not sure the rest of the bungalow is. Think I'll get my deposit back?"

"I'll set Scott on it. Here's something to take your mind off your troubles. An assignment came up, one I think you'd do well. It's a locate and plan for retrieval."

"Seriously? One day of vacation is all I get?"

"This assignment won't interfere with your holiday. Not in any major way." Bruce looked to the side, perhaps pulling up another screen. Were his sideburns even longer than two days ago? "You get your white box?"

It wasn't white, and it wasn't a box. It looked like a big fake opal but really was a sound-scrambler. They'd put it in a "welcome to the team" package delivered to her ship.

Frankie pulled it out of the side pocket of her duffel. Dry at least. "Just flick the switch?"

"Right. It will start blinking red when it needs to charge. Usually after twenty hours' use. Got it?"

She nodded. He waited. She realized he wanted verbal confirmation. "Yes." That was in the instructions, voice start, but in the wake of the Monstrous Deadly Storm, she'd forgotten.

She really needed to eat something. Even she could tell how cranky she was.

"We need you to visit your friend, on Cloud."

"What?"

"Morgan Orr. He's invited you, right?"

How did he know that? Oh right, Spike the not-cat was there, too, when Morgan made his first offer, in the ship's galley. Furry matted tattle-tale.

Frankie grimaced. "I'm not sure the offer still stands. I was kind of rude yesterday."

"He's resilient. And he likes you. We need you to go and see if a certain … person … is there. On the premises."

"And then what? Poison them?"

"Please refrain from sarcasm, especially that which might be misconstrued if overheard." Bruce had puffed up like a university professor whose favorite thesis had been questioned. Frankie hoped the tiny neck hole of his plain charcoal-gray top was stretchy.

"Right, sorry. I take a look around. Take a photo?"

"Ideally, talk to them. We've heard they want to emigrate, but the Orrs have them tied down on Cloud. No one has seen them alone without an Orr in years."

Frankie thought about that. "How do I get them out? How do I even get there? It's kind of a disaster area here."

"You're renting a shuttle as we speak." Bruce looked up, past her. "Scott says get the shuttles are going fast, no surprise. Everybody there wants out. Better get down to the main resort compound as soon as you can, or you'll lose your ride to a higher bidder."

"This is a capitalist economy?"

"Welcome to the World of Orrs." Sarcasm did not suit Bruce. Frankie decided not to tell him that.

"Okay. Assuming Morgan is still talking to me, and willing to bring me to meet his family. How do I find this person?"

"It's someone Spike knows."

"I have to convince Morgan to take on Spike, too?" No wonder she needed her own shuttle. "Can't I just do it by myself? It doesn't sound that tough."

Bruce stroked one of his sideburns. "You are on probation. Best to take the help where you can find it. Anyway, Spike will be the one deciding whether extraction is feasible."

"You mean, Spike will decide if we help the person run away from the Orrs? In a rental shuttle with limited power and a regulator on its speed?"

"When was the last time you ate?"

She waved that away. "Why didn't you tell me Morgan was

an Orr? You know all, so you must have known he was traveling under his middle name."

Bruce tilted his head, waiting.

Frankie came up with it herself. "No competent pilot would take someone unknown and unvetted onto her ship. I should have checked." But it had been such a great chance, to be anonymous herself. Just a cargo pilot, nothing more.

So she made the deal. With one of the worst possible people she could have chosen in the entire universe.

The universe wasn't usually so literal.

"You didn't set me up? Bruce, tell me you didn't."

"I did not." His baritone voice rang true.

"Fine. I'll see what I can do. Assuming I can even get out of this bathroom."

"Might want to change clothes. The Orrs have standards. Dusty and wrinkled isn't going to cut it."

"Thanks, dad."

CHAPTER
FIVE

ONLY HOURS after Alvin's stormy progress had swept much of the White Sands Resort into the nearby town, the glare of the sun had baked the dark pavement of its parking lot warm enough to melt the soles of Frankie's sandals.

She shaded her eyes with a hand while listening to an affronted Purveyor of Business huff and puff and swing her arms about over the use of the little shuttlebus sitting on the pad in front of them. A shuttle that clearly had Frankie's name on the manifest.

"I don't see why we can't both use the shuttle," Frankie said, trying to solve the problem by sacrificing her state of mind. "I can take all four of you with me back to the city."

"That's not the point!" the Purveyor bleated.

Frankie didn't know how to answer that.

The clamor of an incoming vessel was a welcome distraction. Not a shuttle, unfortunately, only a helicopter-style hopper that maybe could hold four people. It homed in on the landing pad one space over from them.

It bounced hard on one of its two long landing gears, with a groan of affronted metal. The second time, it settled perfectly. Pilot must have flicked the switch to auto-land.

Frankie was glad she wouldn't be traveling with that guy. Let the Purveyor risk it.

A head of unmistakable, perfectly tousled hair bounced out of the pilot's door, on the other side of the hopper.

Morgan Orr.

As he came around the hopper's blunt nose, she caught the full effect: A full-toothed grin on top of another one of those tunics that continuously swirled a rainbow's worth of colors. Narrow aquamarine pants tucked into calf-high boots that looked made of antique black rubber. Even the Purveyor swayed at the sight.

"Captain!" he barged into the space between the Purveyor and Frankie. "Care to reconsider my offer?"

"Same terms?" Frankie said.

"No strings, no family. Peppermint every day."

She looked at the blustery Purveyor. The woman had somehow obtained a smallish child, the kind with sad eyes giant in their heads. Sympathy magnet. She had an arm loosely around the child's shoulders. Unfair advantage. She shouldn't get to win.

Frankie let the resentment go with a soft sigh.

"Acceptable," she said. She pulled the shuttle's manifest up, erased her name, and slid it over to the Purveyor. The woman wisely said not one more word to her. The kid ran off.

Frankie picked up her duffle, slung its strap across her shoulder. She walked past Morgan, toward the hopper. It was the kind with only two windowy doors. She'd have to get in to shove the duffle in the back.

"Is that your best outfit?" Morgan said. He must have seen the small stain on her calf from an incident with the soy sauce this morning at the breakfast buffet. She thought she had washed it off to near invisibility.

"I'm on vacation," she said. "What do you want?"

He frowned. What was he so worried about? "Maybe we should stop in the city. Your Systems friends would pay for replacement clothes, right?"

She stopped. She turned back to him. Perfect.

"I'd pick up the tab. But it's a good idea. I've lost my other swimsuit. And we have to pick up Spike."

Morgan actually took a step back. His hands rose halfway, as if to block something. "That one? She's here?"

"What? She's an experienced stowaway, I don't control her. But I can't leave her on one moon while I go to another. At least, tell her I'm leaving."

Morgan opened his mouth, maybe to argue with that, but paused. He closed it again, nodded, and took a step toward her.

An ear-curdling shriek erupted from the side of the shuttle.

A pause.

"Kitty!" screeched a small child's voice.

Morgan put his hands over his ears. Frankie dropped her bag on Morgan's boots and ran toward the noise.

The shuttle's side door was open. The small child careened nearby, holding a bundle of disreputable fur. Angry, disreputable fur.

The Purveyor was bleating something negative. The child's shrieks were starting to sound like pain rather than delight. Was that blood?

"Let go!" Frankie said. "She doesn't like to be touched."

The child flung its arms wide, dropping Spike headfirst toward the molten pavement. Somehow, the not-cat was able to twist its spine and get her front paws under her before she hit.

"This is your. Your." The Purveyor's whole body vibrated; a volcano ready to explode. "Animal?"

"Not mine," Frankie said. Spike did not help by rushing to

hide behind Frankie's calves. She rubbed her cheek on Frankie's knee.

"She's emancipated," Frankie said, weakly.

"That's it!" the Purveyor said. "I'm speaking to the Management." She stalked off, small child scurrying behind.

Morgan had come up beside her. He had her bag on his shoulder. "Think we better go direct to Cloud. Safer that way."

CHAPTER
SIX

UNLIKE SILVA, its twin moon Cloud had not been terraformed. Seen from orbit, it did not have the "Cooperative Planets Look." The one that came about from generations of Cooperative geoneers hewing faithfully to the realm's planetary standard of forty percent land and sixty percent water.

Instead, Cloud looked like marbled chocolate fudge. Black rock covered the parts that weren't under massive polar ice caps, with thick swaths of oddly white water twisting through the landscape. A collection of gigantic domes—Morgan wasn't kidding about the size—clustered at one section of the belly of the moon. Other than a couple of portable bases, probably for mining something or other, the rest of the moon was empty. Of humans, at least.

The cross-moon shuttle dropped them at the biggest of the domes, which looked to house a city of maybe thirty thousand people. As Morgan did not dawdle at the platform, Frankie didn't catch more than a glimpse: Black-and-white stone architecture in pleasing shapes, gray sky above.

Morgan had drawn a bit of attention on the shuttle. Not surprising, seeing as everybody else was in practical working clothes that did not shimmer or swirl, and their hair was not half the height of their head or neon orange. But there was an odd undercurrent of wariness among their fellow travelers. Nobody sat near them. They'd all crowded onto the other row of seats. It couldn't be Spike; Frankie had coaxed the still-ruffled not-cat to sit between herself and Morgan. Was it Morgan's scent? Patchouli was a weird choice for a traveling day.

Whatever, it was his own fault. What did he expect?

On arrival, he ushered her away from the main exit and down a smaller side ramp. Soon they were underground, speeding in a classic limousine-shaped autocar to who knew where. Frankie wanted to pump Morgan for directions—how would they ever get out of here without him?—but he'd sunk deep into his own thoughts.

Sunk was the word for it. With each step on the trip, Morgan had closed off more of himself. First the animation in his face had fled. Then his whole body went so still. She hadn't realized until then that he was such a fidgeter, some part of him always jiggling about. Even his hair seemed somehow tamed.

Now his neck and shoulders had gone concave and rigid. They must be close.

The limo ascended a ramp into bright gray air. It turned quickly before it could plow into a veritable wall of forest-green bushes. They must have been planted expressly to block the view of this two-lane road that ringed the inner edge of the dome. The only way she could tell they weren't one incredibly long bush was that each section was speckled with tiny flowers in different colors: white, red, yellow, blue, pale green. She leaned forward to see how far it went.

"This is the back way," Morgan said, voice reedy. "We're at the edge of the family dome. The main house is nearer the center."

She pulled her gaze from the outstanding hedge and stared at him. "The family dome?"

He winced. "Actually, it's the family moon."

That sent her all the way back into the seat. "You can purchase a moon?" Usually companies bought rights to materials or space on moons from the local governmental entity. Who would sell their moon outright?

"It's edge space. Anything goes." As they turned onto a single-lane road, he gestured out the window. "There's the main lake, excellent for swimming. We'll be on this side of it. In a minute, you'll get a great view of the House."

House was not the word for it. It must be more than a kilometer away, but it loomed over the wide meadow-style lawn aproning down to the lake. The four-story rectangle was softened by the cream-and-gold tones of the stones that made it up, as well as the many wide, glinting windows. The solar-paneled peaked roof had a whimsical flip along the edge, probably hiding the rain gutters.

Frankie was beginning to think the Orrs might be a bit compulsive about hiding every ugliness.

Morgan went on. "Anyway, this was going to be the place Mom and Dad retired to, and a place for long holidays in the meantime."

The limo slid into stillness in front of a cottage that looked as if it had been ported out of a princess and ogre fairytale, even down to the thatched roof. More windows, though.

"Supercute, huh?" Morgan pushed out of the car and came around to Frankie's side, closest to the cottage. He opened the door, and held a hand out to her. She put the strap of her duffel in his hand and got out without his help. He smiled and shook his head.

"Dad had superbig plans and everything. I can show you the scale model if you want. I think it's in storage next to the cabana."

She walked past the cottage to take another look at the big house. Morgan opened the cottage door and set the duffel inside, and then joined her.

"It's on a hill?" she said. "To look so tall?"

"Joke's on us, yes. To get to the house from anywhere in the dome it's uphill. But to leave is always an easy downhill, so I guess it evens out."

"How long do you think finishing the whole moon will take?"

"Oh, it's done now. We lost all our money—well, not all our money—but funds for special projects like Cloud were the first to go. We were Walapped."

"Walloped?" She frowned at him. Could there be a High Galactic word she didn't know?

"No. Wala—the planet. Walapped. Get it?"

Frankie absolutely did not get it. "I'm sorry the murder of everyone on my planet interfered with the plans for your vacation home."

Morgan slapped his forehead. "Right. My very great apologies. What a heedless thing to say." He shook his head. "Looked different from our side. Manslaughter, at most." He caught her look of fury and hurried back to the door of the cottage. He was right: He needed to be gone.

"Okay, so you're here, and I'm three minutes away in a matching cottage. You can't see it from here, but if you take the path behind the cottage and go left, you'll be there in three minutes. If you go right, you'll hit the cabana in forty-five minutes. Or use the bike. Then it's only five minutes."

He was talking too fast again. She couldn't fathom how he had ever had any success as a con artist.

"But maybe wait for me to go to the cabana," he rushed on. "Don't want you to run into any strangers. I'll ring up Mom and see what's up. Maybe she's not here. But the lake is great for swimming. You'll like it better than the pool, I bet. I figure. Yeah."

He leapt back into the limo through her still-open door, and it sped away.

CHAPTER
SEVEN

NOT FIVE MINUTES LATER, Frankie was in her suit and floating on her back in the perfectly chilled lake. The water went deep just a few strokes out from shore. Fresh water, not ocean, so she had to keep a lazy scull going to stay on the surface. But no brine or dead-fish smell, just fresh plants in the gentle breeze. So, a trade up.

The lake was big enough to have a noticeable tide, if the lines on the three mooring posts set a ways out were any indication. Nowhere near as strong as the Pearl Sea, which was just fine with her. She'd had enough turbulence for a while. This trip was enough to put her off vacations altogether.

Still, it wasn't the first holiday that had gone wrong. And you couldn't blame the weather for being weather. Not like someone had on purpose sent a massive bomb too close to a planet's gravity well.

Frankie pushed those thoughts away, into the soft water rippling away from her.

She moved her neck in tiny figure eights, loosening joints, easing the usual tightness along her shoulders. Working down, she gently sways her hips in the same shape. The knots from huddling in a hot tub all night eased out and away. Her knees seemed okay, but her feet must have suffered more than she'd though on the hot pavement. The cold still slapped them, even after the rest of her had accepted it.

She should have gone to a big city for holiday. This water reminded her even more of vacations on Wala. It was harder to push all that away when she wasn't busy doing something. Maybe that was why she almost never took vacations. Lately her excuse was she needed to establish her reliability as a cargo hauler with a new route. But she was the one who had chosen to be a cargo hauler.

And it wasn't like hauling cargo didn't have a lot of dead time. She'd learned to play the guitar. She'd gone through yet another series of sessions with a grief counselor app. She'd re-read all the books she'd liked but had to skim through to keep up in university. What next?

Think about that tomorrow. Or next week.

She shouldn't have come here. There were good reasons—excellent reasons—not to. She knew them all. And yet, here she was. What would her counselor say?

She sculled herself down, dunking her head in the chill embrace so the water could pull her hair back out of her eyes.

Coming back up, she squinted, trying to see the seams in the dome, or at least the rows of lights. The design was clever, with such wide diffusion it was hard to tell it wasn't a single light source. Of course, the sun's being nearly at the horizon gave the trick away.

Why didn't the Orrs time their day with their own main sun? To stay on the Cooperative capital city's time? Frankie couldn't imagine the cost of a real-time call from Zichi.

She should call Beth. It was her turn. But later. And absolutely not from Orr-ville. Beth would surely recognize Cloud when it came up on the location label. Better to call her from the Spear, once the ship was back in service. She would need to test out the new communications array and everything.

Good excuse.

Frankie rotated to point the back of her head toward shore, and slowly sculled in. The cottage had both towels and thick beach blankets, and she'd taken them all. Across the narrow road, she'd seen a meadow with young trees for shade.

Looked like the perfect place for a nap.

Okay, sure, so maybe she was avoiding being inside another tiny rickety-looking building at the moment. But how often could you sleep outside and know—absolutely know—you were safe?

She wasn't going to pass that up.

FRANKIE COULDN'T TELL if it was the flakes of crud dropping onto her face or the angry-teakettle of a hiss that woke her. She really hoped it was Spike, who had snuggled into the bend of her legs almost as soon as she lay down. The shady grass outside the narrow woods had been too soft and inviting to pass up.

As Frankie hoisted herself to a sideways seat, blinking hard to get the sleep out of her eyes, her knee brushed vibrating fur. It was, indeed, Spike, her long, even-more-raggedy coat sprinkled with what Frankie hoped was dirt. The not-cat perched stiff on her haunches, ready to leap at something between them and the road.

In the now-brighter sun, Frankie couldn't see more than an orange shadow shaped like a person. The shadow resolved itself into a woman. Boots, narrow brown slacks, black tank top, tanned arms with hands on hips. Tilted head with all the brownish hair tied behind it. Big dark eyes. Wide mouth.

Not smiling.

"How did you get here?" the woman said in flawless Galactic, complete with patrician sneer. Was that scent Cozumar? Most expensive over-the-counter perfume in the system.

Ten to one it was Morgan's mom.

Great.

"Um," Frankie said. Trying to wake up, she wiped at the hope-it's-dirt off her face. She groped at smoothing her must-be-everywhere hair. The woman snorted.

"Someone's coming to escort you off the premises," she said. "This is private property, as I'm sure you know." She took a step toward them, leaning in as if looking for something. "Where's your photo rig?"

A low growl rumbled out of Spike.

The woman stopped, startled. "What happened to you?" she said to Spike.

Spike didn't answer.

Frankie shook her head hard to wake up her brain, and tried again. "I came with Morgan."

The woman stopped cold. Her arms slid to hold themselves across her belly. She turned toward the cottage. Her long hair was tied in the back in such a tight inverted braid it looked unreal. Like art.

"He's not there," Frankie said. "Turn left on the path and walk three minutes. He said—I haven't tried it." She pulled a towel around her middle and pushed up to standing.

The woman looked back at her. "He's not sleeping with you?" Whatever the expression was on Frankie's face must have satisfied her. "Smart girl."

Frankie hated that she felt forced to explain. "I'm a pilot. I hauled Morgan and his cargo to Smithson Station. My ship got damaged on the run, so I'm stuck here while Eckberg's makes the fixes."

"Smithson, you said? You were the pilot who outran the Skolls?"

Frankie frowned. She hadn't thought of it that way.

The woman laughed, and suddenly seemed a lot warmer. Spike seemed to think so, too. The not-cat plopped her butt on one of Frankie's feet, still tucked under a towel.

"So you're the one I have to thank for keeping my youngest's skin intact," she said. She took a step closer, to the appropriate distance, and performed a semiformal Cooperative bow. "Pleased to meet you. I'm Marissa Cloud-Orr."

"Cloud?"

"Like the moon, yes. Konrad thought it providential when we were looking for a place to settle down. I think the planet's polity saw us coming and changed the name so they could boost the price. Still," she turned, her gaze sweeping across the cottage, water, mansion on the hill. "It is a beautiful place. Now."

She sighed, and turned back to Frankie. "But you can't stay here."

Frankie looked down at Spike. Spike slightly but intentionally shook her head. One of them would not be leaving.

Well, that was easy enough. The not-cat would bound away, into the woods. Spike would keep looking for their target.

And then what? They hadn't set up a system to communicate yet.

Frankie was a terrible spy.

"We're expecting guests soon," Cloud-Orr said. They'll be staying here. For our big annual gala, you know. I'm glad Morgan remembered he was supposed to be here for it."

Frankie seriously doubted he remembered anything at all about it. "I'm still mostly packed," she said. "No problem."

"Oh, so you do have clothes?" Cloud-Orr's voice went silvery when she teased. At least, Frankie hoped it was teasing.

"Sorry, yeah. I saw the water and I just had to be in it. First thing."

"Don't blame you. But you don't have to cover yourself up quite so much. Our domes filter out the burning rays without dimming the intake of the solar panels."

Frankie couldn't help looking up at the dome. "Wow."

"New tech. Konrad's. Cloud is the beta tester for many of his projects." She looked up again, too. "The first filter went green after a couple weeks. We all looked like zombies."

"Now," she dropped her sharp gaze back to Frankie. "Pack up, and we'll walk to where you should be staying."

Frankie shrugged. "No worries. I'll go straight to Morgan's. The transport we came in might even still be there. Which would be easy."

"Oh, you're not going anywhere." A sly look came into Morgan's mother's eyes. "We'll set you up in the cabana, not the main house. Totally informal, don't worry."

That was a fast change. "Okay," Frankie said slowly. "Give me five minutes."

She took three.

It was time enough for a home invasion.

Coming out of the very nicely tiled bathroom, soggy suit over one arm, duffel on the opposite shoulder, she found Cloud-Orr inside the cottage. At the mini-kitchen counter. Writing something on a tablet.

"Just leaving a note for Morgan," his mother said. She looked up. She had that gleam in her eyes again.

"He'll join us when he's ready."

CHAPTER
EIGHT

MARISSA CLOUD-ORR HEADED for the cottage door, obviously expecting Frankie to follow.

Absolutely not. She was not going anywhere with a stranger. Especially without her one contact on-site knowing about it.

Frankie twisted her wrist, powering on her wristcom. As she got to the entrance, she stopped.

"Think I left something in the bathroom. Right back."

As she passed the tablet with its note, Frankie took an image of its screen. She checked the bathroom quickly, to prove her words true. She sent the image to Morgan's line and then scooted out of the cottage.

A gardener's go-cart rolled up to them from the direction of Morgan's cottage. The oversized wheelbarrow of a vehicle pulled to a stop beside Cloud-Orr. It must have just hauled peat, by the smell of it. An older, wiry person in peat-kneed overalls rolled out of its tiny seat.

"False alarm, Mal," Cloud-Orr said. "This is Frankie. Friend of the family." She turned to Frankie. "Here's Mal. He manages the team that makes our gardens grow. And he shuttles invasive plants and people off the property."

Mal greeted her by touching the brim of his sunhat. He apparently did not appear to trust the protective shield above them, or maybe that was a mandatory part of the outfit.

"Usually I'm the one that finds 'em, though." He set a foot on the floorboard of the cart, as if to step back in, and squinted at Cloud-Orr. "Sorry about that, Marissa."

Marissa Cloud-Orr waved his apology away and glanced at Frankie. "Everybody calls me Marissa. You can, too."

"What's up today?" she said to Mal. "Besides false alarms."

"Birds shat up that well again." Mal took his foot off the cart and shook his head. "Flying rats."

"Birds are just as important as your beloved bees," Marissa said.

Frankie frowned. "Don't they need to migrate?"

"Not all birds," Mal said. "These just stay in one place. And shit in one place." He looked toward the woods.

"And keep the ecosystem rolling," Marissa said on a sigh. Must be a familiar tune from Mal.

Mal gestured at the woods. "Why don't they roost in there? Or the bushes?" Suddenly, he went stiff. Then he pointed at something at the edge the woods.

Spike. Staring at them.

"What the blazing worlds is that?"

Marissa laughed, a silvered slice of humor. "Answer to your prayers, Mal. Raggedy monster, out on the loose. Might eat all your flying rats in one go."

Mal climbed back into the cart's seat. "If you say so."

"Mal," Marissa said, stopping him as he reached for the control panel. "Seen Morgan?"

Surprise stretched the wrinkles from his face.

"No ma'am. Not hide nor hair."

"Came with Frankie, here. You see him, tell him to come say hello properly, will you?"

Mal touched his cap, powered the cart back on, and checked his mirrors.

And then grinned.

"Tell him yourself." He looked over his shoulder.

Morgan, hair too far on one side and red in the face, was puffing up the road toward them.

Frankie sidled toward Mal. "Space for one more?" she whispered.

Mal just winked at her and scooted away.

"Mom!" Morgan huffed out. "I'm home!" He dropped his duffel on the road and reached out to hug her.

Marissa submitted to the rather flopsy embrace. She waited for him to finish, and step back. He had already caught his breath, his face returning to its normal creamy tan.

"Something wrong with the house?" she said.

The red came back. "I just needed a nap first." His gaze fled from his mother's face, alighting here and there. Finally locking onto Frankie. "Did Frankie tell you about the cyclone?"

Marissa turned her gimlet gaze to Frankie. "She told me about Smithson."

"Yeah, well. But she was staying at that posh resort on Silva, on the shores of Pearl, you know, with the doves? And a cyclone ripped her hut right away. While she was in it!"

"That explains the bruise, then."

Bruise? Frankie reached for her face. She touched her cheek. Where?

"On the back of your arm, dearie. You probably can't see it. Big purple circle. Size of a sink drain."

Frankie twisted, trying to look behind herself. She barely caught sight of the edge of a bruise. "Hot-tub vent," she said. "Slept in one last night."

Marissa snorted. "Well. We can do better than that."

Frankie wasn't sure what she meant by that. Better, or worse? Morgan's careful, cautious look at his mother did not ease Frankie's mind.

THE CABANA WAS, indeed, far better than a drained-out hot tub. Not a cabana at all, more like a medium-sized house, in a completely different design than the old-fashioned bulk of the main house. One of those short-white-boxes-strung-together setups, a single story with the hall on the non-pool side so every suite would have sliding window-doors directly to the superlong pool. And the pool! More like a lagoon, and no chemical smell. The building's wild-meadow roof, as well as the unlikely desert trees and well-tended underbrush, added to the feeling of being in a gentle jungle. An energizing sense of wildness but actually completely tame.

Most interesting was the way the plantings blocked any view of the main house. Frankie walked the carefully irregular curves of the giant pool and could find only one spot—near a slightly sickly tree—where she could get even a peek at the mansion. Interesting choice. The architects had put the mansion on display for the lowly people in the cottages below, but blocked it from closer friends—or family—who might not wish to have its ostentation slapped in their faces all day. Or maybe it was just an illusion for the family: a trip they could pretend was far away without leaving dome.

The positioning made her wonder why Morgan had chosen the cottages first. She probably wouldn't have a chance to ask him for a while.

Marissa had kept her arm locked with his, outwardly

companionably, for the whole walk. Even as she walked them into the box through the glass door farthest from the house.

At the first of a row of opaqued-glass doors, Marissa had touched a pad. The door slid open. She waved Frankie into a small but airy sitting room.

"Shared areas and kitchen are down the hall. Enjoy yourself," she'd said as Frankie walked through. And she'd closed the door.

At least she hadn't locked it.

Frankie hadn't even dropped her duffel in this room. She'd gone straight through, passing the too-hard looking steel-and-white sitting room furnishings, the too-soft white rattan bedroom set and out the clear sliding door to the just-right pool area. Here was the delicious smell of warmed cedar planking. And the chairs that could stretch you out or prop you up, all with enticing, waterproof cushions. Also white. Impractical and beautiful.

After her circuit of the pool, Frankie did another half-circle and chose a sun-warmed chair on the tree side. She could keep an eye on the cabana complex, at least until the sun lulled her to sleep again. And it would take a while for anyone to get to her. Maybe this time, she'd wake up before somebody's mom snuck up on her.

She hadn't listened to more than a half a chapter of the latest Mon Gviv romance when something landed heavily on the chair beside hers.

Spike.

"Tired of roughing it already?" she said to her not-cat colleague.

Spike shook herself like a wet dog trying to get dry. Dirt, bits of leaves and even pine needles flew onto the decking.

"Where did you find a pine tree? Don't tell me you've cased the whole dome?"

Spike flopped on her side, showing her paw-pads to Frankie. Between the beans was dirt that smelled like peat.

"You hitched a ride? With Mel? Mal?" Frankie frowned. "We need to set up a way to communicate."

Spike tilted her head, ears halfway back. Apparently, not-cats could roll their eyes at you without actually rolling their eyes.

"No. What if Marissa had kicked me out? How would I get in touch with you? How would I know you were in trouble? What if you need rescuing?"

Spike flopped all the way onto her back on that one.

"Fine. Maybe not rescue, but what about if you just need a hand? You know, with opposable thumbs."

That earned her a glare. She'd hit a sore spot.

Spike lifted a front paw, stretching it toward Frankie. Frankie leaned over to set her hand on Spike's lounge chair. Spike flicked her wrist—was it a wrist, on not-cats? She must want the other hand. Frankie sighed and rolled closer to put her left wrist, the one with her comm, on Spike's cushion.

Spike wiped her left-front paw on the cushion, leaving a tiny streak of peat. She set the now-somewhat-cleaner paw pads on the wristcom.

A jolt, and a new window opened on Frankie's main screen. Very slowly, a word typed itself across the screen.

Satisfied?

Frankie stared at Spike. "How? Oh, never mind. Okay, it's a lot of work for you. But maybe less work than talking?" Spike gave her a slow blink, yes.

"And do I send you voice messages? Or can you read, too?"

Spike lifted her paw and rolled entirely away from Frankie. She started cleaning herself, showing her back to her colleague.

"Fine, okay. Stupid question." Frankie wasn't sure she liked being part of this team. Then again, Spike hadn't asked for it, either. And Spike was a pro. It must be doubly annoying to her to have a newbie teammate.

Frankie leaned back, settling in for more listening in the sun.

She would rest a bit, see if Morgan came back, find something to eat.

Let the Orrs forget she was here. Then the real search would begin.

"Thank you for your help," she said.

Spike stopped mid-lick. She stretched, rolled back to face Frankie, and started in again.

CHAPTER
NINE

FRANKIE WAS PULLED out of one of Mon Gviv's famous seduction scenes by the buzz of an incoming message.

Morgan.

Supper soon. Formal casual

So much for laying low.

Not family-only?

Command performance.

Whose command? Had his mom already changed her mind about stowing Frankie away?

Not so good. Frankie had rather enjoyed the idea of being stowed away. Eating dessert first. Playing her music loud. Definitely not dressing for dinner.

U there? Morgan messaged.

Formal casual?

Ask the wardrobe. Pick you up 20 min

Now she was intrigued.

Spike was sleeping like the dead on the lounger. Frankie contemplated the wisdom of offering to help her take a sudsy bath, and quickly rejected it.

"Gotta go, Spike," she said. "Command performance. Hold the fort."

All she got from the not-cat was an ear flick. Such a life.

The wardrobe was a walk-in closet off the bathroom, to the side of the two main rooms. As Frankie entered, lights went on above her and around a triple floor-length mirror on the opposite wall. Along the two side walls hung double rods of tops and bottoms in muted hues. Below sat a range of fabrics and pieces of footwear, the kind that could be combined and molded to fit any foot.

"Hello, wardrobe. I need to look formal casual for dinner tonight."

"Is it a dinner or a supper?" The voice was supposedly neutral High Galactic female coded.

Shit. Was this really going to be a Hi-G meal, out here in the wild moons of nowhere?

"Supper," she said.

A square appeared in the center mirrors. The wardrobe was offering her six similar looks. Tunic hems were shorter this year, but the asymmetrical neck was still a thing. Each outfit was shades of gray and ecru. Ash city.

Frankie was sensing a pattern. "Thanks, wardrobe," she said, looking at the screen in the mirror as if Wardrobe's eyes were there? "Do you have more choices that include brighter colors?"

A second row of six popped up, incorporating navy. But one also had a scarf in muted orange. Might do better to tame her hair than a liter of gel. She touched that picture.

Something behind the mirror started to hum. Fabricator. Arrows on the mirror-screen pointed to the right. Tiny green laser spots lingered above two hangers. Apparently, the tan wide-legged pants and cream undershirt were immediately available.

Frankie left the wardrobe to its humming to do her other prep. By the time she was showered, powdered, hair still wild, there was the scarf. By the time she'd wrestled her hair into an attractive non-bulbous mass, the navy tunic was ready. Frankie hadn't noticed the orange piping along its trapezoidal neck opening. Or maybe Wardrobe had added it on the fly.

She put it on and ran out to get her soft boots. She held them up to the mirror.

"Okay?" An arrow pointed down to something that looked like a boot polisher. So they must be okay.

Frankie had her pants legs pulled up to her shins and was playing with the shoe polisher—the action was like a double-speed foot massage—when a triangle-style bell sounded out. She stomped her boots, dropped her pants hem, and took one last look at herself.

"Thanks, Wardrobe!"

She could have sworn the room's lights blinked.

AS THE HALL door slid open, Morgan took a step back. Frankie looked amazing. Those wild auburn curls lassoed by a shimmery band. Tunic and slacks making complementary angles. And color!

He made a proper Cooperative bow, trying to come up with something to say that would sound sweet and not desperate.

"You clean up good," he said. He mentally slapped his forehead. Some smooth spacer he was.

But Frankie laughed, and it was that "relieved this isn't going to be awkward" laugh. He hadn't made it worse, at least. But the ache was still there.

She spun in place in her sitting room. "It's all Wardrobe. What a great amenity."

No way. "But how did you get it to do the orange headwrap? I never see that in my options."

She shrugged. "I have skills you've only dreamed of."

Morgan's heart jumped. And so did his mind, to that topic Frankie did not want to speak about. She was not interested in him, that way. Or she was, but something about him did not qualify. Or something. He wasn't sure, but he didn't want to push.

But he did want to be sure.

Not tonight, though. They would be lucky to come out of this supper still friends. Frankie had no idea what she was in for.

He held out his arm, inviting her to join him in the hall. The sun's half-light cast a vague rainbow through the glass outer wall and across her middle. His, too, probably.

They started walking. He checked his comm again. "I'm timing it so we get there in time to introduce everyone and pick up a drink, but not enough time to actually drink it. I'd advise just one glass of wine. With the last course—Silva makes a lovely ice wine."

Frankie slowed, gazing out the wall of windows. On this side of the cabana, past the white-gravel access road, a lawn spread wide, greens fading into a giant field of unripe wheat a kilometer or so away. Most of the dome was agricultural, but around the house it also served as ornament.

"Last course?" Frankie touched the ribbon in her hair. He wondered if she knew how often she touched her hair. When she was thinking, worried, off-balance. It was the worst kind of tell. He was grateful for it. "How casual formal is this dinner? Supper," she amended.

"Not sure. We're usually casual casual here." Actually, they almost never ate supper together. Maybe a little overlap at break- fast. But Mom had her gardens and her virtual meetings, and David might not come out of his office until well after dark. At least Morgan had been spared the Eldest Son's nightmare of a life. Then again, at least he would have known what to do with himself. His current act, sitting around being the spare, was dull, dull, dull.

Outside the cabana the day was cooling. The crickets were warming up. The gravel in the road crunched in a satisfying way under their boots. Strange that it always seemed the cusp of autumn here. Frankie had chosen the right colors.

Her head swiveled gently back and forth, trying to take in all the new sights. It was fun to have her here. He wanted to hear what she thought of the rolling lawns (ostentatious water-sponges), the faux-ancient facade (pretentious folderol), the family (less said, the better).

"What do you think?" he said.

"Temperature is perfect. Everything looks so lovely in this light. Why am I going to this supper?

The last one startled him so much he nearly missed a step. She didn't laugh at him, but one of the corners of her mouth did rise.

"Okay, first, it's not about you. It's punishment. For me. For not telling them ahead of time that I was coming. For coming unannounced with a stranger. For hiding from them, even if it was only resting up before the familial onslaught."

"How does this punish you?"

He had to tell her. "They're going to be mean to you. To get to me. I hate it when people are mean to my friends. To anyone. And my family." He searched for the right words. "They're really good at being mean, in that way where you're not sure they really are. Only I will be sure."

Frankie looked out at the wheat. "Maybe they've changed," she finally said.

"The last time I brought a friend home I was thirteen. And we both left crying."

"Left?" She looked at him, startled.

"Left for school, not forever. Although it was forever for my friend." Morgan wasn't sure Celine had forgiven him even yet.

"Okay, so, that was kind of a long time ago," Frankie began.

Morgan cut her off. "Just take care. But at least I didn't tell them who you really were."

"What?" Frankie stopped so fast the cuffs of her slacks carried on without her for a moment.

"No, it's good," Morgan backtracked. "Don't give them any more fodder."

Frankie frowned at him, disbelieving. She started up again.

"Paranoid much?"

She had no idea.

CHAPTER
TEN

UP CLOSE, the front of the Orr mansion took Frankie's breath away. A magical castle from a fairytale past. A wide white-marble ramp led to an equally wide single-slab porch, complete with a granite railing that somehow suggested cherubs. The main entrance, a double-wide wooden door, had something embossed on each panel. An actual family crest?

Symmetrical windows along the porcelain-white-faced wall shouted wealth and fastidiousness. A soft white shone through the windows from inside. Light through sheer curtains? The roof was standard greenery and solar panels, but the flipped edges she'd seen from a distance were actual curlicues up close. A building that couldn't be more than a few decades old instead looked as if it had been built a millennia ago and shipped here.

But as they passed through one of the doors, into a coolly lit hall in whites and ecrus, the illusion fell away. Practical carpeting, sweeping stair-ramps in the modern style. Not a sound but the noise of their passing. Physical artwork, mostly statues, from this century. Lots of pointy edges.

She slowed to gape at one that reminded her of a waterfall,

clear with soft greens and blues shot through it. Morgan put a hand on the small of her back and pushed gently to get her going again.

Down the hall, and quickly past an open door through which she could see a formal table—even down to the silvered legs and white ceramic top. Frankie twisted, trying to see more as they flew by. Could that possibly be a formal setting?

They stopped at the next door, one of the kind with the knob in the middle. White, of course. Morgan did not reach for the knob.

"I've never seen this door closed," he said. As he turned to her, the ease in his expression fled. Hard mouth, sharp eyes, not a shadow of a smile. "Are you ready?".

"What day is it, Galactic?"

He looked at her, eyes widening. "They wouldn't dare," Details of the most-extreme formal suppers varied, tiny but critical changes based on season, day, and time.

"They might."

They both lifted their arms to look at their wristcoms. Morgan bumped her comm with his. The readings matched. "At least we agree."

"Got it." She smiled, ignoring the sneaking flame of panic coming from her gut. "Guess I'm more nervous than I thought. Meeting the family."

"It's not like that," he said. He sounded a little sad about that.

"You smell nice," she said. "What is it?"

His face stayed the same, but his shoulders perked up. "Elegante, the new formulation." Then he deflated. "Too much?"

"Perfect," she said. "I wish you'd made your hair orange, though." She made a moue of sadness. "Then we would match."

That cracked a small smile out of him. Got him moving.

"Next time," he said. He pulled open the door.

IT WASN'T AS bad as Morgan expected.

It was worse.

He pulled the door open to see his brother posed to be framed perfectly by anyone coming into the room. David was in full peacock. He stood, one hip back, with his hand on the mantel of the giant fake fireplace. Young Heir Relaxed at Home. Barrel chest out, his artfully blond hair swept into that bizarre cyclone shape popular this season among the center-right politicians in the Great Senate. Dressed in shades of the family color, insipid white, he glowed as if radioactive.

Mom next to him and lower, as appropriate for the aging matriarch. Straight-backed in one of the two throne-chairs beside the crackling fake fire. At least she was in a light blue, which matched her coloring (and Morgan's) so much better and didn't blind anybody. She had chosen classics, the tunic and trousers he remembered from the celebration of David's taking his father's Senate seat.

Both formal formal.

The invitation lied.

He waved Frankie to enter and followed her quickly to come abreast with her in one step. She stepped through confidently, her eyes open and curious, scanning the room. Seeing David, her jaw clamped tight.

An impulse shot up Morgan's spine into his brain, turning into an idea. Turn around.

He did not break stride. Or break into a sweat. So, already doing better than last time. Of course, Konrad wasn't here, so that made it easier.

He had no doubt Frankie could handle herself. She'd certainly handled him well enough.

He just didn't want her to have to.

David lurched gracefully into motion. He met them at the edge of the white shagged carpet that formed the sitting-room portion of this great cold space. They only ever used the near corner of this giant room, with its soaring windows and rafters three stories away. It was really the ballroom, but since they could always control the weather on Cloud, big events were always held outside. As the daylight drew down, shadows filled the empty spaces, which only highlighted the fireplace tableaux.

The two men bowed semiformally. David came up faster. His body was long and lean, too. They must look like bookends. But David's face looked just like Dad, while Morgan favored Mom. In more than just looks.

Formal greeting performed, David pivoted the proper forty-five degrees and looked down his nose at Frankie.

"David, this is my friend Frankie."

"The cargo pilot." David's voice had a playful, reedy overtone, at odds with the snooty expressions always on his face. Those frown lines probably were already permanent.

Morgan stiffened, a reflex. Frankie only smiled her professional-pilot-at-work smile.

"I appreciate the honor of being welcomed to your home, Senator Orr. Madame Orr," she bowed, correctly, toward Mom, but spoke, correctly, to David. "The Stauffer in the entryway is stunning. I love his blues."

David's bushy black eyebrows crashed down toward his eyes. "It is a fine piece," he said. Pretty noncommittal for a work of art by one of the Cooperatives' most popular contemporary artists. He glared at Morgan. Did he think Morgan had fed her the line?

David's glass was empty, which was a good sign. As if at Morgan's thought, the white wood double doors leading to the formal dining room opened. One of dad's servos pushed both doors open at once, and then retreated back to its corner charging station.

Frankie's attention jumped from the open door to David. "You have bots?"

"Servos. Of course. It is a major part of what Industrial Orr produces you know."

Mom had risen and joined them, bringing the scent of orange and jasmine with her. She'd done something new to her hair that put the bulk of it at the nape of her neck. She took Frankie by the upper arm, leading her in front of the two men, away from David.

"One of the perks of being an Orr," she said. "Fewer people to be always around. But no servo can replace our chefs."

A dark-haired person in Orr tan management dress stood at the side of the lead chair of the aggressively long white oval ceramic table. "And definitely not Samson," Mom said, nodding to the person.

Samson was new. He looked like a rower, upper body well defined. And he'd obviously not gotten the message about blonding his hair. Or maybe not caved in to it? Morgan liked him for that reason alone. And also because his brow was as sweaty with worry as Morgan's.

Then he saw the table, and knew why.

In front of each of the four places, like a vast, ornate flower display, was an intricate collection of small plates. One bite of food sat perfectly on each of sixty-four tiny round white ceramic plates. Some of the plates hung from tiny chains connected to a silver octopus candelabra thing. Other plates sat on white cubes or rectangles, all at different heights. The order of eating was precise.

Dangerously precise. Mistakes could be fatal in the midst of negotiations, whether political or social.

This was the Cooperative Realm's most-formal dining setting, used only for the highest of holidays, or when the Regent came to call.

It was never used here on Cloud.

"Wow," Morgan said in his most-bored tone. "Wasn't sure we even had a set of these."

Samson wiped his brow.

Mom drew Frankie to the left side of the table, while David and Morgan took the right. The rest of the table, which could seat at least forty, sat empty and shadowed. Tall fake white candles illuminated their edge of the table. The overhead lights off, to make judging the distances between similar white platforms tricky.

"It's the first day of autumn," David announced, pride and malice in his thready voice. "We thought we'd celebrate."

He looked across the table at Frankie.

Her professional mask had not slipped. She radiated more calm than either Samson or Morgan.

Or Mom. Marissa's face was stone, a cross between anger and concern. Except for the dagger gaze at David. She must not have been a party to this.

Morgan glared at the side of David's face. What was the point of making Frankie uncomfortable? Nobody could get the order right without reading up first. Even the tableware—spoons, eating sticks, knives, forks, the shrimp thing, that other thing— were impossible.

So much work, just to make someone feel bad?

This was low, even for an Orr.

David caught the tail end of Morgan's glare, and winked. He leaned so close his whisper held a taste of rum. "We'll get you free of her, no worries."

Morgan actually took a step back. That's what they thought? That Frankie was a gold digger?

What a strange way to counteract it.

Frankie's face projected calm, but her gaze jumped from plate to plate. Her lips pressed tight. What were the chances she could follow even some rules of a High Galactic feast day?

She blinked. She glanced at Samson, who had not stopped sweating.

And then she looked at David, and frowned sweetly.

"Beautiful. I am so grateful for this great honor. But—"

"But?" David pushed, voice almost gleeful. Mom glared at him across the table. Morgan groaned silently.

"But," Frankie said. She leaned in to look at the hanging plates, her face all concentration. Then looked up at David. "Shouldn't the shrimp be in the third ring. Not the second?"

David took a look, and then reared back as if slapped. Did he even know what was wrong? He glared at Samson.

Who wilted. "We didn't have any almonds, right? We set the shrimp higher, still protein, and substituted bean paste puff down below."

"What!" David's screech of a roar sounded as if it had been sped up to one and a half speed.

Samson held his hands out as if to block a punch. "Chef did her best! There was no time! Silva was totally out."

"You've ruined it! Ruined. It's… It's… " David seemed to want to say more. His face went from red to redder with the effort. No words came out.

Instead, he stomped his foot. The move made a weak click on the stone floor. He must be wearing heel guards.

The puny sound for such a large movement set Morgan off. He puffed out a soft laugh, surprising himself.

Frankie leaned back and laughed. Her round merry sound set off Mom. Mom's laugh was a cackle, which set them all off more. Morgan loved his mother's witchy-love laugh.

David grimaced, and threw himself into his high-backed white-metal chair. Good thing the seat had a cushion. Mom sat gracefully, still cackling. Frankie looked toward Samson and smiled.

"It is a beautiful setting. It is. And that was a good substitution. Your explanation is perfect. I bet no one at Central's Community Relations would have any argument with it."

Samson's eyes widened. "You know people at CCR?"

Frankie gracefully dropped into her seat. "I took training there. A little bit." She gazed up at the top levels of the display. "These are a lot of work."

CHAPTER
ELEVEN

FRANKIE HADN'T SEEN SUCH a formal setup since she was a teenager. Thank the stars she still remembered it all. She should: Proctor Lizbet had drilled the girls to beyond boredom with all that Hi-G etiquette. Now they could do it without thinking too hard.

Only one of them had actually wanted to. Her best friend, Beth, lived for all the pomp and parade. But knowing the forms had saved Frankie today, and who could say boo to that?

Morgan's brother, what a peacock! And in his own house. They weren't in the halls of the Great Senate here. If David Orr was anything like his father, she never wanted to meet Konrad Orr. Actually meet him, not that formal-apology-in-a-great-hall pantomime back when she was ten.

Just thinking of Konrad Orr made Frankie shiver. And here she was in his house, picking up a piece of ginger shrimp with the scissor tongs. What if he suddenly appeared? Would she flash back to that last day of Wala? Her counselors said PTSD was unpredictable. She might freeze, or faint, or flee.

Or fight.

Let him come, and see her chewing happily at his table. Let him feel regret—shame, if that was possible—at what he'd done. At what her being here would remind him he had done. Even for him. It was hard to talk yourself into thinking you were a hero when one of the critically wounded was standing right in front of you.

But that was just dreaming, thank the stars. Konrad almost never came out here, Morgan said. This was his retirement estate. The place to stow his out-of-style belongings. And his family, apparently.

Although David could make the same argument, and here he was, growling at his single plated shrimp. He must hate them.

The dumbest thing about this extended formal service was its almost-complete lack of smell. Why take half the joy out of food?

The second-dumbest thing about this extended formal service was that at least one of the eight-times-eight plates would be guaranteed to hold some bit of a food that you absolutely loathed, even if you could barely smell it. And each piece must be eaten, unless you were so allergic you'd die on the spot. Sensitive people—or their staffs—often brought epinephrine with them just to be safe.

Frankie wasn't sure what the point of that was. Food should be savored. If David didn't like shrimp, he should be free to give it to her.

She wasn't going to tell him that, though. At least not tonight.

"Senator," she started just as he lunged for the shrimp.

David startled slightly, his tongs bumping into the shrimp instead of snagging it. The slippery piece of seafood lurched off the tiny plate and onto the shiny bright table.

Everything went still. Even the soft chime of the tiny chains holding the plates fell away.

David dropped his hand, tongs and all, into his lap. His face, which had lost that high-blood-pressure red, crept close to that hue again. His gaze burned through the offending plate, swinging slightly, now empty.

Morgan and his mom sat still, staring at him for a moment. And then, as if on cue, they flicked their gazes back to their own food arrays and recommenced chewing. Not commenting. Not noticing.

Samson swept up from behind, reaching past David's chair to swipe the morsel up with an extra linen napkin. White, no surprise. She had one like it on her lap. Not a second later, it was as if nothing had happened.

David let out a long breath, which helped his complexion. Frankie judged it safe to start in again.

"How often do you come out here? It must take a week's travel each way." She knew it was faster than that.

He shook his head, glaring at her.

She opened her eyes as innocently wide as she could. Why so mad? He hadn't wanted to eat it anyway. He should be thanking her.

"Three days, only," he said. "Each way. Come out here between sessions." At her frown—wasn't the session now?—he continued. "And now. For the gala." He looked toward Marissa. "Who's coming this year?"

Marissa waved her eating sticks. "The usual. Plus one." She smiled at Morgan.

Who looked instantly suspicious. "Who is it this time?"

"Your good friend, Celine Brtzo."

Morgan's eyebrows shot up into nearly arches. "What did you say to her? Last I heard, she was never going to set foot on Cloud again."

Marissa did not answer, pretending to concentrate on reaching past two tall columns to reach the smaller column with the next dish, burnt seaweed.

"Mom."

She put the morsel in her mouth and chewed, gazing serenely at her younger son.

Morgan grabbed his seaweed, setting one of the taller columns to rocking. As he pulled the sticks holding the morsel back, he stilled the column with the back of his hand. He tossed the seaweed in his mouth less than graciously, and did not stop staring at his mother.

She looked away first. She set her sticks, white with three silver bands at the non-eating end, against their simple ceramic rest. She dabbed the corner of her mouth with her napkin. She spread the napkin back in her lap. The blue of her tunic somehow warmed the chill of the white marble of the table.

"Celine has grown since then. As have we," she said, looking at David.

Celine? The girl from the time before? The one Morgan had mentioned on the walk over? Frankie couldn't hold back. "There's a story?" she prompted.

Marissa waved a hand. "Oh, it's a tired tale."

Morgan's face showed he did not agree. "Dad and David tried to drown her," he said.

"Bullshit," David said. "We've been over this before. Celine told us she didn't want the life vest."

"The one you'd poured fish guts all over? That one?" The music in Morgan's voice went caustic. "The one you said was the only one left, when we have dozens?"

"Water under the bridge," David said, eyeing the seaweed plate.

Morgan sucked his teeth, as if he was trying not to say anything more. If so, he failed.

"They took her to the whirlpool drain, where the lake water

gets recycled. She wanted to be an agro-engineer, and she was curious. They dumped her in, and the drain sucked her down."

Frankie gasped. A flash of memory. Erik's little face, bewildered, sinking slowly under an onslaught of waves.

Frankie had to put her sticks on their rest and press her chest to get more breath into her body. Her little brother had almost drowned. People who can't swim should be watched like eagles.

"Exactly," Morgan said, nodding at her. "She went into the drain, through the big pipe, and came out on the other side of the lake."

"Just a bit of fun," David said. "We saw her pop out, closer to shore. Easy swim." He started to smile, but stopped as he caught sight of Frankie's face. "She never was in danger. The whole route takes less than thirty seconds. And I knew she was a good swimmer."

Morgan glared at his brother. "The outlet is not so close to the lake bank. Celine had to drag herself over and out of the water. I didn't know where the outlet was, so it took me more than half an hour of running around the lake to find her."

"Raced about like a rabbit, eh, Morgan?" David tossed the seaweed into his mouth as punctuation.

Marissa bestowed a smile on her younger son. "Such a hero. He gave her his tunic."

"She was shivering." Morgan was not smiling. "And humiliated. And mad. So, again I ask, what did you tell her?"

Frankie wasn't sure what that answer would mean. Wouldn't the better question be why did she change her mind?

Marissa looked at Frankie. "The real question, dear, is what will your friend be wearing?"

"You are not," Morgan said, voice rising.

"Frankie dear, surely you'll join us at our annual gala. Saturday." Four days from now.

No. Absolutely not.

"Oh, my," Frankie said to buy time. "What a great honor. And you're right, I obviously have nothing to wear."

"Obviously," seconded David.

"But I'm afraid I must decline. I'm sure my ship will be ready by then. I have to get back to my routes." She was sure it would not be—Eckberg's had said one part would take days to print—but she would bunk in a storage container before she would ever go to another gala.

Morgan's head was shaking no so violently the edges of his hair battered his eyes. He blinked them hard. "You don't know who she is," he started.

"Oh, any friend of yours is a friend of ours," Marissa said.

"She isn't." David was starting to puff up. At least he was consistent. Marissa's apparent plan to shame Frankie by forcing her to stumble her way through a formal social event didn't match her earlier kindnesses.

Frankie frowned. "Why?"

Morgan threw his sticks on the table. "She wants you there to goose Celine into proposing."

"Proposing what?"

A servo swept past Morgan, removing the sticks and replacing them with clean ones. The steward, Samson, must be out arranging the dessert course.

"Marriage contract," Morgan said. "Right?"

Marissa tilted her head, considering. "Why not?" she said with a shrug. "It could work."

"We don't want to marry," Morgan insisted.

"Are you sure about that?" cut in his mother. "People grow and change, Morgan. Look around you this weekend. You'll see."

"It's time," David said in a false tone of boredom.

Morgan turned on his brother, leaning in. "And your contract worked so well. Where is your happy family now, David?"

David leaned in as well. "It's not about me."

"For once."

"Ever."

"Boys." Marissa signaled to the servos to clear the table. She leaned toward Frankie conspiratorially.

"Welcome to the family."

TWELVE

MORGAN COULD SEE that Frankie had had enough. Her face went blank, and then hard. Not concentration hard, like when she was outsmarting the Sculls big-laser gunship. Deadly hard. The last thing in the universe she would ever want was to be part of the Orr family.

Unfortunately.

He had to get her out of here. He looked around for Samson. The steward could change the ice-wine course setting, put it back by the fireplace, and still be formally correct.

But he was missing.

"Ah, no." Frankie sat straighter, away from the edge of the table. "You don't have all the facts about me." She locked gazes with Marissa.

Morgan waved his arms, trying to wrench back the conversation. "Looking forward to the ice wine."

The women did not spare him a glance.

Marissa's eyes were steel. "Tell."

"When Morgan asked me to come here, I said no. It's inappropriate."

"Got that right," David muttered. For the millionth time, Morgan thought about poisoning that asshole's shrimp.

"I am a pilot, yes. Which is not a menial occupation," Frankie shot a glance at David, then returned to Marissa. "But I am also one of the Orphans of Wala."

The people—the very air in the room—froze. Even the soft flick of the candles somehow went silent.

Marissa's face was still. Slowly, her eyelids dropped. Slowly, they lifted again. If Morgan hadn't known better, he would have thought she was having a stroke. But he'd seen this reaction once before. When they were all far younger.

"So you see," Frankie said. "A private visit is iffy enough. A public gala is a step too far. For me to accept your invitation would send a message I'm not sure any of us wants to send.

"So again, thank you, but I must decline."

MORGAN MANAGED to get Frankie out of the house immediately after the meal. They were out the room, out the door, and onto the walk to the cabana in less than fifteen minutes.

Frankie had gone so pale during the discussion of the gala he thought she might faint. But it was his mother who had nearly swooned. Marissa fell back against the hard wood of her chair, fanning herself. Morgan half-stood, to come over to her, but she waved him back down. Hot flash, she said, but no one was fooled.

Frankie had only looked relieved. Less stiffness to her neck, less tension in her jaw. And her gaze was fixed on the steward, who had returned with the ice wine.

So they'd stayed through the last course. It was only polite.

And, as he'd hoped, to fully savor the wine, Frankie had

closed her eyes. And clearly, it was a hit. The tiny blue-crystal glasses, rimed with ice, formed the perfect setting for such a sweet, sly treat. And watching her enjoy food, well, that was always a delight.

Now, out in the mildest of chills, Frankie was sober. And chewing on her bottom lip.

"Should I go?" she said.

He didn't see why. "The harm's done. If there was any harm." The chorus of the crickets buoyed him. "It was all so long ago."

"Seriously?" The moon haloed the bright scarf over her curls. "Do you have no sense of political theater at all?"

"It's not political. It's a party, far away from Central District."

"Sure." He couldn't see her expression, but her tone was cutting. "The Orphan of Wala accepts the kind invitation of the Butcher of Wala—"

"We don't like that phrase."

"And the whole galaxy knows I've sold out. Jettisoned my heritage." Her sigh sounded less mad and more frustrated.

"It's not like that," he insisted. "No, really. Politics is politics. Senators sue each other, cast aspersions, all that. And then they all sit down to dinner."

"Supper."

"Supper. It's done all the time. We are not the roles we play on stage."

Frankie stopped just before the main door to the cabana. "Is there a way to get to the lagoon without going inside? I want to stay in the dark a bit longer."

He just wanted to stay with her.

Morgan pressed a button on a panel beside the door. Tiny lights at ankle height illuminated a path around the side of the building. He wanted to take her arm, but instead followed her. Near enough to catch her if she slipped but far enough to avoid those wide pant legs. What a bizarre style for the Wardrobe to choose for country life.

The same style of ankle lights, bright on the path but hooded so as not to interfere with the night sky, ringed the long stretch of the pool and outlined the stairs to the decks that surrounded it. Frankie looked up.

"Which way will Silva come up?"

"The left. Best view is here, actually. Foot of the lagoon." He checked his wristcom. "Should be soon."

She stepped over to an unfolded deck recliner, ghostly white fabric stretched across bamboolike wooden supports. She sat carefully on the lower part, and then pivoted to lean on the back support.

"I'm going to wait and watch for it. You don't have to stay." Her gaze flicked to his. All he could see was the brightness of her eyes. "If you don't want to."

"You know I do," he said without thinking.

For all it was fall, Frankie reminded him of summer. Cardamom and cream. He walked past her and threw himself onto the recliner to her right. The sturdy cushions held just a touch of dew.

She sighed. "How can I not go to that gala? What even is it?"

"It's a celebration of autumn. The passing of the seasons, even though we don't have seasons here." He leaned his head on the headrest. The stars were sharp tonight. But already fading, as Silva rose. "It's a see-and-be-seen for Dad's cronies and people who want to be his cronies. It's a marriage mart, sometimes. It's a command performance, for people who want something from the Orrs." He grimaced. "It's smaller now. Since, you know."

"Wala." Her chin went high. She must be looking at the stars, too. "What a waste."

He wasn't sure if it was the destruction of Wala that was the waste or the self-indulgent extravagance of holding a gala in the middle of nowhere that she considered a waste.

Probably both.

Something stirred in the narrow barrier of tall bushes around the pool. Better not be that blasted cat. Disreputable, unsanitary, interference unit.

Frankie turned toward the sound. "Spike likes it here. Did you see how filthy she got this morning? I put a towel on the floor in front of my poolside door so she can at least wipe her feet when she comes in."

"She's probably out there unbalancing the ecosystem," he said. "Just like you."

"Ha, ha." Frankie sat up. Her face went shadowed, so she must be looking at him. "Listen, Morgan. If someone wanted to leave here, quit the Orrs, get off Cloud, would that be a problem?"

"You're free to go, anytime." He tried to keep the longing out of his voice. "Call for a cab. They're all day, all night."

A ghost of light touched the crown of her head. Silva peeking over the horizon, reflecting both the sun and Cloud itself, helping Morgan get a reading on her.

Frowning eyebrows marred her face. "Not me. Someone who lived here. Worked here."

He laughed, watching the new night's light shimmer down on her. "Depends who it is. For me? For David?"

"Be serious. An employee. A retainer." Her frown was not true. "What even are they here?"

"They are contract employees who sign draconian nondisclosure agreements and promises not to steal tech secrets. But they are free to go, anytime. Promise."

"All of them?"

She was avoiding talking about what they needed to talk about.

"Yes, of course. We're not slavers." Morgan spit out the last word. The Orrs couldn't always have said that. Their great-grandparents had been ruthless. But the current Orrs lived off the proceeds of their brilliant minds. Or Konrad's beautiful mind. Morgan wasn't sure about David. "But you're deflecting."

"Deflecting?"

"Talking about one thing to avoid another."

"Like space debris, only in conversation."

"Frankie."

"Fine." She leaned back, face up to the stars. She wrapped her arms around her middle, never a good sign. He shouldn't have said anything.

But this feeling had been growing, and not slaking, for days. They were both adults, and free, and beautiful to each other. What was to stop them from getting to know each other better?

"I know you want to knock boots," she started. And stopped. She tilted her face up again, gazing at the stars. He did not take his gaze from her.

"But?"

"But I can't give you what you want."

"A night of pleasure with a lady I'm crazy about?" He tried to make the tone teasing.

She didn't smile. "Put it this way. I'm a mammal, right? So let's say I'm in heat."

"That is the rudest thing I've ever heard someone say about themselves."

She waved that away with a hand. "So what I need is to scratch an itch, right? An itch that happens, only, oh, every couple of years."

"You sell yourself short."

"Now, while this was common—standard—on the world I come from, it's less so here in wide space."

Morgan crossed his own arms. "You're telling me the Walans were all one-night-stand people?"

"No! Well, yes. We partner for life; we usually have sex with the same partner. But not a lot. It's just not that interesting to us."

Morgan took a moment to digest this. If they weren't thinking about sex most of the time, what ever did they think about? "You have a low libido?"

"Sure. That works." She nodded.

"And so we can't have one-night-only-sex because?"

"Because you do not."

"I can respect your boundaries."

"Thanks. But I like you. I'd like us to maybe get to be better friends. Sex with other-worlders always messes things up." Sadness laced her words. She must have learned this the hard way.

But it wasn't true. "Bullshit," he said.

She tilted her head to look at him. Her eyes were luminous. He leaned toward the light so she would not mistake his expression.

"You don't get to make those decisions for me. What do you know of me, anyway? 'A non-serious person.' Isn't that how you put it?"

"Not about this. You'd be serious about this."

"Would not."

"Would too."

She laughed, and his heart eased. "Listen to us."

This was his opening. "I take total responsibility for myself. One and done. Agreed?"

She tilted her head back, considering him.

He held his breath. For a panicked second, he searched his memories for which of his many poses she preferred. Face full in Silva's light? Half-shadow and mysterious? He didn't know.

Actually, he did. No pose.

He opened his eyes to her. Let her see his heart. His soul.

"Fine." She held her hand out to him, palm up.

He grasped it gently. He lifted it to his lips.

The kiss sent a jolt of ice wine happiness from his chin to his toes.

Frankie shivered. The move knocked a soft giggle out of her.

"Here, or my room?" she said.

"Inside," he said. "And lock that cat out."

FRANKIE WOKE IN BLISS. Amazing giant bed, minty-fresh sheets, three kinds of pillows. Sun shining through the sliding doors, glinting off the ridges of softly moving water in the lagoon outside. Vacation day. Nowhere she had to be, nothing she had to do.

Her itch had been scratched, skin shed, load lifted. All the cliches, every single one.

She stretched long, like a cat, her limbs and her senses both.

And constricted. Fast.

Morgan was still here.

He'd said he would leave.

She didn't mind his heft and heat and scent of last night's cologne, sweat, and sex. But he'd promised he'd go afterward.

She didn't want him patterning on her, or whatever it was called. Imprinting? And calling it love. And now that she felt fine, she didn't want a repeat of last night, either. Probably not again for a couple of years.

Morgan lay on his belly, his face smashed into the pillow so deep she would have worried about his breathing if his ribs hadn't been gently rising and falling. The sheet had fallen to his hips. He had a birthmark just under his right shoulder blade. His skin was the same toffee ice cream hue all over. Nothing had wounded it.

Frankie slid out from under the covers silently and ran on tiptoes to the shower. She didn't want to pollute the lagoon. She felt so good, a swim before even coffee seemed possible. Besides, making coffee would wake him up.

The shower apparently didn't. She was in her suit and out the door in a flash. He'd really locked it! Poor Spike.

The water was perfect. Cool, fresh, empty. The sun was the equivalent of mid-day, which made her laugh. Such a holiday lazybones! She started with a slow crawl, waking up her joints, warming up her muscles, practicing her breathing.

When seen from land, the curves of the lagoon were deceptive. Everything looked round and twisty. But here at water level, she could see how the designer had shaped the pool so two entire standard-long swim lanes stretched its length. Perfect for serious swimmers and casual splashers, too.

First thing today was find Spike. Frankie didn't know what to make of Morgan's answer last night. If everyone was free to go at any time, who had they come here to rescue? She'd thought it would be someone close to the family, or a dependent of one of those people.

Already at the far end of the pool, she kicked off the side and switched to a stretchy, easy backstroke. The sun kissed her face, but there was no warmth, just light.

If everybody could all just leave, who was left? A family member? Surely not. The mice? Morgan's horses?

Then she remembered.

Elvin. A synthetic human. An "illegal being," who had special dispensation to remain alive in Cooperative space only because he had the right papers. Papers that said he was part of some experiment. No way would he be allowed to call a cab, get on a shuttle, go anywhere.

She'd met Elvin on the last haul, the one with all the excitement. He was part of the excitement: an undeclared life form riding in the luxury cargo container Morgan had outfitted like a horse stable. Elvin was acting as veterinarian to the two racehorses who were on their way to a famous racetrack near Smithson Station.

Good thing, because he had saved Minnie from certain death. The pale giant snake—the best mouser in the quadrant—had eaten some of the mice the Skoll cabal had poisoned and then loosed on Frankie's ship. Elvin had gotten the mice out of her and patched her up without even a permanent scar. Soon after, Minnie had retired to the planet her first captain had moved to.

Frankie put 'Get new mouser' on her mental ship-fix list.

Back to Elvin. Where would he be on Cloud? Surely not in the horse barn. Morgan said he was out of that business now; those were the last two horses to sell. Was there a laboratory nearby?

Spike would know. Back to the first thing on her list: talk to Spike.

Someone shouted. Frankie tilted, tipping her head above the water. Morgan was up. Or rather sitting, with his feet dipped in the pool water.

"You know, suits are optional here," he said.

She tread water, enjoying the figure eights of her hands through the water, sculling. "I see you are of that opinion." He was bare as a baby, and his hair went in every direction except flat. His dry hair.

"I do like that suit better, though," he went on. "Not so much covering arms and legs. Black isn't really your color though."

Frankie let that go. "You said you would leave."

Morgan didn't stop. "And how did your hair get so long? You look like a mermaid. A Siren. Sunset-red tresses beckoning sailors."

That did distract her. "You've seen my hair wet before."

He looked to the side. "Maybe I wasn't focusing on your hair. No, you were always drying it! Squishing it up."

He didn't understand curly hair? She shook her head. Focus.

"You said you would go. After."

Morgan held his hands up, blocking her words. "I did! But I didn't want to go all the way back to the house, and it wasn't much fun being alone next door to you. I didn't have any of my stuff, and I couldn't sleep. So I came back. Just to sleep."

He tilted his head, one eyebrow raised. "Anyway, it helped you, too. To settle down."

She frowned. She had no memory of that.

"The nightmare. Remember?"

Frankie's mouth dropped so low she almost caught water in it. "Last night? But I went to sleep so happy." It didn't make sense.

"You're very welcome," he said. He grinned so wide she worried for the joints in his jaw. "Care for a rematch?"

This was what she'd worried about. He looked so eager, so hungry.

Frankie's hunger had melted. Dissolved. Vaporized.

Morgan pushed himself into the water. He went completely under, and emerged an arm's length away from her.

"Ugh!" she said. "At least shower off first."

"Don't sweat it. Pool's filters are gold. Literally."

Frankie didn't see how that would help. Before Morgan could get any closer, she sculled backwards a meter.

"We talked about this yesterday," she said. "And before that. And before that, too."

He dipped his head under. She felt the pressure of the waves as he sped past her underwater. She turned to follow the motion. When he came up, the water had washed away his grin. He stood straight, shoulders out now he was in the shallower water, and pushed his hair back with both hands.

"I thought I could change your mind," he said. "I hoped."

Frankie found she was able to shrug, even while sculling to stay upright. She shook her head. "You don't listen."

"I just hope." He twined his fingers behind his neck and leaned back, stretching out his upper back. "More than you do."

Frankie side-stroked to a spot where she could stand, a little farther down from Morgan. "Right. Attack the one you're trying to seduce." She flicked a small spray of water at him. It didn't come close. Why was she so touchy?

She'd told him, that's why. Again and again.

She'd already had this conversation, with every stupid person she'd tried to get serious with. After the first one, she'd been clear as glass. It wasn't her fault they didn't listen.

But it felt like her fault.

"Listen. How about this?" she said. "Let's make a date." She tried to quick set that date into the Galactic calendar, and failed. "Um, I can predict pretty close to the next time I'll, ah—"

"Be itchy?"

"Not helping. Let's put it on the calendar, and ping each other then. See where we are." It was more than she'd offered anyone else. But Morgan was a nice guy, and entertaining when he wasn't being needy. Or sneaky. Or white-lying.

Hmmm.

Morgan looked at the sky. "And in the interim?"

"Um?" Frankie cast about for an idea. "Celine?"

"Now you sound like my mother." He was just disappointed, she knew. But he was trying to hurt her. And succeeding.

"Great!" she said. "What do you think there is for breakfast?"

"Dunno. But watch out!" His attention had been snagged by something directly behind her. Something that made the bushes rustle.

Something that splashed into the pool without wiping off the dirt, the leaves, the whatever-the-hell else.

Spike.

CHAPTER
FOURTEEN

MORGAN DID NOT WANT to be interrupted by some filthy oversized cat-monster, but maybe it was for the best. He didn't want to make Frankie cry.

He didn't want to make himself cry.

Frankie's face had been rigid. Her beautiful eyes outlined in frustration. He just knew she must have this same conversation with every partner. No wonder that she considered paying for a single night of companionship the better option.

But he'd convinced himself he would be different. Of course.

Egotistical asshole.

And who decided this pool should be so blasted cold? His sack was a tiny nubbin tucked close to his skin, warning that if they didn't get out of the water soon, it wouldn't guarantee his later fertility.

Frankie was scolding her monster and trying to collect the biggest pieces of the forest it had been sporting before they sank under the surface. Morgan used her distraction to heave toward the side of the pool and out. By the time he had reached his towel, on the foot of one of the loungers, she had quite the little mound of crap piled on the opposite curve of the pool. He grabbed the towel on the move. He wanted to get away before she noticed.

Slipping through the slider into the room next to hers, Morgan found his requested outfit laid out on the bed so no wrinkles, efficiently servo-delivered like always. At least the family hadn't deleted his access to the servos. The servo had also left a basket of the crap for his bathroom routine by the small box of a shower. A subtle hint?

Blasting the water punishingly hot, Morgan took stock of his life. It was time to come clean, ha ha. He couldn't go through life much longer in this magical world of his mind.

He had excuses for all the bumps his carelessness caused others. They were mild. Collateral damage. And most of them deserved some bumps in their lives, like the Skolls.

But not Frankie.

Did he ever think about what she wanted? What was—not love—caring deeply for someone if you didn't care how your actions affected them?

He'd really thought—had he really thought, really?—that his sweat and his—what? ministrations?—would ease her soul. Help her forget her troubles, especially the one his family had just put her through.

What an ass.

His skin was hot to the touch as he scrubbed the scent of her off him. What little was left, after that stupid dip in the pool. She had been hot, and warm. And far more open than he'd even hoped.

Of course, she would be all thoughtful and reserved the next day. That's how she always was. Well, the two or three times something big had happened to her the day before.

Asshole. Like he was "something big."

He shook soap from his eyes. This couldn't go on. He had to

do something with his life. Scamming bad people turned out not to be it. He needed something with more meaning.

He should go back to school. And study what? Advanced Asshole? Then he could join the family business.

Join the fight against the family business? The disaffected son —that story was as old as the universe.

Frankie's arms were as strong as her legs, and that said something. She'd nearly squeezed the squeal out of him wrapping her legs around his waist.

He ached for her to do it again. Now, not however many years from now.

Maybe there was something wrong with her? Not enough hormones? But who was he to force her to be other than she was. Wasn't that what he loved about her.

Shit.

He could not possibly be in love with her. He'd known her how long—three weeks? And she'd been irritated with him for all but the last few days of it.

But she had liked him, under that. She couldn't deny it. He certainly couldn't, on his side.

He shut off the water and stepped out of the shower into the steam of his own making. Back into the life of his own making.

Something needed to change.

Someone.

Him.

When he stepped out onto the deck, fully dressed and carefully primped, the monster cat was lolling on a nearby chaise lounge. It did not look as filthy, which boded well for the white cushions on the lounger.

No Frankie, but encouraging noises were coming from down the cabana where the kitchen was. That door slid open, and Frankie backed out, apparently arguing with the waist-high servo that followed her out onto the deck. Balanced on the servo's flat head was a breakfast feast.

"I can carry it myself," she was telling it. She'd changed into Frankie casual: close-fitting dark pants, maybe a bit shorter than usual. Yet another shade of blue tunic with side-slit pockets. Her hair was free, and had sprung back to just below her ears and fanning out. Bare feet, pretty toes.

"You're on holiday," he called to her. "Let the servos pamper you."

She stopped to consider that, her head slightly tilted. The servo sped past her, toward Morgan and the monster.

"I get it," she said. She considered him. He was glad she was still at some distance. "Servo knew you needed breakfast too. That's why so much." She nodded. Mystery solved.

Morgan unfolded one of the little tables that matched the loungers and placed it between the two nearest ones. The servo took the hint, and deposited the tray neatly on the table, which, like the servo, was sized perfectly for a large tray. Morgan took a seat on the lounger one away from the monster, turning his back briefly on Frankie. She could sit next to that thing.

Frankie also took the hint, and settled carefully on the middle lounger. Once she was sure it wasn't flimsy, she leaned forward toward the tray. She took a deep breath in.

"Can't decide. Everything smells so good."

It did. Warm fruit tart, cold creamed cheeses, pickled fish, veggies and sauces. Sweet rolls and sour and sesame and plain.

All he wanted was the sharp, bitter tea. Orrs weren't coffee drinkers; another family held that monopoly, and so far their own test fields of coffee beans had not produced a decent drink.

"No coffee?" Frankie said.

He shook his head. "Try this, though. It carries the same jolt. Bitter, but you like that, right?"

She looked at him, wary. Where had that come from?

"I mean, you don't put sugar or anything in your coffee. This is in average plain coffee range." He frowned at himself. What was he saying?

Frankie lifted the curvy silver pot and poured out a quarter-cup into the durable mug. She sniffed it, and then sipped. She closed her eyes.

He tried to guess what she was tasting. Chicory, burnt cinnamon, something floral, homegrown black tea. Whichever, she must like it. Her shoulders eased, pushing the mug toward her lap. Her eyes popped open.

"Wow!" She reached for the pot again. "Family secret recipe?"

"Nah. I can get it for you." He forced himself to take a roll, and slathered it with the softest cheese.

A noise roughly similar to a meow came from the monster's lounger.

"Oh yeah," Frankie said. "Does any of this look like it's good for Spike?"

"Does it like pickled fish?"

Frankie turned to look at the thing. "She. And not especially," she said. Morgan was turning to see if the servo was still here—nope—when she grabbed something from the very edge of the tray.

"Got it." A small, square plate with some meaty stuff in a neat mound in the center. A toothpick with a tiny flag on the end stuck out of the mound as if some miniature expedition had conquered it. The flag was Orr white with a sketch of a cat head on it.

Frankie held it up to her eye level. "Who made this flag?"

"The servo, probably. They like to be creative, when they can."

She turned, and, after a slight tussle about whether the plate should go on the deck or on the lounger, deposited it at the very foot of the lounger. Morgan could have sworn the thing grunted its disapproval before lurching to its paws. It couldn't have any real complaints—the mound was half gone by the time Frankie had settled back and picked up her mug again.

"How many servos do you have, here?"

"Hundreds. They do all sorts of stuff."

Frankie touched the top of an apricot. The fruit popped open, falling to the into a circle of eight neat wedges. She grinned at Morgan.

"Watched Servo set it up. Supercool." She took a wedge. "So, what's on the schedule for today."

Morgan polished off his roll and licked the cheese off a finger. "Relax. Relax. And then, relax."

"Sounds good." She reached for another wedge. "Everything's better with breakfast. Would you take me to see the stables?"

Morgan, startled, stopped in mid-reach. "You want to ride a horse? We only have farm animals now."

Her eyes cast to the side. Another tell. "Thought I could say hi to Elvin," she said, oddly casual. "See how he's doing."

He was surprised she was so interested. To cover his confusion, Morgan completed his grab for a wedge of apricot.

Most people were terrified of synthetic humans, and rightly so. Then again, Elvin did save the life of Frankie's pet snake.

Maybe that's why she thought differently about him.

"Not sure he's still there," Morgan said. He tossed the whole wedge in his mouth. No way he could take a bit like Frankie did and not have the juice spurt out across his chin. Maybe even his tunic. Bronze today, to highlight his newly blonded hair. "Dad might have him on another project already."

That interested her. "He's a laboratory assistant?"

"More like a manager. But not of labs. He's usually running one of the practicals. Practical, meaning in-the-field experiments, like testing new dome tiles. The lab experiments are done elsewhere. Cloud is a big beta test site."

"Marissa said that too," Frankie poured herself more tea. "But she didn't sound as cheerful about it."

"Yeah, well. Mom has more experience with the failures. It makes her mad when dad forgets about stuff, like the gala, and runs some experiment that turns the air orange."

Frankie's eyebrows arched. "Orange?"

"A new plant-grow potion, or something. Turned out it wasn't as stable as they thought, so instead of settling down on the soil it floated up and away. Everywhere." He smiled at the memory. That had been back when Mom held those giant annual picnics. The orange cloud had started just hours before. Mom had pulled out all the stops, trying to cover the whole meadow in netting to keep the air inside clear.

It couldn't possibly work. Blankets, food, people, all left the event early, coated in a fine dust of orange.

"We had to replace all the air filters," he said. "We couldn't wash the orange out of them."

Frankie smiled at the picture. "Is your mom a yeller or an angry-silence person?"

"Yell, then angry silence. Gravely disappointed." Morgan laughed. "Dad never notices. He assumes all is going well until the moment you are standing in front of him, bleeding. Then he assumes all he needs to do is tell you to go to the medic. Typical genius inventor, I'm told."

"How convenient for genius inventors," she said. She leaned back in the lounger, nursing her tea, and turned her gaze to Spike. Who was now stretched out, licking her front paw. The white plate was completely empty.

"So, if Alvin is in charge, does he manage people or work on his own?"

"Oh, he has an army of servos he can tell what to do. Just like the rest of us."

"Really?" She snapped her gaze back to him, eyes clear and open. "Could I have a few?"

"What?"

"Just for a few minutes. Not now, later. Maybe."

Spike stopped licking to stare at Frankie. Morgan felt the same. Whatever for?

Morgan frowned. "I don't know. Have to look up the permissions."

"What if I just ask the servos, straight out? They must have instructions to help me out."

"That they do," he said, relieved. "Right. It should be fine."

"What?" she said to Spike, who was still staring at her. The beast blinked once, and then rolled to her other side, facing away from them, and started cleaning her other front paw.

This was nice. Just being together, no pressure. Making vague plans for the day, which would be sunny and nice, just like yesterday. It only rained in Cloud at night.

He could live with this.

Right?

CHAPTER
FIFTEEN

FRANKIE HAD no clue why she might need a small contingent of bots, but the thought of it made her tingle with anticipation.

She rested her head on the chaise lounge's pillow, and nursed her tea. Surprisingly good, for tea. Not much smell, but something about the mix made her tongue happy. Soft sunlight warmed the cedar-scented furniture. The mildest of breezes kept everything fresh. Nobody else around, not even the sound of anyone.

Now this was a holiday.

She and Spike had to play dumb while Morgan was here, so Frankie had nothing to do but relax. Morgan was in his usual floppy top and tailored slacks, with new black flat shoes to match. He seemed to have taken their Big Talk well, but she knew from experience it would take another talk—at least one—to set the idea firmly in his head. At least his disappointment didn't translate into moping, like last time, on the ship.

He'd called up a screen from his wristcom, looking for Elvin. He hadn't questioned her vague reasons why she wanted to see the synthetic human. Maybe he was still distracted by Big Talk. She wondered what else she could get out of him in that state. Get Spike into the house?

Her not-cat colleague looked the best Frankie had ever seen her. Still scruffy, fur all different lengths, but fluffy-clean and somewhat groomed. A week of whatever that fabulous plate of Spike-food was might even make her coat shiny. Enticing, like those glamourous shots of kittens to adopt that Frankie always quickly scrolled past.

Ervin was apparently hard to find. Morgan grumbled something she didn't catch. Frankie hoped the synth was not out-of-dome. Planetside space was not her idea of fun.

"Got him." Morgan's face stretched into surprise. "Mom's got him. That's why I couldn't find him at the labs. He's running the gala prep."

"Elvin's a party planner, too?"

"You would not believe all he can do."

All the more reason he might not feel able to flee from the Orrs. Frankie still had to confer with Spike, but she was sure they were here for the synth. Their conference was still on hold, not just because Morgan was nearby. Spike's eyes were currently closed, her sprawled body, angled to catch the most-possible light, reached from one edge of the lounger's lower cushion to the other.

Elvin. How would they ever spirit him away?

As soon as the synth stepped outside the protection of the Orrs, he was a walking dead man. Cooperative Realm officers had instructions to shoot synths on sight. Elvin was humanform, neat and groomed like an upper-level functionary, which could help him pass. And his voice—cultured asshole—certainly passed muster. But the slight bronze cast to his skin would be noticeable to anyone looking closely. So they needed to move him through places where people wouldn't look closely.

Problem was the first shuttle. There was nothing else to do on the short hop to Silva but look at the other passengers. Someone would surely notice. Frankie wasn't sure she could look totally calm sitting next to him, either. His personality already set her on edge; his being a synth was extra.

They'd have to ship Elvin as cargo.

He'd love that.

Where to find a shipping container? That was easy: Gala preparations. There must be plenty of stuff coming in for that. They could pack him up and set him aside with the other surplus material to be returned after the gala. He could even put himself on the manifest, since he was probably in charge of it.

What would he call himself? Fragile: Fine Art.

She snorted.

Spike cracked an eye open, took her measure, and closed it again.

THEIR HOLIDAY IDYLL lasted almost half an hour. Frankie's wristcom, which she had left on the bed in her room, boomed the first four notes of the Regent's processional march.

Frankie went from dozy and reclining to full alert and standing between the second note and the third. On the fourth note, she had to stop her sway. She'd moved too fast.

Morgan, who looked as if he was melting into his lounger, opened one eye. "What the heck is that?"

"Command performance."

He opened his other eye. "A Dirda march?"

She didn't want to talk about it. "It's an alert. Call's coming in a couple minutes." It couldn't be good.

She looked toward the bedroom she was staying in. Probably bugged, at least by the voice-command speakers. Where was that not-white "white box," the jammer that her new boss gave her? In the duffel, in the bathroom. Frankie shook her head, trying to get her thoughts in sync. She grabbed a peppermint candy—two—from the cute white ceramic holder on the breakfast tray. One went in her mouth, one for standby in her off-hand.

"Gonna take it in my room," she said. Morgan waved a languid hand.

As she slid the door open, Spike lurched past her. Wasn't she just sleeping?

"No," she said, stepping into the room. "This is a personal call." She stood by the door, waiting for Spike to lurch out the way she'd come in.

The not-cat didn't spare her a glance. She continued padding toward the sitting room. Frankie pulled the door almost shut—a cat's width remained—and stomped after her.

"Seriously, Spike. It's just Beth." She grabbed up her wristcom as she passed the bed and checked it. "Beth," she confirmed. "You know she's not part of the assignment." Beth was Frankie's oldest friend, whose path had taken her so far from where they'd started.

Beth thrived in the Cooperatives' central district. She lived in the Regent's Complex itself. She was famed for her support of the underdog and their causes. But in safe ways, ones that did not cross the Regent or the goals of the Cooperative.

Sellout, whispered a mean voice deep inside Frankie's soul. Beloved, shouted the voice at the top of her heart.

By the time Frankie had pulled the jammer out of her duffel and reached the sitting room, Spike had jumped onto the white rattan loveseat. She spun twice and settled in a circle on one of its square white cushions, her gaze daring Frankie to argue about it.

"Fine," Frankie said. "We need to talk after, anyways." Which they actually did, but still. Frankie pulled one of the flimsy-throne-looking rattan chairs toward a matching short table. She set the amber ovoid jammer on the table and clicked it on. As always, there was no sign the thing was working besides the tiny green light on the device itself.

Frankie strapped the comm on her wrist, arranged herself on the chair, and took a deep breath. She pressed the comm to send the response ping.

Not ten seconds later, the channel opened. The top half of her best friend appeared on a small screen. Beth was paying for the best transmission—near realtime visual and audio. She would have had to request one of the special satellites be moved here, unless the Orrs had one already.

This couldn't be good.

As soon as the connection looked stable—she saw Beth blink —Frankie tried to get the first word in.

"Great new hairstyle!" Beth, always au courant, had braids of her long, straight, dark hair wrapped in circles on the top of her head like an ornate bird's nest. She wasn't wearing one of those heavy court jackets, just a forest green collared blouse that glowed on camera. She didn't have court makeup on either; Frankie could see the spray of tiny freckles across her otherwise perfectly patrician nose. And the glower coming from her eyes and lips.

"Fridrika Faldasdotter, where are you? Oh, let me see what the signal says. The Planet of the Orrs." She paused to deepen her glare. "What the hell are you thinking?"

"It's not what you think!" Frankie wasn't sure what Beth thought. Nothing good. But the reality was too strange for anyone to have thought of it.

"No? The Orphan of Wala, who uses the name Orr as a curse word—"

"I don't do that anymore."

"News to me." Beth continued. "Is spending time as a guest of the murderous Orr family, on their private enclave of Cloud."

"Okay, that sounds bad, but—"

"And not only that. Only a week earlier, she found herself in a deadly firefight."

"I was going to tell you—"

"A ruddy cargo hauler! In a firefight!"

"It wasn't really a firefight—"

"And not only that. She's become a known enemy of the Skolls, the leading shippers in her part of edge space. In less than a year!"

Frankie didn't even bother trying to get a word in. She stuck the other peppermint in her mouth, hoping its minty goodness would help her find the words once Beth wound down.

"And get this. Get this! The Orphan of Wala, who always has to be dragged kicking and screaming to any blasted formal event in Central District. That one, you know her? She has cheerfully accepted an invitation to a gala at the Butcher of Wala's family hideaway. A gala!"

Frankie froze. "How do you even know that?"

Beth's lips pressed shut. eyes still full glare. Of course, she had the whole of the regent's information network at a blink.

Something bumped Frankie's knee. Spike, on her haunches, looked up at her. Without thinking, Frankie ran a hand down her fur from crown to shoulder. The ice in her spine melted a bit.

"Okay, so you're mad. But it's not what you think." She held a hand up just before Beth finished her inhale. "I did not accept that invitation. I turned them down. I offered to leave."

"But you did not leave."

"I can explain!"

Beth crossed her arms and leaned back. And then seemed to realize she was not in a chair, and leaned forward again. She must be on one of those footstool-cushion things in her dressing room.

The room was blurred. Frankie's background was blurred, too, now that she looked at the inset showing her camera's view. Did Beth have a jammer, too?

"Okay. I wasn't in a firefight. I got shot at! I wasn't trying to fight anybody! But my ship got wrecked, so we had to get a tow to the closest repair shop."

Beth looked like she was going to interrupt, her wide mouth pursing. Frankie hurried on.

"Okay, maybe not the closest, but the best in the sector. And they're going to fix her up better than before! Because I got a new job. Not just hauling."

Suddenly, her image of Beth went darkly fuzzy. Spike had jumped on the table, in front of the screen. A warning.

"What in the Regent's galaxy is that?"

"Okay, I won't," Frankie leaned in to whisper to Spike. No talking about the new job, even to someone with an A-3 security clearance.

She didn't quite touch her colleague's butt, but made a motion like she would. Spike huffed off the table and jumped onto the back of the throne-chair, which turned out to be sturdier than it looked.

"That's Spike," she said, looking back at Beth.

"If you say so." Beth shook her head, slowly so she wouldn't topple that hair. "Please continue."

Frankie ran her story through again. "Right. Anyway, I have a new client, and they wanted some upgrades to the Spear. So I'm on holiday! Right? You always say I work too hard."

"Right," Beth said, stretching the word out. "And the only place you could take a holiday is with the people who give you nightmares."

Frankie couldn't argue that. "It's a long story?" she said, which sounded lame even to herself. Spike shifted to lick a paw just above her left ear.

Beth's eyes went glassy for a second, then she focused on the camera again. "I don't have much more time on the satellite. Get to the point."

"The point?"

"How am I going to explain this to the Regent's people? To our people?"

Frankie thought quickly. "How about: In a series of my usual blunders, I ended up a pawn of the Orrs. Luckily, my friends are helping me get away. Maybe before the gala even starts?"

Beth pursed her lips again. "How fast can you get off Cloud?"

Frankie didn't want to get off Cloud. Not without a plan for Elvin. But they might get that sorted this afternoon. "How about I tell them I have to go to Silva for some gala outfit thing that they can't print here? What would that be?"

"Something to do with your hair. Which needs a trim, by the way."

"Wow. Petty much?"

"Just looking out for you." Beth almost cracked a smile. Frankie pressed on. This might work.

"So, I get to Silva, and then just keep going. Up to the repair station, and hide in the Spear."

Beth looked opaque again, and then in focus. "By tonight." She waggled a finger at Frankie. "And you do nothing else media worthy for the rest of the year. You keep saying you want people to forget you, and then you do this." She looked to the side and tapped her chin. "But I could do something with the shooting, to distract. You're the victim in that." She glanced back. "I'm assuming."

"Totally!"

Spike snorted, a sound Frankie dearly hoped would not transmit. She couldn't have Beth mad at her. Never that.

"You know I wouldn't have gone out of my way to do this," Frankie pleaded. "You know me."

Beth sighed, and finally smiled. But it was a smile with a shadow of sadness.

"What I know is that you don't create the chaos. But ever since you moved out there, the chaos seems to cluster around you."

Frankie couldn't argue with that.

SIXTEEN

THEY FOUND ELVIN, as stiff and stern as ever, on the lawn just outside the family's mansion. Rigid and disapproving, he was watching bots as they portered bundles up the hill from the meadow.

Piles of sturdy white material and long poles were starting to grow at regular intervals from the clear sliding doors that led into the mansion's ballroom/sitting room to a white tent with many peaks in the meadow below. Morning dew had not left the grass, which flavored the air with a touch of amber.

Frankie had forgotten that rigid stance. Didn't scream friendly human, our Elvin. Another argument in favor of the plan for him to escape via cargo carton.

Nattily dressed in what must be Orr business casual, tan cotton slacks, tan blouse with collar and cuffs, Elvin had never looked less calm. He was actually tapping his foot, clad in sturdy tan boots, as he watched two bots start do something to the walls around the two sets of doublewide doors.

He did not look pleased to see the three of them. Not Frankie, not Spike, and especially not Morgan.

As soon as they came in comfortable voice range, Elvin started. "Should have known you were here, Cloud." His voice sharp and high, but not nasal. "No one else would have brought up the orange in her presence."

Morgan made his "who, me?" face. "Not I. I told Frankie here, but that's it. Mom must have remembered on her own."

"Well, she did, and at the last possible moment. Now she wants an awning, all the way to the pavilion." Elvin waved toward the meadow. Frankie squinted. It must be a good quarter-kilometer away.

"But weren't we always going to be inside, this time?" Morgan said. "To match the theme?"

Frankie's attention snapped back to Morgan. "What theme? We don't just wear pretty outfits?"

"We do, that," Morgan agreed. "But to match the theme: Fairy Tale Kingdom."

That didn't tell her any more than before. "Whose fairy tales? When?"

"Oh, right. You didn't receive the formal invitation. She used real cards! Or flimsies, for farther away. Do you remember the wording, El?"

Elvin's very stillness communicated how idiotic he thought that question was. Synths probably didn't forget anything.

"Transport yourself into an age of impeccable manners, delicate dresses, and oh-so-fancy footwork," he said, the flatness in his voice a sharp contrast to the flowery words. "An evening spent in The Regency of Yore will surprise and delight you. Come ready to cross wits, not swords. Exclamation point," Elvin added. "I argued against that. It goes on. Promenade along the pond, quadrille in the ballroom, on and on and on."

Frankie had no idea what a quadrille was, or a promenade. "It's an alternate-world regency?" she said.

"Myth, really," Morgan said. "Mom heard about it somewhere, and fell in love with the dresses and the dances. And, of course, the pun on our current regency."

The Cooperative Realm officially had a collective form of governance—every voice heard. But in practice, people (which people? Frankie always wondered) preferred a single face at the top. Thus the Regent, a vestigial touch of royalty. They appeared at functions, signed treaties, and, probably, made secret decisions that affected everything in the galaxy. Whatever, it didn't sound much like this kind of regency.

But here was her opening. "And you expect Wardrobe to pop out one of these—what was it?—delicate dresses for me? Can't be done." She turned to Morgan and put her hands on her hips. "I need to go to town. Maybe Silva, even. I want real clothes, made by people. And something. For my hair." That could get her out of the Orrs' orbit, and away, faster than Beth could say told-you-so.

Elvin snorted in a way both elegant and cutting. "Don't sell our Wardrobe short. She has samples of all the fabrics and styles. And she knows how to flatter every body type." Even yours, he managed to insinuate.

Frankie had forgotten how bitter the synth was. Probably had plenty of reasons to be that way, but ugh. Made it hard to want to rescue him.

She needed to get him alone. Maybe suggest Morgan inspect the tent? Why? Appeal to his design sense? Could there be food there already?

Elvin saved her the trouble. His attention snagged on something behind them. "The Lady approaches."

They turned to see Marissa stepping out of the mansion's central back door. She stopped, gazing out toward the giant tent-pavilion. Dressed in a copy of yesterday, shin-length khakis and walking boots, but a new tank top, this time white. Her hair was still tight in that painful looking twist. Frankie hoped the regency styles were gentler on the head. Going to a gala was torture enough, why make your hair hurt you, too?

"Mother!" Morgan called, waving. She turned, saw them, and started striding purposefully their way.

"Keep her away from me," Elvin muttered.

Morgan started walking toward Marissa. They met a good distance away from the others.

This was the chance. They could talk to Elvin alone.

Frankie looked at Spike. Did she want to lead? Frankie was supposed to be assisting in this caper, not leading it. Spike, sitting on her haunches, gazed back at her, blank.

Fine.

"So, Elvin," she started, moving closer to the synth.

He stepped back, as if afraid she was going to hit him.

Frankie stopped. "No worries. But I heard—somebody told me—someone had the idea that you might not be happy here? On Cloud?"

Elvin's bewilderment was plain, as was his annoyance. "Nobody talks about me to you. What do you really want?"

Spike head-butted Frankie on the left shin hard enough that she had to take a step back with her right to stay upright. Frankie glared down. What?

Spike glared right back. She slowly shook her head side to side.

No?

This was such a stupid was to run a partnership.

Frankie dropped on her own haunches, to get to Spike's level. She didn't want to go on one knee—who knew how sharp that gravel was. "What? she whispered? Isn't he the one?"

Again the slow shake.

Shit. "Who, then?"

Spike didn't answer, of course, that would be too helpful. Instead, her not-cat colleague took her own steps back. By the crunching of the gravel, she knew Marissa and Morgan were walking toward them. Too late to save Elvin, now, but apparently he didn't need saving. Back to where she started.

The steps stopped just behind her.

"Don't talk to that... thing," Marissa said, her voice venom. "It's a spy."

SEVENTEEN

FROM HER NOT-CAT-HEIGHT squat on the graveled walkway, Frankie shot up to standing, somehow also turning around.

Blocking Marissa's access to Spike.

Which was completely unnecessary. Spike shot down the side of the path and in seconds was around the corner of the mansion and away.

"What's wrong?" Frankie said, breathless and a little dizzy.

Morgan's mother was beautiful when she glowered. "That thing. It spies for Konrad," she said.

Konrad? Spike was a double-agent? Frankie rocked back on her heels.

Elvin, behind her—Elvin who hated her—pushed her back gently to keep her upright.

"Not like that!" Morgan said. Clarifying nothing.

Elvin gave an impatient sigh. "Konrad's cyvlossic isn't a spy. It merely assists him in his duties."

"Sigh vlossic?" Frankie said.

"That creature," Marissa said, banishing it with the wave of her hand. "It skulks around watching what we're doing and reports back to Konrad, so he knows he doesn't have to waste his time spending time with us." She looked at Frankie. "I don't know why it's so interested in you."

Frankie's heart stuttered. She couldn't catch her breath. She was thinking too fast.

Marissa didn't recognize Spike, but she knew of a not-cat that Spike must be similar to. A not-cat that always traveled with her husband.

Who was Konrad Orr. The Butcher of Wala.

Panic replaced the dizziness. She had to get out of here. He wanted to kill her.

No, he didn't, the front of her mind shouted, arguing. The back of her mind was not listening. He wouldn't want her here, that's for sure. He'd punish her. Would he hurt Beth? How much damage he could do. This destroyer of worlds.

Take a breath, the front of her mind said, the trained-out-of-PTSD part. He's not going to drop a bomb on his own planet.

Right. Right.

"What's the kitty's name?" Frankie squeaked out.

Elvin gave her a final tiny push, and then removed his hand. He must be convinced she would remain standing. She was not completely convinced.

"Sunshine," he said. "Morgan named them all when he was little."

Morgan.

Another secret.

She swallowed, trying to calm her vocal cords. She shifted her gaze from Marissa, who had already moved on to inspecting the bots that were doing something to the sitting room doors, to her supposedly besotted lover.

"So you know all about the kitty and didn't tell me?" she said sweetly.

Morgan's face pleaded innocence but his body language screamed guilty as hell.

And Spike. Knew Morgan. And also said nothing.

"It's a hybrid," Elvin said smoothly, going into museum docent mode. "Not quite a synth, but close. Vlossics are an endangered species in the sector. Konrad offered to try to save them. But he did it on his own terms."

Frankie barely heard him. She needed to get away. Get off this moon. Get clear of all these people. These liars.

Even Spike.

"Right, well," she started. "Who knows?" She ripped her gaze away from Morgan and smiled at the side of Marissa's head. "Anyway, I was telling Morgan here that I need to go to town. Actually, probably to Silva. This gala, it has me all turned around. I didn't know it had a theme!" She was babbling. But that could be a good thing. People going shopping always sounded like babbling to her.

Marissa frowned, turning to squint down the slope of the lawn to the tent. "That might work," she said. "Elvin just told me the guest gifts are delayed. Morgan can go with you, and whip that candy shop into action."

Morgan ran a hand through his long forelock. "Not the Sweetgrass baskets again."

"I know it's a repeat. But it fit the theme." Marissa cast a glance at Frankie. "You wouldn't believe how hard it is to find actual handwoven baskets. There's long grass everywhere now!"

She moved on to her next victim. "Elvin. Why do these servos dawdle?"

As they fell into a discussion of heights and widths, Frankie sidled away, toward the corner of the house closest to the cabana. The corner Spike had run past. Three steps to the side, and then she turned fully. Not running, but fast-walking away.

Get to Silva. Dump Morgan. Hop to the orbital platform. Get to her ship.

Hide.

Morgan didn't catch up to her until she'd rounded the house and hit the path that led to the lagoon.

"I'm sorry sorry sorry."

"You continue to hide information. Even after," she waved her hand, trying and failing to indicate intimacy.

"I was three! According to the family story, I never even saw the cyvlossics, just a photo of all of them together. Later, one bit me at the lab, and I never went back. For the longest time, I thought Dad kept one of them around to train me out of being scared of them."

She had no time for this.

Frankie grabbed at his arm, captured his wrist. "Tell me, is Konrad here?"

"I don't know. Ow!" He winced.

She loosened her grip, but didn't let go.

"Not yet. David thought he'd skip it, because session is running hot. But apparently, Mother is still expecting him."

"And you didn't think that was worth mentioning?"

"No! Because you overreact every time his name comes up. He's just a man, Frankie. A man whose actions gravely harmed you, but still. Just a man."

She hated Morgan, in that moment.

He winced again.

MORGAN COULD NOT BELIEVE his freaking luck.

He'd lost her.

Frankie started stomping back to the cabana. The hard soles of her soft boots slapped the gravel. The bounce of her curls looked manic.

"I'm not taking you to Silva," he said.

She stomped her free foot down, stopping, and turned. "What?"

"You'll just run away. I know it."

She fisted her hands, pressing her arms tight to body. "Running away is the correct decision. Looking at things objectively."

He dared to take a step closer to her. Her face—her stance—reminded him of those cartoon characters who were steaming mad. But no unusual heat was emanating from her person, just the usual hint of violet and green.

"It's not running," she repeated. "I shouldn't have been here in the first place. It's correcting position."

"I understand," he said, even though he didn't. "We've put too much pressure on you."

Her fingers unclenched, pulled straight. "This is supposed to be a holiday. Not another session of me having to manage other people's pain about my past." She brought her hands together, twisting her fingers together so tight that Morgan's fingers winced.

He reached out and put a hand over hers. "It's not fair," he said.

"It's not fair." Her shoulders eased away from her ears. She looked like she had a neck again.

He put his other hand under hers, cupping her. "You know what will be great? This time tomorrow, there will be almost four hundred people here—strangers—taking all the attention." He half-turned and looked out at the meadow on the other side of the cabana and pool. "Some will come by shuttle from the station, but many will land their own cars down past our row of pool-trees. We can sit on the deck and watch the parade. Comment on the outfits."

She followed his gaze. "Hide."

"Hide. Feel like part of it, but not. And if we don't want to go, we don't."

She cast him a glance full of disbelief.

"Well, yes, I have to. But what I usually do is watch from the cabana, wait for the second set of music, and then suddenly appear at Mom's side like I've been mingling the whole time. I meet the nice lady she's chosen from me, make sure the lady thinks I'm a total dolt, and then scurry away. Takes less than half an hour."

She pursed her lips, considering. "But what about the food?"

"Oh, now you think you're going to be hungry?"

Frankie seemed to deflate. "I can't. My friend from Wala—there's only a few of us—she's so mad I'm here. I don't know what I was thinking."

All of these Walans needed to grow up and see reality. The destruction of their planet sucked, sure enough, but it wasn't intentional. Morgan frowned. At least no evidence that it was intentional had been released.

But today he only cared about one Walan, the one in front of him, the one who had gone back to twisting her fingers. He stepped past her

"Listen. We make a call, to the basket people. Apologize for Mom's scaring them to death. Double their fee."

"You're going to pay?"

"I'll just tell Elvin they demanded it. They'll say yes, ship same-day, and we're free."

"Free," she said, her voice soft, sad. She looked around, past him. "I need to check on Spike."

"So you'll stay? Spike seems to love it here." He couldn't keep the eagerness—okay, panic—out of his voice. She couldn't leave him here alone, not this way.

She allowed him to put his arm around her shoulders. She leaned into him, and he was silently glad. So glad.

They walked that way, so surprisingly comfortable, until they reached the poolside deck.

A familiar pile of disreputable fur stretched along the length of her usual lounger chair.

Way to reinforce the message, Spike.

He might learn to like these blasted cats after all.

CHAPTER
EIGHTEEN

FRANKIE SPENT an hour in the sun on deck by the cabana lagoon, recovering from her adrenaline spike and researching the Regency of Yore. This was the first she'd heard of it, which was a surprise since the pun was right there, plain to see.

Similar to the current regency, Yore had a particular dress code, persnickety manners, and intricate dancing that no one could possibly think intuitive. The dancing intrigued her: groups in multiples of four moving in and out of one another's orbit. To do it, she'd need her wristcom as a guide, unless she practiced. This was probably the sort of gala where everyone pretended like they'd known the steps forever, while really having just learned on the shuttle ride over.

Among all the annoyances and demands of living in the Regent's orbit, dancing was one that Frankie actually liked. Not the frenzied style currently popular, but slower moves, like these. Maybe she sneak in at the back of the party and try a few steps.

Spike, the cyvlossic, slept stretched out on her side, belly facing Frankie, on the chaise lounge beside hers. Her gentle snores were a match with the sound of the wind feathering the water in the lagoon. Frankie had tried to research vlossics and found precious little. And even less on cyvlossics; not even a mention. Interesting that Orr Enterprises had paid for such a complete data wipe.

Frankie rolled on her side to face Spike, stretched out a foot, set her big toe gently on her middle. "Spy-key, spy-key" she crooned. "Tell me your secrets, do."

Spike slowly closed in on her foot claws out, like one of those carnivorous flytrap plants. But she stopped before breaking any skin. She opened her eyes.

Frankie tugged softly, pulling the toe away from Spike's fur. She rested the foot on Spike's lounger cushion, pleasantly scratchy and warm. "It's Sunshine we want, right?"

Spike nodded, once.

Frankie sighed. "I was afraid of that. You think—Bruce and the office thinks—that Konrad Orr is coming home to attend his own party." She pushed away the hair that had fallen across one eye. "You all think it would be easier to get—her?—away from here than Central District, or from the Orr compound there. Makes sense."

"Him," Spike ground out, voice even more ragged than her fur. "Only chance."

Spike was talking! Frankie must have passed the test, whatever it was. She tried not to grin. Be professional.

"So. Plan?"

"Swap."

It took a moment for Frankie to understand. "You stay and he goes? With me?"

"I follow. Later."

Frankie didn't like the sound of that. "You'll be safe?"

The claws came back around her foot. The suggestion of a claw-prick on the side of the little toe.

Frankie didn't flinch. "Fine, fine, I know you know your job." She pulled her leg back and rolled onto her back, pushing back up to lay her head on the headrest cushion. So much white. The dome's sun lights on high made the cushions a shocking white, and even bleached out top water in the lagoon. But she wasn't hot enough yet to dive in.

Spike growled her voice into action again. "Best tonight. Crowds."

Frankie sighed. "Think we can do this without me having to be in the same room with Konrad Orr?"

Spike snorted.

Thought not. Well, if she had to mingle with the Butcher of Wala, better here than in the halls of Central City. Right? She could prepare. She would not be surprised, like that one time. Luckily, he had a face, a shape, that didn't much change. Super easy to recognize.

And avoid. Hopefully.

"Suppose that means we'll need to learn those dances, then?"

"We?" ground out Spike.

Frankie sighed again. And then breathed in something that smelled so marvelous it made her sit up and turn toward it.

The cabana's kitchen bot, that gray boxy one that slapped at her hands when she tried to help, was trundling out. A napkin-covered tray balanced on its top. Brownies! And something else.

Before she could suss out that second smell, the bot arrived, dragging that small table they'd used for breakfast back into place beside her lounger. It sat the tray on the table and pulled the very white cloth napkin off its top of it, exposing two good-sized brownies with colorful flecks and another bottle of water. The bot played an audible "ta-da!"

Frankie grabbed a brownie, moist but not crumbly, and took a bite. Warm. Melty. Chocolatey. Plus. "Peppermint!"

The bot burbled happily. "Added special for you," it said in a husky alto voice.

Frankie nodded to the bot. "Your voice is lovely."

"I am also a music system. And I project visual entertainment." It wiggled in place, preening. "Whatever the guests need."

"That's fantastic. What do you call yourself?"

"You can't pronounce it. Call me Cabana-Prime."

"Cabana-Prime. Very nice to meet you. "A thought occurred to her as she was taking a second bite of brownie, but she lost it in the chocolate. After swallowing, she paused to savor the taste, and to try to lure the thought back.

There it was. "So, Cab-One. Do you get any time off?"

"All servos have downtime. yes."

"I was wondering because I need some help. And maybe you know how to help me."

The little bot wiggled even faster. "Yes!"

"How many friends do you have? Who also have some time off this afternoon?"

IN THE BEDROOM next to Frankie's, identical to hers in shape and style but nowhere near as warm or cozy, Morgan clicked his wristcom off. He lifted a foot to rest on the mattress and rested his chin on his knee. The high sun triangled across the floor through a skinny opening in the long white-canvas curtains blocking the wide glass doors. Even inside with the doors shut and curtains pulled, the warmed cedar scent of the decking sidled in.

The call had gone well. The woven baskets to carry gifts for each guest were being packed up and would be delivered by tonight. It had only cost him twenty minutes of groveling—and cost the estate a hefty new "shipping" charge.

How did these people, this family of his, get along when he wasn't there? They didn't seem to know there was any alternative to superciliously snapping at everyone.

Not his problem.

Most of the time.

His Regency of Yore outfit was ready, most of it hanging in the bathroom. The square black shoe-boots looked comfortable, but Morgan could not believe how tight those half-pants were. He could only hang the one way! But the frills on collar and cuffs of the undershirt beat anything. And the overcoat, a three-quarter length with a double row of brassy buttons and slits in the arms for the undershirt to peek through, was velvety soft. He might spend the night petting his own hips if he wasn't careful.

There were no rules on scent. He hoped Frankie would use her woodsy one, not some fairy-dust floral.

He should tell Elvin the baskets were on the way. Instead, he called up his comm screen again and sent a query to Eckberg Ship Rebuilding. Their estimate to do the repairs to Frankie's ship had been a rather wide window.

Shit. It would be ready in two days.

Well, he wasn't going to tell her that. Although it might make it easier to get over her if she was out of sight.

He didn't want to get over her. He just had to dial down his feelings, into the friend zone. He wanted to make this friendship thing work. He needed her to be his friend.

Problem was, how did one do such a thing?

He rubbed at an itch on his upper lip. He'd forgotten to shave.

He could be useful. Help her.

Tonight. Help her survive the gala.

Keep an eye on her emotional temperature. Keep Konrad away from her.

He could do that, for her.

Problem was, who would be doing that for him?

An odd thumping interrupted his thoughts. Not his heart. Outside, something with a regular beat. Frankie must be playing music loud for the bass to reverberate that much.

She must be swimming. Wanting to hear the music under water.

He quickly shed his clothes and stepped into the slick black of his swim trunks. Not making that mistake again.

He pushed the curtain aside and went to pull the door open.

And stopped.

On the deck directly outside, the chaise lounges and tiny tables had vanished. In their place stood a motley collection of servos, lined up in two rows. All were looking to the right, at Frankie. Who was leaning over the kitchen servo, saying something.

Suddenly, a faded hologram appeared. Overlaid on each servo —squat or tall, spider or rolling—was the image of a person in weirdly familiar dress.

Regency of Yore.

Frankie straightened up. She looked down the row. More than two dozen servos and an equal number of Regency holo-ghosts looked at her. One of the fruit-picking servos stood way out of the illusion, all tall and gangly, there in the middle.

She nodded.

The music started up, and the hologram-people began to move. Only the taller servos tried the opening move, a curtsey. Then all joined in, following the pattern made by the holos' feet.

They were practicing tonight's dancing.

This one was a simple pattern, in to the partner and out. In to the neighbor's partner and out. Spin, step around the neighbor's back, settle. Repeat, on down the row, with the final pair scooting past everyone's backs up to the top of the row. That kept the form in place on the deck, which was lucky since the troupe had already taken up most of the space.

As soon as she started moving, Frankie's smile transformed her entire face. It carried through her movements, holding her arms out toward the hands of a cleaning servo, stepping in, stepping out. As she spun around her neighbor, avoiding its sharp edges, she laughed.

No way she was going to miss the real dancing.

But they weren't through the third pairing before the fruit-servo accidentally kicked a vacuum out of the line.

The vacuum kicked it right back.

Frankie, startled, waved her hands quickly, calling a halt. The music stopped; the ghostly dancers vanished.

The fruit-servo was just too big and bulky. Couldn't it fold itself in or something?

Everyone seemed to be puzzling over that, except for the angry vacuum, when Frankie caught sight of Morgan. Her face lit up as if she'd discovered a vein of iridium.

Her warmth spread into Morgan's soul.

She waved at him to come out. "Perfect timing!" she said. "Do you think you could stand in for Apple Three? They offered to step out, but we have to have an even number of dancers."

"Only if I can pair with you." She needed to practice actual hand-holds, with a right-sized partner, he argued to himself.

He was helping her, really.

The cleaning servo scooted down the aisle between dancers to take Apple Three's place. Morgan took their spot.

The ghosts reappeared; the music started up again. Morgan followed his ghost's arms and legs. The opening bow was surprisingly like the casual-formal bow currently used at Central events.

He stepped in, touching his palm to Frankie's. Warm, but without that almost-painful spark of yesterday. He stepped back, losing her hand.

Her concentration was all on the hands, and the feet, and the turn, and the step to the side.

And then, it was all on him. Eyes so welcoming, so appreciative. Small smile hiding big glee.

He focused hard, trying to reflect it back to her.

This was how he could help her.

And it wasn't that hard, after all.

CHAPTER
NINETEEN

THE BOTS TURNED out to be great dancers. They learned quickly and stepped lively, even when Cabana-Prime sped the music up to standard speed. Frankie loved the thump-swish of their movements, all unique, all together. And after they'd run through five of the dances, their scents of lemon cleaning fluid and noonlight-warmed plastic parts were sweeter than a lot of sweaty humans.

And boy, was she sweaty. Dancing was hard work! Even Morgan looked glowy, and he had all that skin showing to cool himself off. He was ready to hit the lagoon, with that racer-suit on. Frankie wondered if the pool filters could take it if she just fell in, backwards, as she was. Maybe slip her boots off, first.

Morgan rose from the tune's final bow like a Regency Prince of Yore. "You must have done this before," he said.

She shook her head. "No. Would you believe it? I hope Marissa starts a trend; this style is so much better than the solo-frenzy stuff they're doing at Central." She looked up the dance floor, now just bots after Cabana-One turned the hologram off.

She and Morgan had ended the reel at the very foot of the two rows.

"Thank you, everyone. This was great. And thank you, Apple-Three, for letting Morgan here step in." The ladder-spider bot had parked itself off by the pool, but it hadn't left. Frankie curtseyed in her best attempt at Regency Femme of Yore.

As the dancer bots did their best versions, Cabana-One spoke up. "There is another dance."

Morgan mock-groaned. "There's always another dance. Take pity on us."

Frankie shook her head at him. He did look sweaty, now that he'd stopped moving. "I wonder how many there will be tonight. Surely more than five. But maybe they're repeated? Are there sets, or is it continuous?"

"Elvin would know," Morgan said. He looked up at Cabana-One, and then somewhat beyond the bot. "Speak of the devil."

Elvin looked even growlier than usual. The synthetic human wasn't stomping, exactly, as he stepped onto the deck from the path at the side of the cabana, but he gave the impression of stomping.

"Elvin would know what?" he said. "That the reason none of the spare servos are answering my calls is because they've all run away to join the cabana crew?"

All the bots seemed to pull into themselves. The two floor sweepers started to slink backwards, toward the sliding door Morgan had left half-open.

Unacceptable.

Frankie sped up the center aisle between the bots, stepped around Cabana-One, which had molded itself into a featureless cube, and poked Elvin's stiff chest. "They came at my request. I'm a guest, remember?"

"You don't have that power."

Frankie looked away from him, gaze traveling down the row of chastened bots, and then turned back to Elvin. Kinda looked like she did.

"I'm rescinding that power."

"You don't want your guests to be happy?"

"Not when they interfere with important family obligations."

"What is Apple-Three's important obligation?" Frankie was genuinely curious.

"Apple-Three?" Elvin, startled, swiveled his head, searching the deck for that bot. He found it, and gave it a special glower. "Should be in Hangar Twelve, awaiting orders."

Apple-Three swiveled its torso so its main cameras faced away. It started walking away, in slow, careful steps with its six spidery legs. Now all the bots except Cabana-One were slipping away.

Still far down the deck, Morgan, leaning back on one hip, his arms crossed, glowered back at Elvin. Frankie wasn't sure whose was fiercest.

"Well, since you're here, I was wondering," she started.

"I have no doubt," Elvin said.

Frankie plowed on. "How does the dancing work tonight? Is it in sets? How many dances?"

Elvin didn't even look at her. His gaze moved from Apple-Three to Morgan.

"Three sets of four. What about the baskets."

"On their way," Morgan said. "Here by eight."

Elvin pivoted away from her, back toward the cabana path. Frankie couldn't let that go.

"Are you acting such a meanie because you're under stress? We could help you, you know. Ease your load."

Elvin paused, but did not turn back.

"You could not."

AFTER ELVIN HAD STOMPED AWAY, his servos in tow or already gone, the deck felt naked.

And Morgan was coated in sweat. Learning dances took a lot of concentration. Fun, but still hard work. He'd need to rest up for tomorrow night.

He spied where all the loungers and tables had been stashed, on the grass along the far end of the deck. But before he could go grab one, that fruit-picking servo had reappeared, waving him away. With all its arms and legs, the servo had the deck back to order in minutes.

Morgan sank onto a lounger. "Dancing wears a body out." He looked at the cabana servo. "Got anything to eat?"

The servo, which had shrunk into a thigh-high cube during Elvin's Inquisition, popped back up and out. The swinging of its arms as they were freed from its main form made Morgan dizzy. When it spun into action, he had to close his eyes.

He heard Frankie plop onto a seat near his. "That servo needs to learn to meditate," he said.

"Cab-Prime takes their job very seriously."

"They all do, with a taskmaster like Elvin."

"Elvin's a sub. Usually they manage themselves," Frankie said. Morgan opened his eyes to look at her, skeptical.

"No, really. Marissa tells them what she wants, and they organize amongst themselves. With Elvin in charge, there's been a bit of chafing. Cab-Prime says the bots have a countdown clock running for when he is supposed to return to the lab." She pushed all the curls from her forehead, pressing them under her hands. They popped right back, nearly, when she let go. "He doesn't have to be that way."

"He pretty much does. He has to survive. In this family, that means mean." Morgan shrugged. Another reason he stayed away. "I gave him the choice to get away, on that trip to Smithson. But he looked at me as if I'd busted a gasket." Elvin must really like it here. No accounting for taste.

Frankie settled herself cross-legged on the lounger. "Listen," she started.

His wristcom cheeped. His mother's tone.

Morgan held up a palm to Frankie, hold on, and twisted his other wrist to turn the comm on.

Just a text message. "Dad's home," he said.

Frankie shrunk in on herself. Just like one of the bots. He read struggle on her face, and then she relaxed.

"Well, now that's done." She sighed. "I need a swim."

By the time Frankie had gone in and come out again, now in the blue suit that directed attention to her still red-apple-cheeked face, Morgan's evening was fully booked.

"Join me?" she said, walking toward the edge of the pool.

"No time. Command performance dinner tonight. Mandatory family evening. Family only."

She shrugged. "Even better. Not the part about you, of course. But I have some comms to catch up on myself. See what's up with my ship." She stretched her arms high, arching from her shoulders. "A quiet night sounds perfect."

His shoulders twinged in sympathy. "No nightcap?"

"Oh, no," she said, coming out of the stretch. She set her hands on her shapely hips. "You are not coming out here for a family debrief. Save it for tomorrow, when you'll be coherent."

She headed for the edge of the pool, but stopped as something occurred to her. "I will see you tomorrow, right? How much do you have to do for the gala?"

He held onto the glow—she needed him!—and waved her question away. "Nothing, besides the baskets. I'm not necessary to the gala proper until the dancing starts. Plus, my costume is out here. We'll watch the parade together, for sure."

Frankie dove cleanly into the water, barely a splash.

Morgan carried that glow with him like a shield—a Regency Protective Spell—as he headed to the main house.

CHAPTER
TWENTY

THE NEXT DAY, Frankie did not hide, exactly, but she also did not explore the grounds or go anywhere near the house. She spent most of the day—another perfect day, toasty daylight and the wispiest of clouds—alternating between swimming in the lagoon and sunning on the deck. Sitting in her usual lounger with its back tilted up, she couldn't hear any sounds of preparation for the gala, but her mouth watered at all the smells.

Apparently, two of the best ovens for baking from scratch were in the cabana's kitchen. Frankie could only guess at the goodies—Cab-Prime had shooed her out of the room again by handing her a chilled juice concoction and a promise of more later. But for sure, cherry, apple, chocolate, licorice, mint. All the treats. If she hadn't been looking forward to the dancing now, Frankie might just have figured out how to raid the kitchen and binge on all the sweets. Then again, dancing was strenuous. She would surely need to raid the larder afterword.

She ran through strategies for a successful goodie heist while catching up on her messages. Beth was talking to her again, via text if not voice or picture. Eckberg's Ship Rebuilding said the fixes to her ship, the Spear, were complete, and the upgrades nearly so. Another two days.

One day too many.

The plan was to swap Spike for Sunshine during the gala. Apparently, Sunshine was known to love the sound of scratchy violins, so the Regency of Yore music feature was a big draw for him. Vlossics must not have finely tuned hearing, or maybe they heard something in the overtones that eluded Frankie. She would much rather the music be made by thicker strings.

Sunshine would hang around the musicians—real people, not recordings or holos—trying to stick to the twilight and shadows. Toward the end of the second set, the swap would occur. She didn't have the details. That was Spike's job.

Her job was to wait until the end of the set, when everyone would be heading from the dancing hall to the giant tent for the formal dinner part of the evening. She would walk outside with the crowd, and then casually, not drawing any attention to the cabana, step to the side and go to the cabana instead. Blame it on a wardrobe malfunction, if anyone asked. Try to make it so no one would ask.

At the cabana, she would meet Sunshine, probably in the dark next to the gardening cart that was already parked outside in case of emergency. They would take the cart to one of the fancy bespoke guest buses—velvet seats and everything, Morgan said. The bus would roll them through the tunnels to the main dome and on to its cross-moon shuttle pad.

Sometime in the next four hours, according to her boss, Bruce, an atmo-hopper would arrive at the shuttle pad, reserved for her. Hopefully one of the helicopter-shaped ones that she knew how to fly. That would take them up to the repair station in orbit, where the Spear was waiting. Sunshine would hide there until Bruce arranged a handoff.

That was the sticky part. Frankie's ship wouldn't be ready for travel for another day. She had already set the appointment to run through the new upgrades to shields and comms with one of Eckberg's techs, but that wasn't until tomorrow afternoon, when repairs would be in final testing.

If someone came to the station wanting Sunshine back, Frankie wasn't sure how she could guarantee the cyvlossic's safety without damaging the repair base. She could float the Spear away from the base, sure, but if she didn't know how to run the shields that wouldn't be any safer. Besides, the someone who would be searching for Sunshine ran a company that manufactured military tech. If she fought at all, she would be outgunned.

The backup plan was misdirection. Spike, having acted the part of Sunshine for the rest of the evening, would let herself be seen hitching a ride to the cross-moon pad. She would appear on camera at the shuttle pad sneaking into a shuttle headed to Silva, to one of that moon's many stations. A few random hops later, she would reach the repair dock. If really under chase, she would hide out in Silva longer, and meet Frankie back at the firm's home base at Rosing Station.

Except Spike, bless her heart, looked almost nothing like Sunshine. She didn't walk like Sunshine, act like Sunshine, or sound like Sunshine. The cameras would need to be super blurry for the ruse to work.

Too much to worry about.

Frankie shivered in the warm sun. She pulled in her knees and wrapped one of the fluffy white mega-towels around herself. She wasn't some well-trained corporate spy, just a cargo hauler with a Central District pedigree and some diplomatic skills. Wasn't this supposed to be merely an information-gathering assignment?

She rested her face on her knees. The wonderful, sweet smells spilling out of the kitchen tormented her.

When she heard Spike's familiar swish and the thump of a cyvlossic landing on the cushion of the lounger next to hers, she sighed.

"I don't think I can do this," she said. "It's too much."

Spike rumbled, warming up to speak. "Work the plan," she ground out.

Frankie lifted her head, opened her eyes—and gasped.

Spike had been transformed. In place of the ragged tufts of gray-black-orange fur was a long, almost silky coat the color of creamery butter. A range of brown tones highlighted the tips of the pointed ears, the tops of the paws, the last third of the tale. She sat on her haunches, regal, serene, not glowering even one bit.

"Like?" she screeched.

"Marvelous. Beautiful. Shocking. How ever did you manage it?"

Spike shrugged, as if arranging a dye job and hair straightening for a not-cat in the middle of enemy territory was child's play. Maybe it was, for a skilled operative like her.

This plan could work.

She stretched her arms up, toward the mild warmth of the not-sun. So Konrad Orr had kept the prettiest not-kitty of the litter. And Marissa Orr had never taken a good look at it.

Hard to believe Morgan's mom could have mistaken all-natural Spike for this refined beauty. Could be that there were a lot of people who avoided looking directly at Konrad Orr's spy-creature.

Which would only help Spike—and Sunshine—now.

CHAPTER
TWENTY-ONE

FIFTEEN MINUTES BEFORE SHOWTIME, Morgan was fully in costume, pacing the antiseptic white carpet of his cabana sitting room and worrying at his wristcom. The comm was an obvious anachronism in this midst of all his Regency of Yore finery, but he didn't want to go without it. What if Frankie got lost?

The giant frill on the cuff of his silky white blouse almost hid the comm, but not quite. He loosened the band a tick and pushed the piece higher up his forearm. High enough for the cuff to cover it completely, but low enough that he could get access to it with a flick of his wrist. He'd need to push the sleeve of the navy velvet frock coat up a bit, but he had to do that anyway if he wanted to be able to move his arms. Every piece of clothing was cut so tight, especially the three-quarter-length coat. Extra especially the below-the-knee breeches. Definitely not a forgiving style.

He was practicing the comm-exposing wrist-flick—the ruffle-cuff was finicky—when there was a tap on his door.

"Morgan, I need your help." Frankie's soft alto carried an overtone of panic.

Music to his ears.

He pressed the wall panel to open the door and kept his hand there, so she would first see him leaning. Casual, nonchalant. But as soon as the door slid open, he rolled back on his heels, spoiling the effect.

Frankie looked bizarre. And fantastic.

Morgan had to swallow, slow.

Most of her was encased in a forest green velvety gown that exposed her shoulders and all but a tiny stripe of her arms. The deep, rich color set her dusky skin to glowing. Just perfect.

That style, though. Her waist was squeezed into nothing, her legs expanded into giant stiff triangle.

"You look delicious! But isn't that painful?" He waved toward her waist.

"Worse than it looks," she said. She spun around, exposing a gap in the back where the fabric hadn't yet been hooked together. "This torture device," she banged on her belly, making it clack, "is called a korsett. Hooks in the front. When I first put it on, I couldn't even breathe." She still sounded out of breath. "And I can't twist around to close the dress. Help?"

He leaned over the skirt and tapped an exposed part of the back of the korsett. Thumb-wide ribs of stiffness between narrow bands of fabric that didn't look like it stretched. And he'd thought tight pants were a horror. This was beyond horror.

"Do you really have to wear it?"

"Style won't work otherwise, I'm told. 'It makes the silhouette,' Wardrobe says. We argued. Wardrobe finally made me a second one, half a hand wider. So I can breathe, but at the expense of my ideal silhouette."

The hooks slid easily together, thanks to the torture device. Morgan tapped her warm tan shoulder twice to show all-done. "You'll need help getting out of it."

"I think that's the point?" she said, stepping away from him so she could turn without banging her dress into his knees. "These Regency of Yore folk must have been a lusty bunch. I mean, look at you, in those thick tights. No secrets there."

He looked down at himself. "They're pants, actually."

She laughed. "Can you even move?"

"There's a panel of elastic down the inseams."

"I should have chosen that look," she said. "Wardrobe said it would be more fun being the lady. But how do I even sit? My skirt will pop up. It has a rigid korsett, too." She pushed the front of the skirt down. The back popped up like a portal. Despite his best intentions, Morgan glanced at the wall of windows that made up the other side of the hall. Windows that turned into mirrors under the hall's bright light against the evening dark outside. The whole of her shapely legs and tiny-pantied rear was exposed.

"Lusty bunch, indeed," he said. "I'll tell Wardrobe to make you a little slip for underneath. Dark, to match the dress."

"Speaking of dark, what happened to your hair?"

"A wig. Apparently lords of yore had only golden blond hair or ebony dark tresses. I'm always blond, except for when I'm not, so went for the tresses. Bet my hair's longer than yours."

He turned his face toward the inner wall so she could see the tail, bound at the collar by a wide navy-blue elastic band. The door to his rooms was still open. He scanned the sitting room, seeing only the usual rattan furniture. Not what they needed.

"Bet the kitchen has stools. We could lean against those for the parade. I'll ping your servo friend and see. We're supposed to keep clear of all the kitchens. Watch this."

He flicked the ruffle-cuff like a pro, exposing his wristcomm on the first try. Frankie looked suitably impressed.

Almost immediately after the call ended, one of the skinny tall servos rolled into the hall from the kitchen. It carried two stools, thick circle cushions on top of twined metal legs. Morgan had it place the stools in the hall to the side of his door. Frankie took the first seat, or rather, slow lean. The servo had to scoot Morgan's stool farther away to accommodate her skirt.

"It works!" Frankie said. "But don't we want to be on the other side? To look at the meadow?"

"Change in plans." As the servo rolled away, Morgan waved the hall lights off. The glass wall in front of them went clear. The grass had purpled dark in the fading lights. The graveled path glowed silvery white.

"We did a test run last night, and Mom decided the meadow was too fragile to have hundreds of feet and wheels crowding all over it. This morning, she had the path smoothed, and touched up the reflective paint." They'd also had to move all the special gala lights, which now were jammed into the ground to both sides of the path. He'd liked them out in the meadow better. This would be pretty, but when they were set deep in the meadow it had been magical.

All the lights tonight, from the short ones along paths to the tall ones closer to the tent and its side tents, had hoods. No extra light would spill up. Nothing would spoil the view of a skyful of plush darkness and stars.

His comm chimed. "First guests are here." Most would disembark from the bespoke buses at the end of the path and walk or roll up. Some would come up from the cottages. A few, for physical or privacy reasons, would arrive the back way, riding in the extremely well-scrubbed gardeners' carts, transformed by white canvas into their best try at regency steeds.

Showtime.

"A Regency fairy path," Frankie said. The opera-length double strand of giant glass diamonds draped around her neck swung as she leaned forward and looked to the right, watching for the crowd. He'd never noticed her wearing jewelry.

"What's with the necklace?" he said. "Seems a little… busy for you."

Frankie touched the garish bauble. "Comes with the outfit. I think they're fake diamonds? These edges are so sharp! I worry they'll cut into my skin if I move too much." She reached a hand behind her neck, to check by feel.

"Absolutely not," Morgan said. "Too blocky for the silhouette. I don't know what Wardrobe was thinking." He paused, considering. "I might have something."

He ducked back into his room, not bothering to turn the lights on. He grabbed Frankie's new underslip from his Wardrobe printer and went to the dresser to raid his jewelry case. Actually, it was his second-best jewelry case, the one that looked like a paper book and also had a hidden pocket. He wasn't quite sure why he'd chosen it for tonight. It did hold the blue ear-cuffs that matched this blasted jacket. But did it have anything green?

Then it came to him: This was the box that held the necklaces.

He traced the secret pattern along the spine of the case, and the hidden pocket was revealed. From the pocket, he pulled out one of the tiny gray silk pouches, squeezing it between thumb and fingertips to confirm its contents. As expected, two small circles on a fine platinum chain, princess length.

He'd found the necklaces at an artisan's shop on Rosing Station, and bought all six. The artist was so surprised they said out loud how they hadn't sold any for so long, and was he sure he wanted all of them?

For a not-small fee, the artist agreed never to make that style again. It was Morgan's first serious quality purchase, and his first business negotiation for exclusivity. He had been thirteen.

When he stepped back into the hall, Frankie was looking his way. "You're sure this is the route? Nobody so far."

"Running late as usual. But good for us." He heard a servo, down the hall but coming their direction, and all the smooth patter he'd planned about the purview and history of the jewelry fled from his thoughts.

"Hold out your hand," he managed to say. At least his tone seemed okay, jocular and light.

With a slight, quizzical smile, Frankie did as he bid. Morgan set the tiny bag on her palm, behind her strong, clever fingers. She glanced at it, and then back at him, a question in her eyes. She'd expected the slip, which he still held in his other hand.

The big boxy chief cabana servo stopped beside him, nearly banging his hip. Still looking at Frankie, Morgan set his hand, and the slip, on the servo's flat top. He pressed down on it, not pushing, just holding still. The blasted thing better understand. *Wait.*

"For you," he said to Frankie. "It will work better. You know. Match."

Blasted hells.

He shut his mouth.

The small smile lingered as she pulled the strings to open the bag. She took a quick look inside, and then poured the necklace out onto her palm.

She looked up at him, eyes bright. "It's so fine! And the shadowy silver matches the edging on my dress."

Morgan hadn't noticed any edging. He scanned her dress. Still nothing.

Frankie grinned, and held the still-bunched necklace up to the top edge of the gown, where her breasts just started to swell. Now he could see the tiniest piping of silver along the fabric. Why such a quiet touch, when the necklace in front of it was so loud?

With her other hand, she lifted the glass bauble off. Now her hands were full.

"Hold your hand out," she said. She poured Morgan's necklace into his palm. She pivoted to show him her back again. Most of her thick curls had been caught up in a graceful silvered net that ended at the nape of her neck. Morgan unhooked the clasp on the chain. He lifted the necklace over her head, draping it a little so the twinned circles were in the right place. The clasp was easy to close, but his fingers lingered on her nape for another second. That garish necklace had already marked her, little pricks of red. He tried to rub them out with the tips of his fingers as he straightened out his chain.

As she turned to show him how it looked, her hand went up to touch the circles. "Two moons? Like Silva and Cloud?"

"Sure," he said.

Let her think that.

He double-tapped the top of the servo.

"Ahem," the servo said.

"Oh, Cab-Prime! Look what Morgan gave me. And you have my slip. Gifts from everyone." Frankie reached for the slip. This time, she mooned the non-mirrored wall, laughing at herself as she bent to slip it on.

"Perfect," she said to the servo as she came back vertical. "Just above the knee." She looked at Morgan. "Now I'm ready to dance." As she moved her hands into the first position of one of the forms they'd practiced yesterday, the giant fake diamonds clacked in her hand. She looked at them, startled, as if she'd already forgotten them.

"Do I give these back to Wardrobe?"

"They're yours, now," Morgan said. "They're not worth anything. Make an ice castle out of them."

"Trade you," the servo said.

They both stared at the servo. It slowly opened the big box of its torso. Inside were two tall glasses of what looked to be ice cream. "Protein shake," it said. "One is vanilla, and one is—"

"Mint!" Frankie said. "I can smell it from here."

"Peppermint, yes." The servo's voice, always beautifully

modulated, had a strange vibrating undertone to it. "You will need energy for the gala. The supper isn't for two-point-three hours."

"Perfect," Frankie said. She held the double-chain up. "Want it on your wrist? Or inside, to save for later?"

The servo reached both its main arms into its midriff storage, and pulled out the drinks. It handed the vanilla one to Morgan. Then it stretched out its empty hand to Frankie.

Frankie wrapped the chain three times to get it tight enough not to slide off the servo's square wrist. She received the peppermint shake in return.

"Happy gala day," she said.

The servo paused, for all the world looking as if it was admiring its new bauble.

"Clear skies," it said. It turned and headed back to the cabana's kitchen.

TWENTY-TWO

IT REALLY DID LOOK like a fairy tale parade. Along the silvered path strolled people in all manner of fancy. Lords for the night in high boots, or soft-soled slippers, or platform shoes. Ladies with big bells of cloth for legs. All quiet, as if mesmerized by the lights, the path, the starry sky.

Or rather, all quiet because the cabana's wall of glass windows was soundproof.

Frankie sipped her minty icy goodness as she watched. She could see what Wardrobe meant about the silhouette for the dresses. The smaller the waist, the bigger the contrast with the swoop of those mighty skirts. She didn't see why it was called an hourglass shape, though. They balance top to bottom was way, way off.

And how was it appealing? The people of Yore wanted their femmes to suffer? Well, they wouldn't be the first.

She didn't care that her silhouette was off. Especially since it meant she could enjoy food and breathing at the same time.

Since Cab-Prime left, Morgan had been quiet. Frankie, already bored with the parade, watched him instead. His gaze drank in every guest. What was he seeing that she was missing?

"What do you think?" she said.

"You missed out on the ruffles. The narrow outfits like mine win, for accessories." He nodded at one frothy white concoction of an undershirt that seemed to be bursting out of its wearer's chest, aggressively pushing aside the poor man's burgundy frock coat. "Also, why so many white-on-white dresses?"

"That is the preferred style," she said, disgusted. "Virginal, you know? When I said I wanted color—dark color—Wardrobe said I would have to go as an aged matron. Unqualified to dance." On the other hand, all these many white dresses, floating above the reflective path, did add to the night's magic.

"Of course you'll dance." Morgan frowned. "But hardly anybody looks good in all white." He'd already finished his drink, and was idly flicking his cuff, exposing his wristcom, not looking at it, and then hiding it again. "Those folks have to slather on the colors to look alive. Everybody else seems to be no-makeup makeup tonight. The Clash of the Palettes."

He peered farther down the path. "Here's a little more color coming. Cornflower, maybe a paler blue?"

Suddenly, he leaned back, as if not wishing to be seen. Frankie turned to look.

A pretty, tall, planet-born person in fancy plaited hair and a dress cut much like her own. "You're right, the light is washing people out. That could even be navy."

"That's Celine." Morgan choked the word off.

His old friend? The one his momma liked?

"Gorgeous dress," she said. "Her necklace looks real. Those are her family?" A collection of tall, pretty people in complicated hairstyles accompanied her, their narrow suits neat, their wide dresses pale.

"The whole stable," he agreed. "She's got a big family. More people to hide behind."

"Speaking of family," Frankie said, watching them pass. Such a graceful group, all of them. "How did family dinner go last night?"

That distracted him. Morgan grimaced.

"Less said, the better."

He then proceeded to tell her about it for ten long minutes.

"Sounds awful," she finally got in.

"Yes." He paused. "But one thing was different. A bit. You know how you know that a thing is going to go a certain way—Dad's going to needle Mom, David's going to stand up for Mom, Morgan's going to try to smooth everyone's feathers by making a joke that falls flat, that kind of thing? These last few dinners, I've been able to watch from a distance, hold my emotions in check, at least in the moment."

Frankie glanced away from two people in parallel wheeled chairs, one dressed all in white, one all in black, to look at Morgan. His gaze was firmly on the parade outside.

"That sounds healthy?" she said.

"Yes, but I still couldn't stop myself from playing my part. Being the clown." His head tilted, and then he met her gaze. "But last night, I could. A little. I couldn't change what I felt like saying. Couldn't change wanting to fix things. But I didn't actually say anything out loud."

He had her full attention. "What happened?"

"The pattern stopped. Everyone froze, like they were waiting for me. David just stared at me. Like I'd missed my cue." He shrugged. "And then they went right back to sniping at each other."

"But you were out of it."

He nodded. "But I was out of it. For that go-round, at least."

"What does your mom do? The rest of the year, I mean."

Morgan waved his hand, as if stirring up an answer. "She's into seeds."

"Seeds?"

"You know, in the ground. She's an agrochemist. Agrobotanist? Mostly she tries to find ways to make seeds stronger. Plants hardier. Able to live in different climates. Like that. You know, you've probably carried seeds she's made among your cargo. She's done a lot in the worlds around Rosing Station. Dad picks at her all the time about it."

"He hates seeds?" Konrad Orr was a real peach.

"How does he put it? She leaves good value on the table. Mom patents her work, so no one else can monopolize it, but then she doesn't sell it. She gives it away. Of course, we don't need the money. Or we didn't used to." He shrugged, gazing out at the fancy tableaux. "We still don't."

They watched the rest of the parade in companionable silence. In her mind, Frankie went over and over the plan. How did real secret rescuers do it? She was a puddle of nerves.

She'd left Spike cat-napping on the wide woven sofa in the sitting room, next to Frankie's already-packed duffel. The now-glossy-blond cyvlossic wouldn't come out until full dark, and would stay outside until just before tradeoff. It wouldn't do for anyone to see two Sunshines. The real one had the run of the house; he wouldn't step outside until after swapping places with Spike. Then, run.

The swap was the diciest part. Every time she got to that part in her mental rehearsal, Frankie found herself touching her new necklace, as if for luck. Superstitious like her dad, her mom would have said.

Always had said. Watching the families pass by was like a gentle, relentless, punch to the heart. Her own family was long, long gone. Frankie had convinced herself she was perfectly fine alone, with her small collection of friends. Seeing other people's families, happy, reminded her how that ache would never really go away.

Then again, seeing Morgan's family in action made her feel perfectly fine. Next time she felt the emptiness, she should make sure to visit a family like his.

"What?" Morgan said. Frankie realized she had chuckled out loud.

"Just thinking about families," she said. The parade was thinning, and now the stragglers hurried by. "Why are they running? Do they close the doors?"

"Actually, they open them. People will be coming in all night. But if you're here now, you don't want to miss the grand opening, when Mom throws open the big doors and all the lights inside the ballroom click on. Everyone wants to say they saw it first."

Didn't make much sense to Frankie. She tipped herself up to standing, catching her balance against the powerful swings of her skirt. She loved the fabric, fuzzy and so, so rich. Maybe she could make a blanket out of it later.

"Shall we go?" she said.

Morgan stood. He crooked his arm like in the holos so she could set her hand on his forearm, very proper.

He smiled at her briefly, but something past her head drew his attention.

He froze. "Shit!"

Frankie turned as fast as the dress would let her. A streak of pale cream dashed across the road and into the long meadow grass.

"Sunshine. Spying on us."

He didn't recognize Spike. First test passed.

Frankie held back a smile. "Who cares?"

"Dad told me to leave you alone. Bad press, he said." He smiled at her again, but this time it looked feral. "He doesn't know the worst of it."

"Morgan."

He started down the hall, Frankie in tow. "Oh, I forgot. You know the dancing?"

She rolled her eyes. Of course she knew the dancing. As they passed, the cabana's kitchen lights dimmed. The bots' work had moved to the tent kitchens.

"Where's your card, then?" Morgan said.

"Um. What card?"

"Your dancing card. The one that says who your partners will be." He hit the panel to open the cabana door with a little too much force. Night-dew and a dozen kinds of perfume greeted them as they stepped out. Her gentle violet scent would never compete.

"Our partners are chosen for us?" Frankie said. That sounded terrible.

"Not exactly. Most dances, the one playing the lord asks a lady ahead of time and the lady taps in their name on her card. Yours should be on your comm."

"My comm is tucked inside my korsett."

"Awkward. Better skip this part, then. It's only important for the first dance, really, and you're already taken for that."

"By whom?" Then she knew. How best to thumb his nose at his father's command to stay away? "Morgan…"

"Regency of Yore rules say the eldest unmarried member of the house has to lead the line for the first dance," Morgan said with too much glee. "And he gets to pick anyone he wants."

"And I've picked you."

CHAPTER
TWENTY-THREE

FRANKIE HAD to skip to keep up with Morgan's quick steps along the path from the cabana to the mansion. She gave thanks to the bots that had smoothed out the bumpy gravel. Even this easy, silvered path slapped at her way-too-flimsy dancing slippers. No way she would forget her boots, set out right in front of her duffle. She'd debated packing them, too, but she was definitely going to need them tonight.

The movements and murmurs of hundreds of people drowned out the evening song of the crickets. The night crowded the air. Only the small lights along the glowing path were lit. The mansion was dark, even the main floor, where the dancing and politicking would be.

The path cut toward the back a little earlier than she expected. The sharp turn had been eased, to make it easier for people to travel. A mild but almost strong breeze threatened her hair-net, but Frankie was confident the bot Marissa had sent to do her hair had done a good job.

Marissa was a puzzle. On the one hand, sending her helpful bots and telling her to keep all the clothes Wardrobe had made for her. On the other, telling Morgan to stay away. Or had that been only Konrad?

No matter. After tonight, no Orrs or Cloud-Orrs would want anything to do with her.

And that was fine.

And that would be fine.

Totally fine.

People were always popping into Frankie's life and popping out just as fast. She knew she was a prickly one—she'd been told that often enough. After all, what did one do with a girl who was now a woman, who was most famous for being a victim?

Konrad Orr's bomb had destroyed her planet. The news gatherer from the Sun-Times had captured that perfect instant of Frankie's grief.

That stupid image ran alongside every anniversary story. It appeared in reporting during the trials, as well as the reparation talks. It kept her forever seven and a half years old in the eyes of the galaxy.

And yet here she was, grown.

But now she could do something good for someone else.

This plan had to work. She wouldn't make a victim of Sunshine.

As they neared the loose-knit crowd, which stretched the length of the mansion and halfway to the giant tent in the lawn below, Frankie scanned for lenses. She saw none. Morgan said the event was officially closed to images, except those approved by the Orrs. Scofflaws could not be punished legally, of course, but they would be shunned by every Orr and all their subsidiaries. Not worth it, apparently, at least to friends of the Orrs. Not-friends weren't invited.

Morgan skirted the far edge of the crowd. "The effect is actually better the farther back you are," he said. Now off the path, Frankie's feet were starting to describe to her the many irregular surfaces they were encountering. Turned out, real dirt had real stones in it.

"Let's not go so far," she said. "My shoes are getting wet."

Morgan stopped instantly. "Here's good enough. Come stand on my feet. These shoe-boots can take it." He set one foot ahead of the other, so she could balance in front of him without her skirt sproinging up. Her feet registered the weird buckles at the top, but at least they weren't sharp or wet. He set his forearms out horizontally. "Lean on these. Pretend I'm a stool."

"You are not a stool," she said. "You're a good friend. Who just might be fishing for a compliment."

He chuckled. "Nobody's called me a prince all day."

Except for the small lights on the paths nearby, the mansion was nearly black on this side. Not even reflections in the windows.

"Black curtains," Morgan said, as if hearing her thoughts. "Heightens the effect."

A bell rang out, a single clear tone. The troubadours along the path earlier had gathered to the side of the mansion. They started up a stately overture, careful half-steps in warm tones slowly building toward a climax. As the music hit that chord, a solid wash of sound, all the windows in the house uncovered at once.

Light blanketed the crowd, highlighting all the whites and silvers. Lots of oohs and aahs. The three sets of double doors leading to the giant sitting room thrust themselves open as one. Marissa Orr stepped into the light of the center doors.

"Welcome to the Regency of Yore! Gallantry, pageantry, virtue, and love. Come in, everyone, and dance!"

Half the crowd immediately turned toward the food tent.

"Always happens," Morgan said behind her.

"Won't Marissa be disappointed?"

"Nah. Part of the plan. No way more than a hundred of us will fit on the dance floor. Especially all of you in circle skirts."

So that was what they were called.

Inside, the giant room Frankie had first seen as cold and forbidding was bright with warmth and sound. The white carpet and bulky chairs where she had first met David Orr and formally met Marissa Cloud-Orr had vanished. Even the fireplace was cleared out. Except for narrow benches made of metal filagree and topped with white cushions placed along the two walls, the entire room was open for dancing.

Light fell on them all from six glassy-diamond chandeliers that hung from the rafters three stories above. Triple-globed sconces on the lower walls chased the shadows away. In the corner farthest from where the Orrs' sitting area had been, a different set of musicians was perched in an overhanging balcony. She hadn't even noticed the balcony last time.

Fragrant parquet now covered the cold stone floor, easy on her shoes and not at all slippery. Frankie hadn't realized she'd stopped to stare at everything until Morgan tugged her gently away from the doors. Once safely out of the stream of guests, he stopped to let her look her fill.

The curtains that had blocked out the light were pure white on this side. Now tightly rolled, they stretched from the top of the third set of windows all the way to the floor. Probably meant to mimic ancient columns of yore. The only thing that was familiar from Frankie's last visit here was the underscent of hemp. Somebody here was a smoker.

People were still flowing into the room, but about half of them weren't lingering.

"Family greeting is in the dining room. If you go in there and expose yourself to the family, you get a glass of the finest bubbly."

"I'll be fine out here."

She heard Morgan smile. "After that, the room will be

converted to a serving station for snacks and drinks," he said. "Our protein drinks can hold us until then."

But not everyone was headed toward the dining room. "Where are those people going? What's in the hall?"

"Fantastic art, as you know. And also, across the way, Konrad's formal office. His real office is upstairs, but this one downstairs is more impressive. People feel like they are making headway with Konrad Orr when they're allowed in that office. Fools."

Morgan drew them closer to the open doors to the dining room. From the side of the doorway, he leaned in to look.

"Knew it. Konrad isn't doing the family greeting. He's left David and Mom to go it alone. David is going to be pissed."

"You're doing the same."

"Yeah, but it's different. David doesn't want me there, so when I'm not around he's glad. When Konrad isn't around, David is the one who has to deal with all the sycophants and deceivers."

"Wow. Your words?"

"Dad's. Wait till you meet him."

CHAPTER
TWENTY-FOUR

"YOUR DAD?" Frankie drew a little closer to Morgan at the side of the doorway from the great hall to the dining room. Not that his skinny person would be much protection anyway. People in pairs and clumps glanced at them as they passed into the room and joined the greeting line. Frankie drew even further back. "Does he dance?"

"Not to worry," Morgan said. "My bet is he doesn't even show until the main supper seating. Where he gets to play the king, of course."

Good, good. She'd be gone by then. Their paths would never cross. Then she registered Morgan's tone of voice.

"Not that you're bitter," she said.

"I'm not bitter." He turned away from the door and back to her. "Caustic is what I am." He flicked his ruffled cuff, smiling at his success as he read his wristcom. Forearm-com. "Ten minutes until the dancing starts. Who can I introduce you to?"

No one. She needed to be seen and not heard tonight. Not quite remembered.

"You know, I'd like to go back to the hall," she said. "See the art for longer than five seconds. Especially that Stauffer."

They spent so much time in the entryway that the family steward, Samson, had to come fetch Morgan to open the dance. Frankie followed in his wake, hoping the gazes of the people would stay on him. They should: He was one of the few, famed Orrs. And unmarried. Eligible, in Yore terms.

The dancers made up four sets of eight couples, with space remaining for at least two more groupings. In the candle-warm light, the undertones of the white dresses glowed forth. Many ladies who were wearing the gowns made of that white superfine fabric—a weave so scanty that Frankie had been afraid it would shred on her in the first dance—had wisely chosen to wear another layer underneath. Those layers of rose, gold, blue, gave the dresses an individuality they had lacked in the parade during early evening's light. Brilliant. She should tell Wardrobe.

She would not be telling Wardrobe anything, Frankie reminded herself. She was working the plan. Not a moment to waste. No time to deviate.

But all thoughts of the plan vanished when the music started. Practicing the steps on the deck with the bots and the holograms had been so fun, but here it was enchantment. Real human-made music, just for this moment alone. Real human hands, clasping and unclasping. Stepping in, stepping out. Spinning around your neighbor, barely getting to the right spot in time. Laughing as everyone had the same problem. Getting in synch with your partner, then your foursquare, then the whole set.

Making shapes out of nothing, not to keep, just to feel.

Heaven.

When the music stopped after six dances, Frankie woke up.

Oh, no.

"Welcome back," Morgan said. His grin looked real. He must not be too upset.

"I forgot to change partners," Frankie said.

"Only by the most severe of definitions, my lady," He did one of those ostentatious Central District bows so enthusiastically his ponytail flicked over his shoulder to the front. "You may have partnered with me alone, but you smiled at every other dancer in the group. People jockeyed to get into our set, after that first dance."

"Because of you," she said, blinking, trying to come back to ground. Expensive scents rose past her, the smell of violin rosin came down from above. They were standing where they had started, just in front of the musician's balcony.

"Because of you." Morgan did that elbow-bend thing. She put her hand carefully inside. "Your generosity to your partners helped them learn faster," he said, "and feel good doing it."

"I wanted us to get to that harmony. Where we were all moving together." She swayed at the thought. Morgan set his free hand on hers.

"You know what? You stay right here, and I'll go get you some punch. Or something stronger?"

No drinking, Spike had said. "Juice, plain," she said. "Or water." Morgan smelled really nice.

"Good idea. There's plenty of drinking at the supper."

He was gone so long that Frankie finally woke up to the fact that she was hot. She moved closer to the last doors to the lawn outside. The slight breeze had picked up a bit, perfect for an easy cooldown.

With her back to the wall, she watched the guests who had chosen to stay inside. Most stayed in the same clumps, with one or another person breaking orbit and gravitating to another clump. Frankie caught some people looking at her, but no one came close. Her gravitational pull must not be strong enough.

Outside, the guests lingered in the light of the mansion or stuck to the well-lit walkways. The starry sky gave the lawns and meadow a new depth, as if they were made of the same fabric as her dress. Everything looked soft, safe.

Deceptive.

At the sound of violins starting to tune up, Frankie turned back to look at the balcony. There was Sunshine, on the ledge closest to the door, sitting as if he owned the place.

Stick to the plan.

Maybe she shouldn't dance this next set. Stay focused. But that might make her overfocused. She needed to stay loose, cool, unaffected. Not look anxious, or guilty. Work the plan.

"What's wrong?" Morgan appeared at her elbow, carrying a crystal goblet. Frankie had to untwine her hands to take it from him. Luckily, the glass held only water. What could she tell him? Why would she be nervous now, in the middle of everything? She looked deep into the now empty goblet, which reflected vague colors from the lights and the dresses. More people were coming in. They were starting to form sets again.

She shook her head. She needed to tell him something. What?

They' forgotten this, in the plan. Leaving Morgan in the lurch. Of course, he'd expect to sit near her at the supper.

The supper. That was it.

Frankie pulled Morgan away from the door, all the way to under the musicians' balcony. No one would hear them here.

"I can't go to the supper." She whispered to boost the effect. "I just can't."

Morgan's face set hard. "Dad."

"It doesn't feel right. Thinking about eating in the same room with him makes me woozy." She was playing it up for Morgan, but saying it out loud made it feel real. She really didn't want to be in the same room as Konrad Orr. It didn't matter that he was just a man who made a mistake. For all her heart knew, he could make another mistake at any moment. And people would die.

"Shhh. It's all right." Morgan held her hands, rubbing them a little. They'd gone cold. "We'll go back to the cabana and eat some snacks. Then come back."

Frankie was prevented from pushing back on that idea by the opening chords of the first dance. Morgan pulled her into place at the end of the last set of dancers.

CHAPTER
TWENTY-FIVE

FRANKIE HAD NO BETTER success at focusing than during the first set of dances. Dancing was just too distracting. The music was faster this time, as the musicians assumed everyone had already learned the steps. The ladies' skirts whirled. The lords' shoes stomped. Everyone spun and spun and spun.

Too soon, it was over. Morgan took his time with his final bow, giving Frankie time to catch her thoughts.

She must find more places to go dancing.

The hair on the edges of Morgan's wig were plastered to his temples, but Frankie felt merely warm. These stiff wide skirts offered plenty of venting. Her cheeks were oddly sore. She lifted her hands to touch them, puzzled.

"You've been grinning for the last half an hour," he said.

"You're grinning, too."

"It's infectious. Look around." He swung his hand out. Her gaze followed.

He was right. Lords, smiling. Ladies, fanning themselves with their hands, talking with friends, giggling as their skirts swam around each other.

A tall lady in blue smiling at her.

As their gazes met, Frankie recognized Celina, Morgan's friend. She stood alone, off to the side of the door, out of the flow of people heading out to the dining tent. The tall window behind her added a silver glow to her hair.

A possible friend.

A possible way out.

Frankie swept her skirt toward that window, and both her feet and Morgan followed. She stopped a Central District social distance from Celine, and waited.

Celine looked at Morgan. It took him a second to remember the etiquette.

"Celine! I'm so happy your allergy to Cloud has lifted."

"Your mother is quite persuasive," she said in a clear soprano. She must have had musical training. She had reversed the layers of fabric: a fine, lacy white underdress peeked out at wrists and covered the rather deep cut in the front of her thicker, dark cornflower dress.

"Did you dance?" Frankie said.

"I did."

"It was wonderful."

"I wasn't in your group, but even from halfway down the floor I could see how much you were enjoying it." Even her smile was graceful.

"Celine, this is my friend Frankie. Frankie, Celine."

They did the Ladies of Yore curtsy, carefully, slowly. Laughingly.

"Morgan has told me so much about you," Frankie started in before they'd finished rising. She needed to direct this conversation. Celina, mildly startled, looked mock askance at Morgan.

"And what ever did he say?" she said.

Morgan raised his hands, mock surrender. "All good, I'm sure. All good."

"Yes," Frankie agreed. "He said you were clever and kind." She stepped to the window, not-quite-subtly forcing Celina to take a step toward Morgan. "And look. You match. Such a pretty blue."

Morgan's gaze swept Celina appreciatively. Then he winced. "Mom told you."

Celina's smile included her eyes. "She's no dummy. Besides, we both look good in blue."

Morgan looked sheepish. "Should have known. Bring a lady home, and it's open season."

Frankie didn't hear Celina's reply. Her attention was snagged by a blur of movement above them, one only she could see. On the railing of the musician's gallery.

One cat, staring at her. Jumping down.

One cat, jumping up. Observing the crowd, regal. Catching her eye.

Work the plan.

Frankie scanned the room. Nobody else seemed to be staring at the balcony. She forced herself to focus on Celine, who was chatting away, something about horses. Morgan looked rapt.

"Oh, but we must be boring poor Frankie," Celine said. She reached for Frankie's arm, and stopped. She changed the movement, and reached out to touch one of the moons on Frankie's necklace.

"A friend," she said. "A good friend."

Frankie looked at Celine, ready to say something nice about her necklace.

And stopped.

Celine was wearing the same necklace.

They both looked at Morgan. Who shrugged. "Can't help it. I love the style."

Before she could say anything in response to that, Frankie's chest buzzed. Everybody looked at her middle.

"Oh! That's my wristcom. It's been sliding slowly down the korsett thing. I don't think I can reach it now."

"Don't try, here," Morgan said. The room was emptying, but not empty, and someone could come in at any time.

"Try the ladies' retiring room," Celine said. "It's always next to the dining tent, right?" She looked at Morgan.

Frankie shook her head, making the hair-net sway. "I think I'd rather run down to my room and rearrange everything altogether." She looked meaningfully at Celine. "Do you think you could take Morgan here to the supper?"

Celine's eyes went wide. "You're positive?"

Frankie nodded vigorously, testing the hair-net even further. She pressed her hand to the front of the korsett, where the comm had finally stopped buzzing. "Who knows what this call is. I might have to answer it."

She took Morgan's arm and gently formed it into that lordly teapot shape. With her eyes, she sought permission from Celine to touch her. At her nod, Frankie took Celine's hand and set it in the crook of Morgan's elbow. Then she took a step back and posed. An artist, judging her work.

"Yes," she said. "Perfect." She took another step back, toward the open doors.

Morgan tilted his head toward Celine, but looked at Frankie. "Did my mother put you up to this."

"No comment," Frankie said, winking at him. Celine chuckled.

Frankie's chest buzzed again. Spike was so impatient. At this rate, the comm really would fall out. She set her hand back on her chest and took another step back.

"Catch you for the next set," she said.

And escaped.

CHAPTER
TWENTY-SIX

CONGRATULATING herself for being able to think on her feet, Frankie loped to the cabana. The silver walkway was a long stretch of empty. Perfect. She could hear the crickets now, in the dark beyond the small lights along the path. The dew didn't disturb the gravel; her footing was good the whole way.

She burst into the cabana hall and ran to her room. Shoes off, socks and boots on. Pull up the weird side-of the shoulder straps to keep the stupid dress up. Duffel strap on the shoulder and go.

She was out the cabana's far door in less than two minutes.

And there she stopped.

No go-carts.

And no Sunshine.

Not ideal. Frankie headed around the cabana to the long deck in the back. Maybe the cyvlossic was hiding there, waiting for her.

Or not.

Light triangled from the kitchen sliders onto the deck. Didn't all the bots leave hours ago, to staff the supper service? Frankie, not panicking, not at all, slunk toward the kitchen.

Elvin was in there, his back to her, along with her boxy bot friend, Cab-Prime. The bot looked a little grimy. It was handing tools to Elvin, who was slicing up something at one of the worktables.

Something furry.

Something that looked like a cyvlossic.

Frankie shoved the glass door open, took a step inside. And tripped.

Sunshine—no, Spike—growled at her.

"What is going on?" she asked her colleague. "Aren't you supposed to be up at the house? Is this part of the plan?"

Elvin finished what he was doing, which now looked like wrapping a paw in clear gauze and not cutting into anybody. He turned, surprised. Unhappily surprised.

"You? You're the crack rescue team?"

Frankie pushed her skirt out of the way and ran to the other side of Elvin's table. "Nice to see you, too. Why aren't you up at the house? Isn't this your event?"

He immediately got puffy. "As if any of those…people…could stand to be in the same room with a terrifying synthetic human."

She'd forgotten that part. Of course, guests of the Orrs would know about synthetic humans, since the Orrs had a history of working with them. But after all the horror stories—synths refusing to work, synths demanding rights, synths shutting down life-support systems—hardly any civilians dared go near one.

"How infuriating," she said.

"Don't pander," Elvin said. He set the roll of gauze on the table. Frankie got her first up-close look at Sunshine.

Who looked like a disreputable, tufty, gray-striped not-cat. Angry. With a wound in his paw.

"You made him into Spike," she said, wonderingly.

"Not I," Elvin said. "I just cut out the leash." He picked up a bloodied piece of tech—a tracking chip—and dropped it into a tiny clear bag. Spike came forward and took the bag in her mouth. "Now Spike really is Sunshine, according to the dome's scanners."

Frankie reached toward a tuft of not-Spike's fur. They must have just dyed it. Was it already dry?

His hiss stopped her.

She turned to Cab-Prime instead. "Do you know where the go-carts are? Was there an emergency?"

Elvin answered. "They were all rounded up to transport guests. Your plan is shot through with holes."

"You're welcome," Frankie said. "And why are you helping us, again? I thought you were happy here."

"I never said that." Elvin crossed his arms and made his agile face scowl. "And all of us here help one another. I'm not going to stand in the way of anyone else's happiness."

"This is more than not standing in the way. This is aiding and abetting."

Frankie hardly had the words out when the outside door to the cabana banged open. Angry voices raced toward the closed kitchen door.

Elvin swiped all his instruments and the extra dyes up and into the closest big sink.

Spike was gone, out the open door.

Sunshine stared at her, wide-eyed.

Cab-Prime popped open the door to the big box of their torso. Brilliant.

Frankie gestured to Sunshine: *Get in*. Sunshine balked, but at what must have been a familiar voice in the hall ("Get the blasted door open!"), he jumped to the floor, and then up into Cab-Prime.

The bot's door didn't close all the way. A tuft of hair was caught. Frankie dropped her duffel, and as gently yet speedily as possible, pushed the fur inside. As she shut the little door, the main kitchen door burst open.

The one behind her.

Frankie pivoted so fast her korsett couldn't keep up. It twisted violently, making her gasp and spilling her wristcom to the floor. Off-balance, she sank to her knees. At least she was able to pick up her wristcomm.

A small man with a face like David's stomped in, three taller people behind him. He gave Frankie, still down by the floor, the briefest of glances, and focused on Elvin.

"Where the hell is Sunshine?"

Elvin shrugged. Frankie really wanted the synth to say, "in your heart." Like the song. Maybe because Konrad Orr's voice carried the same rhythm.

The korsett must have squeezed her brain, too.

"Isn't he with the string players?" Elvin sounded amazingly bored. He would make a good secret agent. She could take lessons from him.

"The readings say he's here."

Frankie rose to standing, trying so hard not to look at Cab-Prime. She looked at Konrad Orr instead. Felt no hitch in her heart. No pain, just the memory of it.

Just a man, like Morgan said. A small man, bitter.

Looked like the decade of grief counseling worked. Didn't mean she ever wanted to be in the room with him, though.

She looked away, out the window. Saw a lump of cream sitting on the other side of the lagoon, near the trees. Staring at her. She took the hint.

She pointed to the window. "Is that your kitty?"

Konrad Orr took one look, and stomped the rest of the way through the kitchen and out the door. "Sunshine! Dammit, get over here."

The lump turned into a flash, and the kitty was gone.

"Tracker says he's headed to the well," a tall person said.

"Mice." Konrad Orr said the word like it was the absolute

worst swearword in the galaxy. He looked into the kitchen and waved at the tall trio. "Get me a blasted go-cart! Supper has already started, dammit."

Frankie thanked her guardian ghosts that the man didn't return to the kitchen. He stomped around the building instead, looking for all the world like a miniature slamball player.

"I didn't realize how tiny he is," she said to Cab-Prime. "He was taller than me back when I was nine."

"Proton bombs are small too," Elvin said, "but just as deadly."

Frankie's breath stopped.

The synth seemed to realize what he'd said, and who he'd said it to.

"My apologies, Fridrika Faldasdotter. That was uncalled for."

Frankie told herself she had heard worse. Elvin was helping. Don't push people away when they're walking toward you.

"You're welcome to join us," she got out. "Guess we'll be going on foot."

Elvin shook his head, not mussing his perfect hair. "Travel faster without the duffel. I can ship it overnight. Where's your ship?"

"Still at Eckberg's repair platform. Thanks."

Cab-Prime's door opened. Sunshine, managing to look almost as disgruntled as Spike always could, hopped out.

"Go," Elvin said, soft. "Quickly."

CHAPTER
TWENTY-SEVEN

THE SILVERED path did not feel magical now. Frankie wanted less light. Less fanfare. Sometimes, there was safety in darkness.

She fast-walked down the path, away from the mansion, toward the spot where the shuttle buses were supposed to stop. Sunshine matched her pace, but in the grass about a meter away from the walkway's lights. No one else was on this part of the path, which just made her more nervous.

"Where is everyone?" she said, mainly to herself.

"Everybody else knows the shuttle schedules," Sunshine said. His voice was shockingly lovely. He might have been a musician. "We have only five point five minutes before the next one departs. It is one kilometer away."

The delay at the cabana had already bogged them down. They couldn't afford to wait another twenty or thirty minutes for the next shuttle. Frankie lifted her skirt from the sides, hopefully not mooning anyone this time, and started to run. Sunshine stayed a few steps ahead of her.

A ways ahead, a giant bot seemed to be settling down directly in the path. Frankie squinted, trying to see if she could get around it. It stretched out, taking up all the space. One of those fruit-picker bots.

Apple-Three?

By the time they reached the bot, it had locked its spidery legs and stretched its gangly torso so long the tip of it reached above the wall of trees or bushes behind it. The picker-claws of two of its long limbs lay on the path, forming a rather frightening nest.

Sunshine streaked across the path and onto the nest. Frankie slowed down to step carefully among the alternating saw-sticks and soft fingers on the hands.

"Ready," Sunshine said.

Apple-Three thrust their arms up. Frankie closed her eyes and held tight to one of the soft paws until the hydraulic express elevator action stopped. The bot's torso squeaked as it swiveled. Frankie had time enough only to see that the bot was saving them from having to run down and back again, a switchback on the path. Instead, they were taking the straight route.

And then the express elevator was diving down.

A shuttle was in sight, just ahead.

It wasn't as nice as Morgan had described. Except for a small ring of seats along two walls, everyone was standing, holding onto straps or poles. And it was packed, mostly with wide skirts.

Frankie took a breath to catch her balance. Sunshine slipped under her skirt. Rude. But probably safer.

"Can you send thanks to Apple-Three?" she whispered toward her feet.

"Later." hummed out. "Now move."

She took long steps, trying to make the most space for the cyvlossic. The gait was slower, but covered more ground. At the ramp up into the shuttle, she paused, trying to figure out where she could stand so Sunshine might hide under a seat.

A young human in Orr colors appeared at her side. "Ticket?" they said.

Frankie looked at them, so young. Regulation-short hair. Barely peach fuzz on their upper lip. How long ago had their voice changed?

"Ticket?" she said.

"On your comm. Came with the invite. Page Four."

Frankie looked at the inside of the shuttle. She looked at the young person. She'd never received a formal invitation.

She was getting on this shuttle.

Or one of them was.

Frankie stepped between the young person and the shuttle, blocking their view of the ramp. She lifted the back of her skirt to not-cat height, hoping Sunshine would take the hint. She set her expression to vacant. Blinked hard to make her eyes moist. Tensed her vocal tract.

"I have not the invitation. Maman does. She keeps it all from me. Maman is so cruel. She keeps everything from me."

The youngster held up their hands, already overwhelmed. "I'm not supposed to let anyone on without a ticket," they said, pleading.

"And now I have the stomach-ache, and there is nothing for it here. I must be home. Right now." Frankie stomped, and felt Sunshine shoot away. "I must!"

The youngster had their hand up by their ear. "Okay, okay, I'm calling for permission. But they are very strict. I already had to send someone back. And they were in a go-cart!" The voice broke. "Maybe call your mama, too?"

"Oh!" Frankie blinked hard again, shook her wristcom awake and stepped away.

Blessed guardians, Morgan answered on the second ring.

"Frankie?"

"Oooh, nice trick," Frankie heard Celine say in the background. Morgan must have done the ruffle right.

So that was going well.

Frankie took as deep a breath as she could, and started in. "I'm at the shuttles. I have to get to my ship. There's a problem. With my ship. I have to go now. But they won't let me on. The shuttle."

"What?" Morgan interrupted. "Why won't they let you on the shuttle?"

Frankie was already out of breath. "Ticket," she got out.

"She needs a ticket," Celine said. "Give me her address. I'll send her mine."

"Then you won't have one," Morgan said. "How will you get home?"

Frankie felt the ping. Saw the ticket. Breathed a small sigh of relief.

"Guess I'll just have to stay over then," Celine was saying.

"Stay over?"

Morgan could be so dumb.

"Let me talk to Celine," Frankie said, walking back to the shuttle ramp. The young ticket-taker still had their hand to their ear. Their forehead was shiny with sweat. When she showed them the ticket on her screen, they looked as relieved as she had felt. They waved her aboard and headed toward the front of the shuttle.

"Frankie?"

"Hey, Celine, thank you so much. Tell Morgan you want to stay out at the cabana."

"The cabana," she repeated. In the background, Morgan moaned. It didn't sound like he was in pain, though.

"Right. Then ask the Wardrobe to make you all the clothes. And then the Orrs will give them to you."

"Golden," Celine said. "Call me anytime."

As she walked up the ramp, Frankie closed the call. New-bus smell fought with eye-stinging perfume for dominance inside the shuttle. What had she said? Would anyone who overheard her be able to piece out what was really happening?

Then she took a good look at her fellow passengers. The ones who weren't dozing in their seats were deep into their comm screens. Behind her, the ramp was drawing in, tucking under the floor of the cabin. Soon the doors would swing closed.

Sunshine didn't have anything to fear.

She didn't have anything to fear.

"Wait!" the ticket-taker said. Frankie heard his footsteps rounding the back of the shuttle.

Her entire body slicked with sweat.

Not now.

Frankie turned to look out the still-open back of the shuttle. She set her booted feet in boxer's stance. They were not getting her out of here without a fight.

The youngster came into view, panting slightly. They held up a woven basket with a single handle.

"Forgot your parting gift."

Frankie took the basket, and even managed to nod a thank you. It held fancy soaps in a variety of too-strong scents that were all fighting for dominance.

The doors slowly folded in and locked. Frankie pressed her forehead into the cool of the back window.

"You're taking up a lot of space," said a voice behind her. A rather small person, dressed in very precise lord's clothing had looked up from their comm. Had to look up, since the comm's screen was blending into the back of Frankie's skirt.

Frankie wasn't sure what she could do about that. Moon the back door?

"Help?" she said.

The tidy person reached toward her waist and stopped, eyebrows raised. Asking for permission. Frankie, tired and relieved and confused and just plain spent, nodded yes.

Somehow, the person found a kind loose string near Frankie's waist. They tugged at it. Air started releasing from around her legs. Soon the bottom quarter of her skirt puddled on the floor of the shuttle.

She'd had no idea.

"There are two sets of ribbons under, by your calves," they said. "Bunch up the hem, and you can tie the extra up."

Frankie followed their instructions, leaving the dress a shade long in case Sunshine needed protection again. "You're a lifesaver," she said.

"It's nothing. They leaned close, which they could do now that Frankie didn't have a giant triangle for legs.

"You know, none of these costumes are anywhere close to period." They sniffed. "Not a bustle to be seen."

TWENTY-EIGHT

FRANKIE ACTUALLY HAD a seat on the bus by the time it reached the cross-moon shuttle terminal. Nearly half the passengers had departed at one or the other of two hotel stops. She used the space to pull up her own comm screen. She hadn't checked since she sent her boss the barely-coded message, *Vacation is a go! Meet up?*

A return message from Bruce was waiting. *Terminal 2, berth C-74. Atmo-hopper. You do remember how they work, right?*

Very funny. Bruce knew the whole story behind Morgan and Frankie's hasty exit from Smithson Prime last month. She'd had to push that atmo-hopper to its limit to avoid the wrath of one of Morgan's unhappy customers. At least Morgan was out of that racket now.

When they finally reached the cross-moon terminal, only a dozen passengers were left to straggle out into the airy, over-bright station. Frankie stayed seated, waiting for everyone else to leave. Sunshine had tucked himself under Frankie's deflated skirt, amidst all the extra fabric.

For most of the trip, he'd hidden under the bench in the

darkest corner. Dressed in Spike's colors, the cyvlossic was nearly invisible there. At least to someone not expecting him.

Nobody would be looking for him here. Yet.

Frankie stood and did the slow-wide walk down the ramp. It was harder to hide a full-grown cyvlossic under the skirt's now-much-skinnier silhouette. She felt a lot of fur—and a lot of grumbling—against her legs.

The young ticket-taker hadn't come back to help with disembark. No one was around as she stepped onto the black-and-white tile of the station proper.

"You know," she said to her skirt. "Spike is known for prizing her independence. Half the time, she walks ahead of me. The rest of the time she pretends she's not even with me."

"Just keep moving," her skirt grumbled.

Frankie checked the map for the fourth time. Nothing had changed. "Terminal Two is to the right. C-74 is surprisingly close."

"So, move."

"Always a pleasure," Frankie said.

Her skirt didn't deign to answer.

A half an hour later, Frankie was almost done with the hopper preflight check. The hopper was a boxy bus orbital shuttle, standard version. The kind every pilot practiced on first.

She cleared her route with the control tower. Not that she'd really be flying that route. She wouldn't be going to Silva, but would veer up, to the repair platform in Silva's orbit. This was the second time in a month she'd lied to control about her destination. Better not make it a habit. Better not get caught.

A quick-burst message pinged on her comm. Bruce again. *Delay. Six minutes.*

"Expecting someone?" she asked Sunshine, meatloafed on the second pilot's seat in preparation for strapping in.

"I should hope not."

Frankie frowned at the cyvlossic, so like Spike and yet not. "Your voice is so lovely. Why is Spike's so scratchy?"

Sunshine opened one eye, judging her. "You don't know?"

Seriously? Frankie was beginning to think that rescuing people really was not its own reward. "Duh," she said.

Sunshine's eye closed. "Not my story to tell."

Fantastic. This was going to be a great trip.

"You know, you might eat something," Sunshine said.

Blasted comets. No wonder she was frantic and cranky. With all the planning and running and panicking and vamping, she'd missed dinner. Protein shakes only stretched so far.

Frankie swiveled her seat around and peered into the shallow drawers built into the half-wall between the pilots and the passengers. Three big chocolate bars, two with flakes of peppermint.

Maybe this trip wouldn't be so bad.

At one minute to go, Frankie got another message. *Open the doors.*

She scanned all the screens showing views outside the shuttle. Nobody was anywhere around. Just the dull gray of the standard-issue docks and transit tubes.

And a flash of cream.

Before Frankie could be sure what she had seen, she heard the door starting to close.

"Spike?"

"Go!" rasped one of the passenger seats.

* * *

THREE HOURS LATER, they were tucked into the public dock for Eckberg Ship Rebuilding. Frankie had let the autopilot fly most of the way, after she cleared the transit-center's dome herself.

She'd spent a good fifteen minutes fighting for freedom from first that beached boat of a dress and then, thank the stars, that blasted korsett. All there was to wear on board were the soft gray pants and top emblazoned with her new employer's logo—a stylized winged horse wearing a halo. Already getting the good swag.

It took another good hour to wipe all the Sunshine off her Spike, using the special wipes that also happened to be in the pilots-wall drawers. Vlossics turned out to have both an overcoat and an undercoat of fur, both of which easily absorbed liters of dye.

Once the cream and browns were gone, her colleague still didn't look quite like herself. The blowout would have to wear off on its own. For now, Frankie used some of the shuttle bathroom's hand lotion to form a few of Spike's signature disreputably raggedy tufts.

So, already halfway through the trip, there were no apparent Sunshines on board anymore. Still, Frankie hadn't been able to make herself relax.

She'd heard nothing from Bruce during transit. She understood need-to-know, but it wasn't only her plan that seemed to be full of holes. Sections, connections, critical moments that one simply vamped through.

But here they were, touched down and apparently ready to vamp again. How was she going to move two healthy-sized cyvlossics across the station, which she knew was peppered with cameras and other monitors? Wrap one in the giant velvet dress? Which one? Neither seemed the type to volunteer.

As she chewed on that puzzle and ran through the shuttle's post-flight check, another pilot stepped on board. Frankie hadn't let them in, so they must be known to the shuttle. And to the vlossics: Neither twitched a whisker.

The pilot smiled at her, all teeth.

"Scott." He made the hand signal for male-presenting. "Great to meet you. Our mutual friend says hello, and well done. I'll be finishing your planned route."

He threw himself into the second-pilot's chair, startling Sunshine onto the deck. "The story is, one of the landing systems threw an error, and you weren't sure you could land in gravity. But it's fixed now." Again, that grin.

She had to admit, it was a pretty good plan.

Frankie grabbed the last chocolate bar and hoisted herself out of her seat. Before she took a step, Sunshine was on the seat, circling to settle in. Couldn't blame him; no good wasting the already-warm cushion.

Spike led the way out of the shuttle and across the shadow-dark dock to the airlock. They both sped up their pace, kicking it even higher when they saw The Spear through the repair bay's window. Walking up its peaty-smelling so-called temporary connection tube, banging on the door panel twice to get it to open, Frankie smiled.

Home.

CHAPTER
TWENTY-NINE

FRANKIE STYLES NURSED her second mug of morning coffee and sighed.

She tucked her feet sideways under her butt on the center orange cushion of the three-sided nook bench in The Spear's cheerful, generous kitchen. Fleecy blanket around her shoulders, thick warm socks on her feet, her new corporate-logo sweats over her sleepwear. She wasn't getting any more dressed than this all day.

She'd just finished the last act of the new Mon Gviv romance —so, so sighworthy—and was contemplating what next to dive into. Mon's trustworthy backlist or something daring and new?

She flicked her wrist and pulled up her list of Mon's works. Maybe switch to video from audio format, that was daring enough for today.

No alarm had woken her. No absolutely critical chores that had to be done right this second. Nothing potentially fatal—physically, politically, socially, or emotionally—lurked in the background. All was calm.

The kitchen's counters and cupboards, its round tables and chairs—even the reheater—were spotless. The breakfast cupboard and the snacks cubbies fully replenished. Same for the drinks fridge and the cold storage bins. She'd switched to the kind of cat food (cat food!) that Spike preferred, one that could be easily opened by cyvlossics. No more waiting for the human to remember it was dinnertime.

She thought about getting up to fix something to eat. Nah. She wasn't really that hungry, and she still had half a cup of coffee.

There was no rush.

Frankie liked the soft blue of the walls in here. Good contrast to the warm sepia of the kitchen setup. These bright orange cushions, though, ugh. Two nooks, six orange cushions. She would make new ones. Put these in the greenroom. Make a little hideaway in there, over where Minnie the snake used to sleep. Great place to relax.

She pulled up a screen and tapped a furniture app, the one with the fun color wheels. Maybe try forest green velvet? Did she have enough? She pinged one of the little ship-bots, the one that always helped with stuck things, and set it to measuring the dimensions of the cushions in the other nook. They were the same as this nook, and Frankie didn't feel like moving.

Strangers were in the ship. Known strangers, the Eckberg team, doing final tests on the upgrades, down in the controls room. They wouldn't come up here. They might not even be onboard that long today, Brigid Eckberg's message said. Frankie's training session on the new shields and buffed-up comms array wasn't until next shift. Just to be sure everything was ready.

No rush at all.

Message: A shipment at the end of the connection tube. Frankie sent one of the little bot's twins out to look at it. Her duffel, and a square white box that looked about the size of her head. They'd been shrink-wrapped together, to count as only one package. She told the bot to bring it to the kitchen, not her rooms. She'd need a blade to cut through that clear wrapping.

A droopy-eyed, scruffy Spike slowly followed the bot through the open door and into the kitchen.

"Good morning, sunshine!" Frankie couldn't stop herself from saying.

Spike groaned. She looked toward the cupboard with Spike-food, and then decided against it. She jumped onto the nook's cushion to Frankie's left. The place Frankie usually sat. Until she met a cyvlossic.

The little bot set the double package on the nook's cushion to her right. With a flick of its arm, its scissor-hand popped out. The bot neatly sliced away the wrapping, collecting and carrying it away, probably to large reclamation. The bot over by the next-door nook had one of the orange cushions propped up, measuring something. Frankie considered the bot.

"Bot Seven-X-three, do you like to chat?" she said.

The bot stopped. It turned its main lenses toward her.

"No," it said.

Okay, then.

Frankie started to go back to her color wheels, when she smelled it.

"Brownies!"

She pulled the white box toward her. Nothing was written on it, just a plain white box.

That smelled delicious.

It better not be more of Marissa's fancy soap.

Frankie lifted the flap. It was not soap. More than a dozen of the brownies with peppermint flakes, piled into a pyramid.

Now she was starving.

One corner of a tiny paper card was set into the top brownie. It was blank. Frankie took the card between her forefinger and middle finger and used the rest of her hand to grab the brownie.

She took a healthy bite—heaven!—and then scanned the card with her wristcom. There was the message, in one of the bot-languages.

"Cabana-Prime sent the recipe, too," she said through a mouthful of brownie. "What can we do nice for them?"

"Stop talking," Spike squawked.

"Such a ray of sunshine," Frankie said, mouth now clear but ready for more brownie. "Sorry," she said looking apologetically at Spike. The cyvlossic turned away, evidently to clean her paw. She knew Frankie wasn't sorry.

And why was Spike so cranky anyway? The operation was a success. Sunshine the cyvlossic was away. Everyone was hale and healthy. Sure, Spike still looked like a small-bear sized ponytail, but her fur was already starting to recover from the blowout.

Nothing new in her duffel, no sweet message from Elvin, ha.

Frankie took another brownie from the box and closed the lid. Like that was going to stop the binge. A trusty Mon Gviv story, peppermint brownies, real-bean coffee.

Bliss.

Video call: Morgan.

Maybe she shouldn't answer. Let him leave a message.

He didn't usually do that, though, just called back later.

Curiosity won out. Frankie raised her call-screen, noticed the brownie on her lip and wiped it away, and made the connection.

"Captain. Are you okay?" Morgan's worried face blocked most of the background, but she could tell he was in a cabana room. Good on Celine.

"Fine, fine," she said. "Just a weird switch problem. I added the fix to the bots' programming so they can handle it next time. How was your evening?"

She heard another voice. Morgan looked up, and then nodded. He ran his hand through his hair. It was actually lying flat.

"Fantastic," he said. "Dad lost his cyvlossic and ran around everywhere, all red. He missed supper! David had to take over."

"Poor guy."

"Not the least of it. David was mad—already mad—so he started to drink. All night long. He was hilarious waving goodbye to the guests! Finally, after everyone was gone—almost everyone—Dad got back to the house. Empty-handed. Then David accused him of loving Sunshine more than he loved his kids. Since that's the truth, Dad couldn't really argue back. So he just got redder. Then the medical servos came, and everyone had to go to bed."

"And Celine?" Frankie had to know.

"She's in the shower," Morgan whispered. "You know, she's even smarter than when she was a kid. And way sexier. She's been working in the family business. They're going to need a new chief attorney—like a decade from now, bunch of planners—so she's going to law school next semester. She's almost got me talked into going, too."

Frankie couldn't picture it. "You mean, like a body man?"

"No, like a fellow student." He rolled his eyes. "She's sure I'll ace the test. I test really well. And, well, it might come in handy. You know, for people like you."

Frankie wasn't keeping up. "Like me?"

"Yes! Small businesspeople who suffer under odious oligarchies."

"You did not just say that."

"I'm serious. It was wrong for Skolls to push you out of the market. You should have had recourse. And what if your insurance company really had said no to the repairs?"

He straightened his shoulders "You need an advocate. Somebody on your side." He leaned forward, eager. "The Kagan University on Zichi has this specialty track, intersystem relations, that would be perfect."

Zichi. The home planet in Central District. Where Frankie never wanted to be.

Well, she wanted Morgan out of her hair, and he surely would be on Zichi.

"U of Zee is a great school."

"No way," Morgan's eyes widened. "You went there?"

"Just for undergrad. The campus is beautiful." And the politics deadly. For the younger son of a loyal benefactor, though, it would be a breeze. "Send me pictures of the South Lawn flower beds. I loved watching the seasons. And eating the berries."

"Mom designed it."

Of course she did.

Morgan looked up again. "She's almost done. Have to wrap up. Oh—you haven't seen Sunshine, have you?"

Frankie swallowed. She'd practiced this.

"The tan one? Not since last night. Spike's the only cranky cyvlossic here with me."

"Shoot. Spike's with you? I was hoping they ran away together. Hiding out, making more cranky baby vlossics, that kind of thing."

"That's you, Morgan."

"Could be." His eyes expressed amazement but his mouth quirked in sly cockiness.

Frankie managed to get the brownie box safely stored in the snack cupboard before eating more than three. Or four. She certainly was not hungry now. Spike had stared at her the whole time, as if she couldn't believe a human could eat three brownies at once. Or four.

"Look, I'm saving some for later," she said to her colleague. "Eating in moderation."

"Wipe face," her colleague softly screeched. "Call Bruce."

So that's what the Spike stare was all about.

"You call Bruce." Frankie didn't care that Spike looked

disgusted. She was relaxing. "Your way is probably more secure, anyway. Ship's comms are in flux." Frankie's wristcom pinged. "Okay, they're done. But still."

They stared at each other. Frankie was not going to break. She had a Mon Gviv telenovela loading on the big screen in the media room, and she wasn't going to miss it. In fact, now that Eckbergs had reported the work done, Frankie was going to turn the comm off.

Spike was the first to break the stare. She did something weird with her front paw. Frankie was still trying to figure out what she'd done when her comm buzzed.

Video call: B at SA

"You did this," Frankie said.

Spike moved down the cushion, leaving the minimum space for Frankie to sit beside her. Frankie plopped down, wiped her mouth, and opened the call. Spike put her front paws on the table, to get her head into camera view.

Bruce had not changed in the past week. Even his charcoal-gray ensemble looked the same. He was stroking one of his luxurious sideburns as the call connected.

"Frankie! And Spike as well. Glad you called."

"Ha, ha," Frankie said under her breath. Spike snorted. "Check out my new sweatshirt," she said aloud. "Now I really feel like part of the team."

"Looks good on you." Bruce could have been a sports-caller in another life, he rolled into his sentences so smoothly.

"Thanks," she said.

"Thank you for your gift, too," he said. "Delivered to the station just this morning. All contents intact."

Spike pushed back onto the cushion, banged her hip against Frankie's, and started to clean a back paw.

Frankie did not forget that she was on camera with her boss. Her expression did not change. Blasted rude not-cat.

"Heard your ship is ready to go." Bruce should know. Systems Analysis was paying for it. "You've got your training?"

"Tomorrow."

He stroked his sideburn again. "Might want to push that up."

"We're on vacation," Frankie said, slow.

"Glad you could take some time off. Get rested up, and all. Because I have a rather big project for you—"

Frankie ducked out of the picture. "I told you!" she spat in a whisper at the back of Spike's head. "We couldn't do this tomorrow?"

The blasted not-cat shrugged a shoulder.

"What was that?" Bruce said. "Connection sounds a little choppy. Anyway, once you get fluent with your new comms array, send a message and I'll send you the details. Sooner the better, team."

"Wait!" Frankie said. "Spike wants reassignment. Could we do that now?"

Spike stopped, mid-lick.

Bruce frowned. He looked to the side, at some other screen. "Didn't include that in her report."

Spike returned to her rude, rude grooming.

"And I haven't seen sign of your report, either, Frankie. First thing you do, post-mission. Obviously, Spike has more to show you."

Obviously. Spike was sandbagging her. Why, Frankie couldn't guess.

"On it," she said to Bruce, trying to sound chipper. Spike snorted softly. Frankie refrained from pushing her colleague off the bench and onto the floor. "Catch you later."

Connection off, she messaged Eckbergs asking to move the training forward half a shift. No problem.

Frankie shuffled to the coffee pot, poured another mugful.

Took only two brownies out of the magic brownie box. Shuffled to the media room. Plopped in front of the big screen.

And spent the next three hours swept away amid Mon Gviv's gorgeous people, heightened passions, and glorious implausibility.

Now this was how to relax.

ALSO BY NICKY PENTTILA

Reading order: Frankie

Cargo & Chaos (this book)

Frankie Takes a Dive

Frankie Finds a Dot

Frankie Takes a Bow

More Cooperative Realm: Arkhide

Tales of Arkhide

Hidden Planet

The Listeners

The Elders of Arkhide

Other Space Opera

Cosmic Weave

Historical Fiction

A Note of Scandal

An Untitled Lady

The Spanish Patriot

ABOUT THE AUTHOR

Nicky Penttila wrote her first story, a Mayan murder mystery, in seventh grade. But then came gymnastics, math team, and boyfriends. Later came husband, car payments, and a sleep-depriving work schedule at newspapers across the country. Then came a second career as a science writer. But the fiction kept trickling out, a story here, a novella there, and finally, a real live novel. And she hasn't stopped.

Find more great reads at nickypenttila.com